Jamaican
Me Crazy

Jamaican Me Crazy

A Christmas Escape

A Novel

Debbie DiGiovanni

Revell
Grand Rapids, Michigan

© 2006 by Debbie DiGiovanni

Published by Fleming H. Revell
a division of Baker Publishing Group
P.O. Box 6287, Grand Rapids, MI 49516-6287
www.revellbooks.com

Printed in the United States of America

All rights reserved. No part of this publication may be reproduced, stored in
a retrieval system, or transmitted in any form or by any means—for example,
electronic, photocopy, recording—without the prior written permission of
the publisher. The only exception is brief quotations in printed reviews.

Library of Congress Cataloging-in-Publication Data
DiGiovanni, Debbie, 1960–
    Jamaican me crazy : a Christmas escape : a novel /
Debbie DiGiovanni
        p.   cm.
    ISBN 10: 0-8007-3107-7 (pbk.)
    ISBN 978-0-8007-3107-6 (pbk.)
    1. Christmas stories. I. Title.
PS3604.I395J36 2006
803′.6—dc22   2006020071

I dedicate this book
to my friends at the Senior Center,
who inspire me.

Acknowledgments

I would like to thank some special people who have been there for me.

First, to my family—each and every one of you. Your joy, understanding, and compassion mean everything to me.

Next, to my old friends—too many to name, but you know who you are. You are never forgotten. We just keep getting better.

Among my old friends, I feel compelled to mention a few, however. Phil Higgins, whose eagle eye has been particularly helpful in my writing. And Mike Faughn, who deserves a dinner in his honor (which I cannot afford at the present time). Mary Johnson, still the same after all these years. And Cathy Claxton, you're an old friend, yet our friendship has been strengthened through a series of life-changing events this past year. You are as true as anyone I've ever known.

And now to the new additions in my life that deserve mention.

Barb Barnes, my editor and new friend. Your beautiful spirit can be felt across the miles.

Mary Lee Woods, you have been a splendidly loyal friend. And to the rest of you by first name only to shorten it . . . Amy, you were from Day One a kindred spirit. Nancy and Tonya, you are talented women with the gift of hospitality. Izzy, the instant I met you I knew you were great.

Some other special souls who have impacted my life recently are Mary, Sherrie, Ivy, Diana, Leah, Virginia, Jo, Linda, and Claire.

And last, but definitely not least, is dear, sweet Pauline.

Hugs!

Prologue

Who would have guessed that the ladies dipping their toes in the turquoise waters of the Caribbean on the twenty-fifth of December were the once-predictable ladies of the Lakeside Baptist Christmas Club? Imagine a group of normally sensible, conservative women sporting Sponge Bob T-shirts and orange flip-flops, with their hair braided Jamaican style.

The congregation of Lakeside Baptist Church couldn't envision it. The news of the last-minute getaway was a complete shock. Peggy Wiggins had to play the piano two Sundays in a row, and let's just say the piano is definitely not her calling.

Jennifer Baker didn't know she was going to start a revolution. All she knew was that Christmas was getting to her, and if she didn't do something about it, she was afraid she was going to lose her mind.

If it had been any other day, the truth might not have spilled out so honestly. If Jennifer had spoken to her best friend about her frustrations first, Claire would have reasoned with her. She would have told her life is tough sometimes. And if that didn't help, then Claire would have purchased Jennifer's favorite chocolates over the Internet and had them Fed Ex'd to her doorstep. Jennifer would have munched right through her restlessness.

But Jennifer didn't talk to Claire first. And Claire thanks her for it. All the ladies in the Christmas Club thank Jennifer for convincing them to take up Becky's generous offer. Every time they see her they thank her profusely, do this jig they made up at the beach house, and say, "No problem, mon!"

This drives the other church ladies mad.

The membership of the Christmas Club has doubled since January. Suddenly all the ladies are feeling charitable. They're pulling out their holiday sewing patterns and cookie recipes for next year's underprivileged children's party.

"We want to go with you guys next time!" they say. The same ones who called them "terrible" and said *they* would never do such an unspiritual thing.

"There won't be a next time," Jennifer says assuredly. But the women don't understand . . . it was just one of those one-time things. You had to be *there* to learn the lesson.

The pastor's wife is starting a new Bible study on contentment, and Jennifer and the other bongo beaters are talking about more outreach to the community. Martha is wearing her hair down these days, and Lillian has incorporated an inordinate amount of beach illustrations into her Sunday school lessons. Claire and her husband are planning a Hawaiian cruise; Dawn is perfecting the Tropical Coconut Chicken recipe; and Becky, the only single of the group, is going back to Jamaica in the spring. Jennifer . . . well, she's looking forward to next Christmas already.

Just to assure you, the husbands and children sustained

no permanent damage. In fact, Casey learned to tie her shoes while her mother was gone, and Trevor learned to make scrambled eggs. The husbands learned some valuable lessons.

There were many small miracles that came out of Jennifer's dance with Christmas discontent.

1

To understand how Jennifer overdosed on Christmas, you have to know about her morning that first week in December. She had just flipped an egg and broken the yolk after a poor night's sleep filled with puzzling dreams. In the dream she could remember, she was lumbering under a load of cumbersome packages, which may have been related to the previous day's bad shopping experience.

She was feeling the pressure.

Jennifer noticed her son's gourmet chocolate Christmas calendar lying on the counter. She wondered what beautifully shaped chocolate was behind the cardboard door for December third. She wondered, and then she did an unthinkable thing. She tore it open and stole the chocolate. It was a reindeer, and she bit off his head and then followed it with his brown, milky body.

Jennifer jumped as her fourteen-year-old son walked in the kitchen, his dark hair spiked full of sculpting gel. Trevor's big blue eyes widened as they took in her expression and then fell to the skinny box with an upturned flap she was holding. "Mom, is that the chocolate calendar you bought me?"

With the evidence in hand—and mouth—what could she say? She stared at him blankly.

"It's okay; you can have it," he insisted.

"I'm so sorry, Trevor, I'll buy you another one; I'll buy you three."

Trevor smiled. "That's okay, Mom. I'm getting sick of chocolate."

"Sick of chocolate?" Jennifer swallowed the last of the delicacy, thinking it was impossible to ever tire of chocolate.

"They're serving chocolate pudding for dessert at school, and I'm sure there'll be even more at today's party."

"Party?" She slid the calendar back onto the counter.

"Yeah. This afternoon."

"And I'm supposed to bring . . ."

"Rice Krispies treats."

She sighed. These parties were getting earlier every year.

At least they packaged Rice Krispies treats now. Would she be a horrible mother to buy packaged goods instead of making them herself?

"Oh yeah, I'm supposed to bring some canned stuff for the food drive." Trevor walked to the cupboard and swung open the door.

"Take the cranberry sauce. I bought too much."

"I don't think people eat cranberries after Thanksgiving."

Jennifer gazed at her son's tall form, then eyed the canned goods on the shelf. "Take the green beans then."

Trevor pulled three cans from the lazy Susan and rearranged his backpack to squeeze them in. Throwing his pack over his shoulder, he said a hasty good-bye that Jennifer only half heard.

He was out the door and headed for the corner bus stop before Jennifer realized he hadn't had breakfast, which most of the time, lately, had been Cocoa Puffs or Cap'n Crunch.

A quiet fell over the house. Jennifer leaned against the counter in her blue terry robe. She stood there motionless, staring into space, until her husband's entrance caught her attention. She grimaced at his mismatched outfit.

Eric was wearing a red-collared shirt under a heavily patterned argyle sweater with a bulging belt underneath. The suit pants he'd picked out were too formal and his leather slip-ons too casual. You'd think a forty-year-old man could dress himself, but the ladies at his insurance office assured Jennifer he needed her help.

"What are you burning?" Eric looked toward the stove and then at Jennifer.

"Burning?"

The smoke alarm went off in the hall.

Jennifer rushed over to the stove where her eggs were smoldering and turned off the gas. She dumped the burnt eggs in the overflowing trash can.

Eric turned on the exhaust fan and waved his arms at the smoke.

The alarm petered out as Jennifer scraped off the pan. She offered to fix him another egg.

"Just pour me a cup of coffee," he said sharply.

"I haven't made it yet."

Eric gave a dismissive shake of his head. "Have you planned the office Christmas party menu yet?"

Jennifer choked. "I forgot about your Christmas party."

"How could you forget?"

Maybe because I want to forget. She shrugged.

"I don't know what's wrong with you, Jen. You're living on some other planet these days." Eric searched for his briefcase, which was in his hand.

Jennifer sighed. "Can't you just cater the thing?" She tightened the belt of her robe.

The disappointment was evident on Eric's face. "I want to have the employees here, in our home. To let them know that even though I'm the owner, we're real people."

"If I host the party, they'll know we're real people. Trust me."

"Okay. Okay. I thought you'd like to do it."

The injured inflection in his voice told Jennifer he expected her to feel guilty.

She stared at him, saying nothing.

"I'll have my secretary plan it, then." Eric paused. Jennifer didn't respond. "I'll pick up a Krispy Kreme for breakfast—again." This time he added a distressed look to the injured voice and pecked Jennifer on the cheek instead of kissing her on the lips. He went to the coatrack, grabbed his big jacket, and left abruptly through the side door to the garage.

Jennifer stared out the window at the gray Minnesota skies for a long time. She knew she was forgetting something. It was on her lengthy to-do list. The one that seemed to grow by the hour.

Krispy Kremes. Jennifer shrank with dread. "Oops. I was supposed to order the doughnuts for the ice hockey Christmas fund-raiser," she said aloud. And then she remembered she had agreed to babysit her friend Ann's parrot over the holidays and had promised Marge from the nursing home she'd talk to her children about them visiting her for the holidays . . . and that she had to pick out the best of the terrible family pictures to be printed on the Christmas cards . . .

Jennifer glared at the clock. 7:55. For all the trouble she'd had this morning, it had to be later than that.

The doorbell rang.

Doesn't anybody care what time it is?

Jennifer opened the door with an unenthusiastic swing. It was her meek little neighbor girl, Chloe. Jennifer couldn't help but smile at her sweetheart face and pigtails under a white wool hat that accented her baby blue eyes.

"I'm collecting money," Chloe said.

Jennifer wasn't sure what she was talking about. The cold air was blowing in, and she hugged her body to warm herself, still trying to remember. "Money for . . ."

"You bought one of my Christmas wreaths, and the money is due to the school today."

"I did?"

"Yes."

"Come inside, Chloe." Jennifer directed her into the entryway and shut the door. Chloe's boots left a mess all over her tile floor. "How much do I owe?"

"Forty dollars," Chloe answered as she pulled on her hand-knitted scarf.

"Forty dollars," Jennifer murmured as she shuffled over to a brass box on the entertainment center. It contained what was left of the dwindling Christmas money. She pulled out two twenties.

"You'll get your wreath next week," Chloe declared with a wide grin as she took the bills from Jennifer and stuffed them in her pocket. Then her eyes traveled around the room for an unnaturally long time.

"Is something wrong, Chloe?"

"I don't see pigs."

"What?"

"My mother says you live in a pigsty."

Jennifer felt the arteries in her neck expand.

"Thanks for dropping by." She ushered Chloe's small frame onto the snowy porch. Closing the door behind her, she leaned against it and looked down at the puddle Chloe had left on the floor.

Jennifer remembered the one time Chloe's mother, Ellen,

had dropped by. She had been getting over the flu and apologized for the dishes in the sink, the messy counter, and the laundry basket with bright red underwear (as red as her face) hanging off the side. Ellen had smiled. She understood, she said. Her house got like that too sometimes.

Jennifer kicked off her now damp, fuzzy slippers, collapsed on the couch, and pulled a blanket over her weary body. She closed her eyes and tried to relax, but she felt frazzled. And all this with not one Christmas decoration up yet.

She picked up the *Good Living* magazine and opened it to the middle.

"Do you ever think you're the only one not having fun?"

It was an ad for a nutritional supplement, and the gray-haired models looked to be having a blast.

"Yeah, I do. I really do."

Jennifer tossed the magazine on the floor and pulled the covers over her head, feeling aged, at thirty-seven.

2

Two hours and fifty minutes after her meltdown, Jennifer sat with the other members of the Lakeside Baptist Christmas Club as Martha, the self-appointed leader of the group, finished reading the mission statement.

". . . to coordinate the charitable efforts for the underprivileged children's party."

Jennifer looked around the room filled with holiday reminders. The rectangular working table was covered with seasonal fabrics and sewing paraphernalia. Since it was a Sunday school room, Christmas pictures painted by the children plastered the walls. A banner with an angel blowing a trumpet read BE OF GOOD CHEER.

"Lillian, will you pray for us, please?" Martha asked ceremoniously.

Her prayer was going to be long. Jennifer knew because Lillian's prayers were always long. She wondered if anyone else was feeling as miserable as she was. If they were growing tired of sewing these rag dolls. The underprivileged children didn't want them; they wanted the loot that would be distributed after the party. CDs and toys and electronic games. These dolls would end up in their closets. Sometimes she'd see the mothers of these underprivileged kids in the store buying cartons of cigarettes when they probably needed laundry soap. *If they wouldn't buy cigarettes . . .* She ended her irreverent thoughts three minutes later, as Lillian ended her prayer.

". . . and bless the children who will benefit from our efforts."

The perfunctory routine began. The ladies took up their crafts to sew.

Dawn hummed "Joy to the World."

Jennifer stared at her doll. The buttons on her dress were crooked and her smile was twisted. She struggled to pursue her project, but it seemed a hill to climb just then. "Claire, do you think raiding your child's chocolate Advent calendar is a sign of desperation?"

Claire turned to her, dangling bells swinging from her ears. "I think you could say that. Why? Do you know someone who actually did that?"

Jennifer didn't answer. She felt hopeless. She wanted it to be summer again. She wanted warm air and green grass and brightly colored flowers. But more than that, she wanted the holiday season over with. She felt empty and unbalanced and unfulfilled. But since all these emotions were ambiguous and complicated, she reduced it all to Charlie Brown simplicity. "I'm beginning to despise Christmas," she mumbled.

Claire was deciding between red and green fabric. "What?"

Jennifer's frustration overtook her sensibility. "I think most people are miserable at Christmas!" she said, louder than she intended.

Everything suddenly stopped. The ladies put down their craftwork. All eyes were directed at Jennifer. Her cranberry-colored lips formed an insecure smile.

"I wouldn't go that far," Claire said, wrinkling her nose.

Jennifer hesitated. She looked at the ladies for a moment and decided she might as well finish what she started. "Well, think of it," she said, elaborating on her theory. "How many people can't make it home for the holidays? Like loved ones in the military and broken families . . . and elderly and sick people. That's half the population right there."

"Those poor kids who have to live by visitation schedules," Lillian interjected.

No one said anything for a long and suffocating moment. And then Dawn, who looked suddenly depressed, added, "And mother-in-laws. Don't forget mother-in-laws who ruin Christmas with malicious comments."

Jennifer hadn't known that Dawn had ill feelings toward her mother-in-law. She hadn't known that Dawn had ill feelings toward anyone.

No one said a word. Bodies stiffened, eyes stared straight ahead.

"And the wives and mothers who do all the work are unhappiest of all!" The voice came from the hall. It was Lisa, who cleaned the church. And that was all she said as she and her cart whizzed by.

Martha rubbed her heart-shaped chin, looking mortified, at a loss for words.

Weariness showed in Claire's eyes. "My daughter is the sugarplum fairy in the *Nutcracker,* and I'm about to collapse from exhaustion from picking her up and dropping her off at practices." She stared down at her French-manicured nails and looked up again with a wistful smile. "But you should see Lexie glide across the stage in her pink satin costume and ballet slippers. She is so beautiful!"

The women smiled with her.

Lisa passed by again with her cart and yelled from the

doorway. "Don't forget to add dysfunctional families to that list of gripes. My family anyway."

Martha cocked her head and removed her spectacles. "Ladies, we are here for a benevolent cause. Not to complain about our lives."

Lillian agreed with Martha. "That's right."

The women picked up their crafts and started sewing again.

Surprisingly, it was Dawn, known for her long-suffering character, who would not give up the subject. "You know, I bought my mother-in-law an expensive cameo for Christmas last year, and she didn't even try it on. She asked if Tommy helped pick it out. When I said no, she put it back in the box like it was nothing."

"Alex's family is impossible to buy for," Claire said.

"I baked fruitcakes for twenty of our friends and neighbors," Lillian bragged.

"You really don't need to go to that trouble, Lil," Jennifer said, holding back a smile.

Lillian's expression turned vacant.

"What she means is that most people don't eat them," Martha said.

Lillian's jaw dropped. "Yes, they do!"

"Do you eat yours?" Martha put Dawn on the spot.

This was going to be good; Jennifer knew Dawn couldn't lie.

"Uh-h-h," Dawn stammered. "No. I never do."

Lillian looked hard at the wall.

"You go right on making your fruitcakes if that's what you want to do," Claire said, always the encourager.

Lillian toyed with the large snowflake pin gracing her bulky red sweater as she looked directly at Jennifer. "You guys are massacring Christmas, and I love Christmas! I get out my

Christmas movies the day after Thanksgiving, and I love it when they put the animated toys out at Sears."

Her words resonated in the stillness.

"I'm sorry, you guys; I really am. I love Christmas too. It's Jesus's birthday, after all." Jennifer picked absentmindedly at the doll she still held. "I suppose what I've lost is the true meaning of Christmas. It's so hard to strike a balance."

"Thank you for that appropriate confession," Martha said as she straightened her collar.

"Don't feel bad, Jen," Claire said, touching her shoulder. "We all feel the pressure. I think Lisa hit it on the head. We do too much around the holidays."

"Becky has a good time at Christmas," Dawn pointed out.

"Because she's single and does what *she* wants," Jennifer said, surprised at her own reply.

"Where is she anyway?" Martha asked.

"Call her on her cell," Dawn suggested just as Becky sauntered in the room. She was wearing her nurse's uniform, and her straight brown hair was neatly pinned in a bun. Her hazel eyes probed the room. "Where are the lemons? You guys look sour."

"We are collectively depressed," Claire stated flatly.

"I'm not depressed," Lillian insisted.

Dawn's stricken expression spoke volumes. "It's just family stuff."

For a moment, Becky looked at the group. "What's wrong, ladies? Trouble in paradise?"

The group sighed in unison.

"You're always bragging about how your husbands are so supportive." She tilted her head, waiting for a response. "How they're always telling you how beautiful you are."

No one said anything.

Becky tried again. "How they send flowers . . . and write little notes with hearts they leave on the mirror."

"That was Tommy with the hearts," Dawn said with a slight smile.

Jennifer's eyebrows went up. "We weren't even discussing the men. But now that you mention it, my loving husband has been on hiatus."

"The word I'd use for Alex is disconnected," Claire said.

Dawn's expression changed to a wilted look of confusion. "With Tommy it's been a tug-of-war of wills."

"Derrick bought me flowers once while we were dating." Lillian smiled.

"Pay no attention to any of it, Becky," Martha said with an edge to her voice. "Jennifer was compelled to share her peculiar thoughts on Christmas with us, and things went downhill from there."

"Whatever the problem is, it doesn't matter. I have the solution in my purse." Becky smiled as though she could barely contain her excitement. She patted her secret.

"Ah, chocolate," Jennifer said excitedly.

"I think you should give up chocolate," Claire said to Jennifer, and then her voice dropped to a whisper. "Did you steal Trevor's chocolate?"

"Yup!" Jennifer grinned at the absurdity of her deed.

"It's something better than chocolate," Becky said. "And much too special to share here."

Jennifer was anxious to know what the surprise was. She was aware of the apprehension on Martha's face, however, and tried to conceal her enthusiasm. "That sounds great." She tapped her right foot nervously.

"How about Oliver's for French onion soup, and then my surprise," Becky suggested. "Daring, I know. But I have breath mints."

An echo of agreement passed over the table.

"After we finish our work, of course," Martha said in her typical domineering tone.

The ladies agreed, and needles flew. More work was accomplished in the next thirty minutes than in the past two meetings, and the box of rag dolls piled so high that another box was needed to hold the overflow.

When the table was cleared, six women stood in reverence as Martha ended the session in a prayer overflowing with adjectives illuminating the joys of this season of selfless giving.

3

Martha waved her arm emphatically as though she were a desperate commuter hailing a taxi outside Grand Central Station.

The busy waiter at Oliver's, a quaint café tucked inside a shopping center, dropped what he was doing, sped over to the table in his Converse tennis shoes, and attempted a smile. "Are you ladies ready to order?"

"We have been for some time." Martha gave her thinning, auburn hair that needed touching up an irritated pat.

"I'll start with you then," the skinny, dark-haired waiter addressed Martha.

She ordered French onion soup for the gang.

The waiter was thrown for a moment. "French onion soup all around?"

Martha nodded. "That's correct."

"May I suggest the blackened salmon or prime rib?"

"You may suggest whatever you want, young man, but we're having the French onion soup!" Martha proclaimed.

The waiter surveyed the conservatively dressed women. Several looked uncomfortable at Martha's abrasive manner. "I'll be back with your . . . ahem, big order," he said and scurried away.

"We're saving ourselves for desserts!" Dawn called to his backside, then turned back to the group. "I think he was hoping we'd order an entrée so he could get a bigger tip."

"It's all their fault. They shouldn't be making award-winning soup if they don't want you to order it," Jennifer said, still in her straightforward mood.

"We'll leave him a nice, big tip," Claire reassured Dawn, who looked worried.

Becky took a sip of ice water, cleared her throat, and was about to speak when her cell phone rang. She excused herself.

"Rats. She took her purse with her so we can't peek at the surprise," Jennifer said.

"I'll bet it's tickets to something." A smile spread over Lillian's round face.

"Tickets?" Dawn scratched her blond head.

"I know . . . to Michael Bublé's concert," Lillian cried. "Last week I saw Becky buying one of his CDs."

Claire stared at her. "I saw him perform live on *The Today Show* last week from Rockefeller Plaza. I doubt Lakeside is on his tour."

"My veterinarian is going to see him in Hershey, Pennsylvania, in July."

Jennifer sighed. "Isn't that where Chocolate World is?"

Martha was quick to discourage the nonsense. "Don't get too excited, ladies. The surprise may not be for us at all. It may be a shopping spree for the children. We must think of the children."

The ladies nodded.

Jennifer secretly hoped it wasn't for the children.

"A girlfriend weekend at the Mall of America," Dawn speculated. Evidently, she, too, hoped it wasn't for the children.

The guesswork continued as Jennifer daydreamed.

At the top of her list was a long weekend at a day spa, the kind to leave fine chocolates on your pillows. But she didn't share her fantasies aloud. That could be seriously overreaching.

Becky returned to the table with a toothy grin. Her eyes danced.

"Tell us the surprise," Claire said, leaning closer.

"Michael Bublé, right?" Lillian was still hoping for the impossible.

Becky sat down in the cushioned dinette chair, her calm and composed body language giving nothing away. "So you know I won on *Who Wants to Be a Millionaire*," she started.

"The fact that you were on the front page of every Minnesota paper was a huge clue," Jennifer said.

"You caused the biggest media frenzy since Sara Blakely invented Spanx." Lillian's proud grin indicated she thought she was very clever.

"Spanx?" Martha asked.

"You know, the footless pantyhose that hides unwanted panty lines." Claire smiled and crossed her legs. "It's a big thing in New York City. My sister loves them."

"Save your fashion analysis for later. Becky is trying to tell us her surprise," Jennifer scolded.

"Thank you," Becky continued. "As I was saying, you all were partially responsible for my big win on *Millionaire*. The twenty-five-thousand-dollar question Meredith asked was one of the dozens of answers you drummed into my head with your cute little rhymes."

"'Methuselah lived to be nine sixty-nine. The oldest man

lived a very long time!'" Lillian recited, and then added, "I made up that rhyme, you know!"

Jennifer almost rolled her eyes. Lillian got on everyone's nerves sometimes, but she got on Jennifer's nerves almost all of the time.

"I think we should give God the glory," Martha said.

Lillian hung her head but quickly recovered and resumed her lively dialogue as though she'd already forgotten Martha's admonition. "I'll betcha Meredith Vieira wears Spanx. I know Spanx are a favorite of Oprah's."

"Why are you so stuck on Spanx? I sure would like to hear what Becky has to say." Jennifer's brown eyes narrowed at Lillian.

"Sorry! I have adult ADD."

Becky splashed her good news without further ado. "I'm taking you all to Jamaica with me!"

There was total silence at the table. The women were obviously shocked.

Becky broke the silence. "It's a great deal. One of my patients is a travel agent, and she made the suggestion."

There was another long, tense pause.

"When would this be?" Martha finally asked.

"Here's the thing," Becky continued. "It would be over Christmas. It's the only time I have off."

"Christmas?" Martha looked like she could use some oxygen.

"I'm a head nurse. I don't exactly have flexible vacations." Becky shrugged.

Dawn's sweet face registered surprise. "Christmas . . . as in three weeks from now, as in the time of giving we are supposed to spend with our families."

"That's the Christmas I'm talking about, alright."

Claire and Jennifer smiled at Becky's news, but neither spoke.

The timing seemed impossible to Jennifer. In fact, so impossible that it must be providential, she thought.

"Wouldn't that be selfish, expecting our husbands to watch the kids while we lie on the beach?" Claire asked, as though she wanted permission to go.

"They don't seem to have a problem going hunting and leaving you to watch the kids," Becky countered.

"She is right, there," Jennifer affirmed.

Martha jumped in with a quote from Proverbs. "'A man's folly ruins his life.'"

"Amen," Lillian said on cue.

Jennifer ignored the rebuke. "Be honest, you guys. If your family said, 'Go if you want' and really meant it, you'd go. At least I know I would."

"So would I," Claire said, giving in.

Jennifer was happy her best friend was in agreement.

"A week away from my mother-in-law would be a dream," Dawn said. "It would be at least a week, wouldn't it?"

Becky nodded. "Actually, it's over a week. Nine days and eight nights." She held up her hands at the looks of hesitation on the ladies' faces. "I know that sounds long, but two of those days are mostly travel. It's an eight-day package, and I added a day so we don't have to fly home on Christmas."

As her friends passed tentative looks to each other, Becky enticed them. "A whole week at the Sea View Resort on a white, sandy beach. No schedules, no responsibilities . . ."

"No Christmas stress." Jennifer was already sold.

"Please, let's not go through that again." Martha's face pinched unattractively.

Lillian blurted, "C-c-come to think of it, I've never been anywhere besides Minnesota."

"Lillian!" Martha spewed.

Lillian stared hard into her water glass.

"We'll never convince the guys," Dawn said as she twirled her long hair around her index finger, clearly collapsing to the pressure.

Claire sighed. "My husband can't imagine why we'd ever want to leave our paradise here. We used to travel all the time. Now his idea of fun is me standing next to him holding his toolbox in case he needs a hammer or nail."

Becky shook her head. "It never occurred to me that you would need to ask permission to go."

"You obviously missed my Bible study on submission," Martha said.

Lillian and Dawn nodded.

"I guess so, Martha, since the only male I have to submit to is Felix," Becky stated matter-of-factly.

"Felix?" Martha said, eyes bulging, mouth agape.

"Felix, her cat," Jennifer said and tried not to laugh.

"Thank goodness." Martha closed her mouth.

Becky sighed and pulled the brochure out of her purse, displaying the glossy vacation photos. "All you need is a birth certificate and driver's license."

The brochure was passed around the table and drew *oohs!* and *ahhs!* and *wows!* until it reached Martha.

"It would be unethical," she spouted. She twisted her linen napkin as she spoke, so forcefully her knuckles turned white. "We have a party to run."

"I don't care. My sanity's at stake," Jennifer said in a voice strangled with emotion.

Claire clung to the brochure. "Let's do it!"

Becky looked pleased.

Martha did not look pleased. She stood up without warning and put on her thick coat, fur hat, and knit scarf. And then, looking like an old maid missionary to Siberia, she preached like one. "Ladies, this is an offense to your families . . . and the Lord, and I will *not* be a part of it."

"But what about your soup? You can't waste it," Lillian said, and ripped at her cuticles, revealing her insecurity.

"It's worth a bowl of soup to keep my dignity intact." Martha opened her thick wallet bulging with outdated pictures of nephews and nieces and Sunday school students with families of their own. She threw a five-dollar bill down on the table.

Jennifer stared at Martha, thinking her bout of hysteria was extreme.

"When you come to your senses, let me know," Martha said after a churchlike silence. She grabbed her purse and turned to Lillian. "Are you coming?" she asked, an angry wobble in her voice.

Lillian smiled weakly. "I think I'll stay."

"Good day then, ladies." Martha stomped away, her black snow boots clumping toward the door. When she stepped on the holiday doormat and it played a tune, she jumped, turned around, and snorted in disgust, as though it were a mean prank someone had pulled on her.

No one laughed, though Jennifer was tempted.

When she was out the door, Dawn waggled her head. "You realize the news of our planned escape will be on the prayer chain by this evening."

4

I can see the headlines now"—Claire's outstretched hand panned across the air— "'CHURCH LADIES ABANDON FAMILIES FOR FRIVOLOUS GETAWAY IN THE CARIBBEAN.'"

"Let her put us on the prayer chain. We need the prayer! At least I do," Jennifer muttered under her breath. The stress of the past few days seemed to have tightened her resolve and loosened her tongue.

Claire unburdened her heart. "I'm sorry, but sometimes that woman thinks she is our spiritual policewoman." She caught Lillian's astonished expression. "And you, Lil, be sure to tell Martha we talked about her behind her back."

Lillian's face scrunched. "What do you think . . . that I'm not my own person or something?"

No one answered Lillian's question.

Claire finished her analysis of Martha. "Martha is a great Bible teacher, but I think we're past the stage of needing to be told what to do."

"Well, starting right now, I'm my own person," Lillian said.

Looks passed back and forth.

"Soup's on!" Jennifer announced, saved by the waiter who arrived balancing his jam-packed tray.

❧

Less than a half hour after her brave statement about how she was going to be her own person, guilt overcame Lillian. "You don't think Martha will stay mad, do you?" Before anyone could answer, she claimed she had a sudden headache, scooped up her outdated green tweed coat and big black plastic purse, and left Oliver's Café in a tremendous hurry.

"I wouldn't be at all surprised if the aspirin she went out for is in Martha's purse," Becky said, sucking on a breath mint.

"Me either," Claire said.

Jennifer was too into her decadent chocolate dessert to comment.

Becky motioned for them all to pay attention and launched into her planning session. "So we need to show your husbands how much you need this getaway. I don't feel like watching a beautiful Jamaican sunset all alone."

Jennifer savored her last bite of Triple Chocolate Fudge Cake and smiled. She didn't want Becky watching that beautiful sunset all alone either.

"So, here's what I'm thinking," Becky said, sounding determined. "I'll come to your respective houses and take movies of you looking stressed. And hopefully that will convince the guys some R&R is desperately needed."

Dawn exhaled slowly. "You can start with my house. Five minutes with my mother-in-law and you'll see why I'm a shadow of my former self."

"Why do you put up with her?" Claire asked.

"Can I think about it and let you know in a few weeks?" Dawn's voice cracked.

"I'll be chilling out with a fruity drink on a Jamaican beach by then," Claire said.

"You hope," Dawn replied.

"We hope," Jennifer said.

"I think I'll start with Lillian. Her house is a stress breeding ground. Three kids and four dogs." Becky wrinkled her nose.

"Four kids, five dogs . . . and a hamster," Dawn corrected.

Becky pinched her face in horror. "That's even worse!"

"Three of the dogs are puppies," Dawn added.

"I only need about three minutes of exaggerated stress from each of you to show how burned out you are," Becky went on.

"Who needs to exaggerate stress?" Jennifer laughed tensely. "I am near the edge. In fact, one good push, and I'll be over the edge."

Becky's index finger traced the snowman on the plastic tablecloth. She bit her lip. "I can visualize the video presentation in my mind."

The group allowed Becky some quiet to concentrate.

After a reasonable length of time, Claire drew her back to earth with her practical question. "So when would we show the tape to the guys?"

"Hmmm, I don't know, but it'll have to be soon," Becky admitted.

Jennifer tossed her cloud of soft brown hair off her shoulders. "It would be more effective if we had all the guys in one place at one time so the 'holdouts' could be crumbled by the peer pressure."

"But first they have to be in a great mood," Becky said.

"Getting five guys in a great mood all in the same week may be difficult," Claire noted.

Jennifer watched Becky's intent expression.

Becky smiled slyly, tripling Jennifer's confidence in her. "There is only one way it can be done."

"You mean . . .?" Claire gave her a sideways glance.

"Yes, I mean . . . ESPN and hot chicken wings." Becky beamed in triumph.

Jennifer smiled back in admiration and wonder.

In the background, Bing Crosby sang "I'll Be Home for Christmas."

∽◌∾

It was Friday night at seven, and the women of the Christmas Club would find out soon whether they would be spending their holiday in sun-soaked Jamaica or blustery, gray Minnesota.

The men were in front of the Baker's big-screen TV watching the Hemlock/Taylor fight on ESPN, stuffing their faces with an all-things–Super Bowl party; the women were gathered in the kitchen, all talking at the same time; and the children—eight of them, ages five to fifteen—were in the basement, playing.

Jennifer peeked into the living room. She could see Lillian's husband, Derrick, perched on one side of the sectional sofa. Alex, Claire's husband, lounged in the La-Z-Boy across from him, playing with his Rolex. Dawn's husband, Tommy, sat near Eric on the longer sectional piece. Each was holding a bowl of chips.

"We have them eating out of our hands," she announced as she stepped back into the kitchen. She was dressed elegantly in a light blue cashmere sweater she'd paired with a long, pleated white skirt. On her feet were sparkly slip-on sandals. All the ladies were overdressed. But Lillian was pushing the envelope the most in a chiffon bubblegum-pink dress she'd told Jennifer—at least three times—she'd bought at the red tag sale at Goodwill for the special occasion.

"Where is Becky with the tape? She's late," Lillian complained.

"Hey, she organized this get-together to convince our husbands to let us go to Jamaica—plus she's paying for the trip. We can't really be mad at her," Jennifer said, sounding harsher than she meant to.

"I was just wondering," Lillian said.

"You're right, you can't be mad at her," Becky said as she walked in the kitchen.

All heads turned. She set a stack of videos on the counter, next to a pile of cookbooks.

Greetings and hugs were exchanged. Dawn took Becky's coat and purse, and Jennifer handed her a cup of hot apple cider; Claire rubbed her cold shoulders, stiff from the single-digit weather.

Lillian's curious brown eyes gazed at the tapes on the counter. "Why are there so many tapes?"

"I had copies made for each of you as a little souvenir," Becky answered. "I thought it would be fun to look back at our foolhardiness years from now after we go through some major life changes." She warmed her hands on the mug and took a sip of hot cider.

"Let's start the tape now," Jennifer said, holding up one of the tapes.

Becky laughed. "The way to get a man in a good mood is *not* to turn off the TV in the middle of a fight. Don't you married women know anything?"

"We'll do it at halftime then," Claire suggested.

"They have rounds in boxing, not halftime," Becky said. And then she went on to review for them every frame of drama she had captured on film in Steven Spielberg detail. As she summarized the details of the video, Jennifer cringed.

༄༅

It was a short bout, as far as fights go. Twelve minutes at the most. Five minutes of those twelve minutes were taken up with Becky talking. Another five minutes were spent picking up the Red Hots Lillian knocked all over the red linoleum floor.

The men were wound up about the early knockout. Which led into a discussion of left hooks and TKOs . . . and bantamweights and featherweights and middleweights.

Without a word, the women replenished the food and ice, gathered trash, and restocked the napkins.

When the job was complete, they gave their best Stepford Wives smiles.

"Are you guys in a really good mood?" Jennifer asked in a voice as warm and sweet as fresh-baked cookies.

Eric flashed a smile. "You betcha, honey. This was a great idea!"

"What warm-blooded American male would argue with that?" Becky said.

Jennifer popped an olive in her mouth and chewed furiously to keep from laughing. If Eric only knew what she was up to.

On Saturday, she had suddenly agreed to the forty-two-inch widescreen, high definition TV her husband had been nagging about since football season started. "An early Christmas present," she had called it when she handed Eric the Best Buy credit card that was in an envelope in a drawer (for emergencies only) as he stood bewildered for two seconds before grabbing his keys and rushing out the door into the frigid air without his coat.

Jennifer felt the timing was perfect. She smiled at Becky and winked.

Becky and her pointy black boots marched over to stand in front of the TV, and the ladies filed in behind her, standing to one side. Jennifer could feel a knot forming in her stomach the way it did when her nerves got the best of her.

5

Without hesitation on her part, Becky started her sales pitch. "I have something to say to you concerning your wives."

The men were still squeezed together on the long sectional sofa after watching the fight. They looked at each other; the women standing nearby looked at each other. Then all eyes present gazed at Becky, and a momentary silence settled over the room.

Derrick was the first to speak. "I knew there had to be a catch to all this!" he objected with his mouth full of food. "Wives always have something up their sleeves."

"Maybe they want new furniture," Alex said.

"Hey, honey, if you want us to build the Christmas set for the play, just say so, and we'll say no," Eric told Jennifer.

"Ha. Ha. Funny," she replied.

"Tommy, what's your take on this?" Derrick asked.

"Nursing not paying enough these days, Bec? Are you peddling beauty products?" Tommy said, in his dry humor.

"Oh, my wrinkles!" Derrick touched his rough face and laughed boisterously.

Her self-confidence dissolving, Jennifer sat down in a side chair attempting to get a grip on her emotions.

"This tape will answer all your questions, gentlemen."
Becky inserted the tape, pushed some buttons, and gracefully
moved out of the way as the screen turned fuzzy gray.

"I get it. It's one of those marriage tapes about how to love
your wives," Derrick said, leaning back into the sofa with a
smug look.

No wonder Lillian is so annoying, Jennifer thought to herself.
I'd be daffy too, if I were married to that jerk.

"'Ten Thousand Mistakes Husbands Make.'" Eric joined in
on the wisecracking again.

Jennifer's faith in her husband started to crumble. *What's
he doing? Trying to impress the other guys by being macho?*

"Haven't you heard the latest?" Alex said. "There's a law
in Spain that requires men to share household duties with
their wives."

That news got a good laugh from the men.

"And I thought your husband was the quiet type," Jennifer
said to Claire.

Claire harrumphed.

Becky ignored the rude comments, looking confident that
all her hard work would pay off in the end.

The assembly waited for the tape to start, which seemed
to Jennifer to take forever.

Finally, the action started.

Eric was the first to catch on to the subject matter, made
obvious by his shout, "Whoa, a hunting tape!"

Jennifer's brown eyes grew big as she looked away from the
TV to see smiles spreading across the men's faces.

All the women gasped.

Tommy turned around, looked at Dawn, and smiled. "We
underestimated you gals."

Claire borrowed Martha's expression. "Good gravy!"

The men were clearly entranced by the wild caribou flying across the frozen tundra.

All female eyes bounded for Becky's perplexed face.

Jennifer barreled out of her chair and pulled Becky by her shiny green blouse into the kitchen. "What's the bright idea?"

And then all the women joined them in the kitchen, snowballing Becky with questions.

The confounded look on Becky's face intensified. "Obviously I have the wrong tape," she said, her index finger in a thinking pose.

"Obviously." Jennifer wrinkled her forehead in dismay.

"There was this guy in fatigues at the video store making copies of his tape too. Old Mr. Barney must have switched the tapes," Becky concluded.

"Mr. Barney is eighty-six. He needs to retire," Dawn said in his defense.

"The hunter can't be too happy either," Claire said.

"Someone give me one of the extras I made," Becky ordered.

Jennifer whipped a tape off the counter and handed it to her.

Becky read the label aloud: ALASKA HUNTING GUIDE CAMP. Her head went back and forth in a series of speedy shakes.

Jennifer grabbed it back and read it too. "What?"

"We're supposed to be showing them how stressed we are, and so we throw them a boxing *and hunting party*." Claire looked down at her long, black velvet dress and Prada shoes and laughed edgily.

Becky sighed. "The video store is closed, and I have to make a decision tonight on the tickets. My friend called me before I walked in the door. Rooms are filling up fast."

Lillian's lip wobbled and she got misty-eyed. "Maybe Martha was right. Maybe this is a sign we shouldn't go."

Dawn patted her shoulder tenderly, even though she looked like she might cry too.

"Well, you better go in and tell them our scandalous plan before they come up with one of their own that involves us watching the kids while they go hunting," Jennifer said in a daze.

Becky took one last sip of cider and jauntily strolled into the other room. This time the ladies did not follow her in. Jennifer moved toward the doorway and watched as Becky positioned her thin body in front of the men's engrossing entertainment. Taking a deep breath, she said, "I'm turning off the tape. Nobody throw food."

Click.

"Hey, what is this?" Eric bellowed.

Becky leapt into her dialogue. "Your wives are very stressed from all the holiday preparation."

"And so you turn off our tape?" Judging by his frown, Alex was very unhappy.

"You can have the new furniture, Lil. Just tell your friend here to turn the tape back on," Derrick yelled in the direction of the kitchen.

"Stressed from what?" Eric pointed at the walls. "Do you see any Christmas decorations up?"

The comment infuriated Jennifer. "I was going to hang Chloe's wreath next week," she mumbled.

"I'm telling you that your wives are about to have nervous breakdowns," Becky said dramatically.

"Women don't know stress," Derrick claimed. "Try my job."

Jennifer turned to Lillian, who was breathing down her

neck. "Al's Auto is high stress? How stressful can an oil change be?"

Lillian gave her a goofy look.

Alex voiced his complaint. "My secretary must have had me sign a thousand cards this week."

"Poor baby," Claire said. She caught Jennifer's eye and shook her head in mock sympathy.

"And I'm planning my own office Christmas party," Eric said.

"You mean your secretary is," Jennifer pealed, this time wanting Eric to hear.

"I know what you mean, buddy," Tommy said. "I've been out to lunch all week with clients. It's killing my figure."

Jennifer turned and made eye contact with Dawn. "That's a harebrained interpretation of stress."

"It's his mother's fried chicken that's killing his figure," Dawn alleged. "The main ingredient in her cooking is fat."

"I can't take it anymore," Jennifer said and stomped into the living room, eyes blazing, hands on hips.

The others followed, overtaking the mostly blue Ikea-style living room and surrounding their husbands, once again.

"We are, too, stressed!" Jennifer retorted.

"Hey, don't look at me. I hang my coat up and pick up my socks," Eric said.

Jennifer was not impressed.

"It must be those phantom children we haven't heard a peep out of all night." Derrick's comment continued to fan the flames.

"Those little monsters," Tommy said sarcastically.

Jennifer suddenly wondered why the children were so quiet but dismissed the thought, figuring Trevor had things under control. It looked like Becky was about to make her brave announcement, and she wasn't about to miss it.

Becky got right to it. "Guys, I want to take your wives to Jamaica over Christmas!"

Jennifer's nervousness elevated as she observed the expressions on the male faces as their brains slowly connected the dots.

"Because they're so stressed?" Tommy displayed his agitation by tapping his chest with his fingertips.

"Yes." Becky nodded.

"Let me get this straight. You want *us* to stay home with the kids at Christmas while you go gallivanting around with *our* money," Alex said, as though he were missing something.

"Not your money, my money," Becky explained. "Don't you think your wives deserve the R&R?"

"You are stay-at-home moms," Tommy objected.

"Forget it, ladies," Becky said. "Men don't like to do something they're incompetent at. That's a proven fact."

It was obvious by the off-in-outer-space looks on the men's faces that Becky's simple statement had an immense effect.

Jennifer knew Becky had mapped out a new strategy.

"Incompetent?" Derrick was the first to protest. "Why, I could do your job any day of the week." He puffed his chest out.

"It would be a piece of cake," Tommy agreed.

"Go ahead then," Becky dared them.

"Okay, we will," Eric said.

His words caused Jennifer's hope to rise like a hot air balloon.

"We will?" Alex asked, his eyebrows rising in uncertainty.

"Oh c'mon, just agree so she'll put the hunting tape back on," Derrick whined.

"Give the angry housewives their way," Tommy said.

Becky forced the issue with an extended stare. "So we're on then?"

45

Eric stood up and made a commanding gesture with his arm. "We're on!" he shouted. "Now, turn the tape back on!"

Jennifer sighed happily. All the idiocy that came out of Eric's mouth this entire evening was instantly forgiven.

Becky's shaking index finger pushed PLAY.

The caribou traipsed across the screen, and the men displayed their pleasure with male noises—grunting and yelling and cheering.

Becky reunited with the Christmas Club members in the kitchen, who were huddled like football players.

Jennifer's pulse was racing. She pulled Becky into the circle, and they all held hands and bounced up and down in glee, burning a few of those calories they had ingested while preparing the feast.

"Are they shallow or what?" Claire said. "A Jamaican vacation in exchange for a hunting tape."

"It's like Esau selling his birthright for a bowl of soup," Dawn reflected.

"They'll regret the decision in the morning," Jennifer said, shaking her head.

"But by the time they feel the regret it will be too late," Becky said, relieved. "I'm calling to purchase the tickets right now!"

6

Dawn's mother-in-law pounced into Dawn and Tommy's flowery, yellow bedroom like a tiger. Invasion of privacy was becoming a bad habit of hers.

"Tommy, how do you want your eggs?" she asked her son.

Tommy was sitting on the antique brass bed enjoying his wife's shoulder massage.

"Would an omelet be too much trouble?" he asked and abruptly pulled away from Dawn and moved to the other side of the room.

Dawn was used to Edna's blatant disrespect, but Tommy's curt manner was a recent development.

"An omelet would be no trouble at all," Edna said. She shot a look of insolence at Dawn and exited, slamming the door the way she had been screaming at her grandchildren not to do all week (while Tommy was at work).

Dawn looked at Tommy with a distressed expression. "You know I like to fix you a big breakfast on Saturday morning. I like to be the one to take care of you, not your mother."

He laughed mockingly. "So that's why you're leaving us for Jamaica . . . because you want to take care of us?"

"You agreed to it last night."

"I did?"

"Yes! You said it would be a piece of cake to do what I do. Remember?"

Tommy gritted his teeth. "So tell me why you're stressed again, because I sure don't get it."

Dawn stepped to her dresser and brushed her long, blond hair.

"You really don't, do you?" she said. Her shoulders sagged under the weight of disappointment.

"What, you mean my mother?" Tommy blared a second later. He paced the room like a caged animal.

"I'd like to do my own shopping, my own cooking, my own cleaning."

"She's trying to be helpful. And she just lost her husband, for goodness' sake."

Her fourth husband . . . over a year ago, Dawn thought, but didn't say it. "I feel like I've lost my husband too," she whispered and wasn't sure if Tommy heard. And if he did hear her, if he cared.

The door swung open again and Dawn dropped the hairbrush. She suspected that Edna had been listening at the door.

"Son, do you want Velveeta in your omelet?" The skin around her eyes was drawn and her wrinkled lips were too red. She had lived a hard life, and it showed.

Dawn took a few steps toward her adversary and wiggled her pink-painted toenails in nervousness. "I'm sorry to tell you this, Edna, but Tommy doesn't care for Velveeta. He prefers sharp cheddar in his omelets."

Edna glared at Dawn. Then Tommy glared at Dawn. "I don't know what you're talking about, sweetheart. I love Velveeta," he said, jittery.

"I knew you did, Son." Edna huffed and gave Dawn a self-satisfied nod.

Tommy followed his mother out the door as Dawn stood alone, feeling abandoned.

Six months ago, before her mother-in-law came to live with them, they had been a very happy family.

❧

In Lillian's disorderly household, the Holmes children were typically active. Simon was pulling the puppy's tail, Israel had just dumped a bag of dog food on the floor, and Jacob was swinging on the battered pine cabinets. Casey, the only girl in the family, was drawing a picture of the chaos.

Lillian stepped down the cement steps into the heated garage. She carried a small plate of doughnuts to Derrick, where his greasy fingers were working their magic under the hood of his latest clunker.

Lillian offered a day-old doughnut that Derrick took without a thank-you.

"So you think you can handle the kids while I'm gone?"

He took a bite and spoke while chewing. "I'll just get out the duct tape."

Lillian taught third grade Sunday school and had heard enough duct tape jokes to write a book on them.

She was having second thoughts about leaving her children under their father's care. Jacob, in addition to being a hyper child, was diabetic. And Israel was hanging around this older neighbor boy who was bad news. Simon had some makeup work to do over Christmas vacation, due to his learning disability. Casey would be no trouble at all, she knew.

"So you're going to take the kids Christmas shopping while I'm gone?"

"Yeah, sure."

"And what about meals . . . do you think you can handle it?"

"Pizza, pizza, pizza," he said.

"I'll post the emergency numbers on the fridge."

"I'll just dial 911."

Lillian tried to laugh, but she didn't think it was all that funny.

Derrick stuffed the remainder of the second doughnut in his mouth. "Got any more of these?" he asked and licked the sticky sugar off his fingers.

"No. But I guess I could drive to the store and get some more," Lillian offered reluctantly.

"Okay," he said and smiled. "But take the kids with you."

∼⌒∽

Claire's luxurious residence overlooking the lake was as orderly as a palace.

The Parker family had a housekeeper who came in one full day a week and put everything in its place, though most of the time it was already in its place.

The couple's only daughter, fifteen-year-old Lexie, was quietly reading her worn copy of *The Princess Bride* and toasting herself in front of the carved stone fireplace in their formal living room.

Maybe Lexie was upset about her leaving, and especially missing her *Nutcracker* performance, Claire thought in passing as she observed that solitary look Lexie sometimes got. If so, she hadn't mentioned it. She had stopped mentioning things that bothered her long ago. Claire knew this; her husband, Alex, did not.

Alex was relaxing in his favorite brown leather recliner reading his paper. He was an intelligent man (and former dreamer) who was consumed with running his two techno-geek businesses.

The world was bleak and quiet here in Lakeside. Too quiet. Funny how Claire hadn't really thought much about it until all this talk of Christmas discontent.

Lexie excused herself, and then it was eerily quiet.

The Christmas decorations were lively, but something was missing.

The tree, she realized.

Alex would not have a tree. Not since their son David died.

Was it actually four years ago . . . at Christmas? Claire gasped in horror.

"Don't choke," Alex said, never looking up from his *Wall Street Journal*.

Claire wanted to talk about David now. But bringing up David stirred bad memories in Alex. Why bad memories? Claire couldn't understand.

David would have been sixteen. He would probably look even more like Alex than he did at twelve. Everyone had said he was 99 percent Alex.

Alex shifted uncomfortably. "Why are you staring at me that way?"

"I was thinking, I guess."

"About what?"

"David."

His dark eyes shot back to his *Wall Street Journal*.

"What about planting a tree in his memory?" Claire suggested timidly.

"In the middle of winter. Nobody plants a tree in December," Alex replied.

Claire sighed heavily.

"Bay's Hardware is having a sale on tile cutters. I think I'll

51

pick one up and tile the mudroom so I'll have something to do while you're gone."

"Lexie is something to do while I'm gone."

"What?"

"Lexie, our daughter."

She couldn't believe his apathy.

"Oh, sure. I didn't hear you."

And suddenly Claire longed for Jamaica. Anywhere far from this barren wilderness of a pretend marriage.

∽

Jennifer had started the whole thing, and she was a happy housewife after getting her way. She made chocolate chip pancakes for Trevor (eating a few chips herself) and called Eric twice at his office to tell him how much she loved him, though his "I love you" back sounded like a forced recording from someone being held hostage.

Trevor was relaxing in his beanbag, immersed in *Adventure* magazine, his head bent forward, his normally styled hair a messy mop even though it was close to noon.

Jennifer hugged him before sitting on his unmade bed. "So, you're sure you'll be okay spending Christmas with just you and your father?"

"Sure, Mom." He stared at her, his blue eyes thoughtful. "I figure your stealing my chocolate was a cry for help and you need this trip."

"That sounds serious."

"It's okay. I figure it has something to do with me growing up and Dad spending so much time at his office. You know, feeling a sense of loss because things are changing so fast."

She patted his broadening shoulders. "I see you have me all figured out."

"Not all figured out. Dad says I'll never have any woman all figured out."

Jennifer laughed so hard she cried, and then grew serious. "You are right though, Dad is spending too much time at the office. I wish he would spend more time having fun."

"Like what kind of fun?"

"Not hunting, for sure." She scratched her head. "Bowling, maybe."

"Bowling. How boring." Trevor pointed to a full-size photo in his magazine. "How about a challenging traverse of the South Patagonian Ice Cap in Argentina?"

"Your father scaling a mountain." Jennifer's eyes widened. "He'd be lucky if he could run a mile with all those doughnuts he's been eating."

❧

The thing Becky did the most was work. Mostly because there wasn't much else for a single woman to do in Lakeside. Becky certainly did not need to work. Her wealthy businessman father had set up a trust fund prior to his death. Her house was paid for. Most people in Lakeside worked hard to make ends meet. They had trouble understanding why someone would work when they didn't need to.

Single men were common in Lakeside, a sportsman's paradise. But they were not the type of men that interested Becky. They were mostly what she called "Paul Bunyan types" with sandpaper hands and dirty fingernails. At least that's what Becky saw. She preferred soft, smooth skin like she remembered her father having.

Most anyone who knew Becky thought she led an exciting life. After all, she bought her groceries at the gourmet market, rented new releases, and drove a red Lexus.

Contrary to popular belief, Becky did not have as exciting

53

a life as she would have liked. On Friday nights, she stayed home reading, doing laundry, or watching the Hallmark Channel with Felix the cat on her lap and a box of Kleenex at her side.

When she started her nursing profession ten years ago, she was filled with purpose and expectation. However, in her seventh year she began having terrible nightmares. Sometimes in the middle of the night she would find herself searching the cupboards of her house looking for babies she had cared for during her shift. Some who had died. Watching the children suffer became too much for her. She gave up pediatrics to become a floor nurse in the cardiac care unit when the in-house promotion was posted eight months ago.

Becky was sipping on chamomile tea, cozy in her black silk pajamas, when she was filled with unexpected doubt and anxiety about the trip. Had she made the right decision by inviting five women on her only vacation in three years? She wasn't much for ladies' events like women's retreats. For one thing, she didn't find talking about husbands and kids a retreat at all (and for some reason, women couldn't help but talk about their families). The clincher, however, was that inevitably the conversation wound around to why she wasn't married. The general rule, it seemed to her, was that single women were to be pitied. She was certain the women of the Christmas Club were different. They loved her for who she was. Married, single . . . a doctor, nurse, or candy striper.

After all that heavy contemplation, she was convinced she'd made the right decision.

∽⚬∾

When female members of the church body needed marriage advice, they called Martha. She considered herself an expert in the field, having been married thirty-nine years.

Martha could quote long passages of the Bible, knew Greek, and had the happy privilege of owning the entire collection of *Through the Bible* books (a gift from her Bible study group) authored by the late Dr. J. Vernon McGee, and a Bible tape collection any pastor would have been proud of.

No one questioned whether Martha was spiritually equipped.

Yet, despite all this intimidating knowledge swirling around in her competent brain, her marriage suffered its own inadequacies. Her husband, Harry, hardly noticed if she was home or not, as long as his farmer's breakfast was served before she left for the church office, where she spent most of her time. On a voluntary basis, of course.

Most of the people bought Martha's little act, including Martha. She'd even convinced herself that if she didn't do all the charitable work she did, nothing would get done. And most people respected her for that (or, at the very least, put up with her).

Martha gave the oak desk in the church office another solid whack for emphasis. "Imagine, leaving their families for a fling in Jamaica."

"Fling?" The pastor's wife was definitely concerned.

After a long and prejudiced explanation, Martha ended with an exasperated sigh. "So, I'm afraid, Donna, I will be coordinating the underprivileged children's party alone this year."

It wasn't true. The cookies were already baked, the dolls sewn, and the presents purchased and wrapped. The decorations were the ones they used every year, and there was an overabundance of volunteers offering their talents, large and small.

But it made Martha feel better to say it. She needed to feel better. Especially since Harry had told her that no way would he let her go to Jamaica—not in a million years.

"Who would retrieve my newspaper in the morning?" he had teased.

"Retrieve?" she'd said, hurt. Dogs retrieve.

And then she went to dutifully refill the flowered cream pitcher, telling herself again what a ridiculous idea Jamaica was.

7

In the short span of fourteen days, all the travel arrangements had been made. Houses were scoured (or at least vacuumed and dusted), doctor and orthodontist appointments were postponed to the next year, and well-thought-out instructions were left with the men so the women could, hopefully, return to find their houses in one piece.

Alex promised he would cancel his important business meeting to attend Lexie's *Nutcracker* performance. He would bring red roses and pay her compliments.

Tommy promised he would not allow his mother to boss the girls around to the point of tears and frustration.

Eric, after two days of guilty persuasion, agreed to drop by and see Marge at the nursing home "sometime during the holidays," since Marge's children had not returned Jennifer's calls. Chloe, the neighbor girl, would watch Ann's parrot for forty-two dollars and fifty cents (she was quite the negotiator).

Derrick laughed at all of Lillian's long-winded directives. He promised, again, to keep the duct tape handy.

Good-byes had been said the night prior to avoid waking the families up early. There were not half the tears one might have expected of the children. The men hugged and kissed their wives, but with far less passion than when they went off on their hunting excursions. All the men said they hoped their wives would have a good time and not to worry about them—except Derrick, who only said not to worry about them.

There was one little rule the husbands had come up with that the ladies had complained about.

NO CALLING HOME.

It would only upset the children, the men agreed.

All of the ladies had sent note cards to friends and family on their Christmas lists, saying they would be giving no Christmas presents this year and they expected none in return. Postcards would be sent from Jamaica highlighting their trip, time permitting.

∽✶∾

Martha's Ford Aerostar came to a halt at the curb outside the check-in counter at the Lakeside Airport, by the sign that said a vehicle should not be left unattended. It was 5:20 a.m., and the place was deserted.

She gazed up at the dark sky. The glare from the streetlights obscured the impressive array of stars she had seen on the drive. The sunrise wouldn't come for a couple more hours. Still, Martha could picture it in her mind. A perfect winter postcard with the snow-dusted trees in the distance silhouetted against the rising sun. As the luggage was being amassed, she stood on the icy sidewalk, musing.

Why on earth would anyone want to spend Christmas on a hot, humid beach? What kind of Christmas would that be?

Deep in her thoughts, Martha lost her footing as she stepped back to let the porter pass. Claire caught her by her big coat, preventing her from slipping.

58

Martha straightened her body and stood in an almost military stance. "I agreed to bring you here, but I am not condoning your behavior, you understand," she said to Claire, her pride overriding her manners. She tucked a few strands of stray hair in the fur hat she always wore all winter.

"Yes, Martha. We understand," Claire said, though by her good spirits, Martha doubted she really understood.

Dawn came around to the front of Martha and rested her hand on her shoulder. "Are you sure you can handle the party without us?" she asked for the third time.

"I have the matter completely in hand," Martha assured her.

Claire warmed her hands in her pockets. "Who's doing the face painting?"

"Mary Sharp."

"Why, that poor lady shakes so much she has trouble putting on her own lipstick."

"Yes, she does." Martha smiled, hoping Claire would feel bad.

"Who's playing the piano for me?" Dawn asked.

"Peggy Wiggins," Martha said in a light voice as she felt a smirk working the corners of her mouth.

"Tell her the C on that old piano doesn't work very well." Dawn's strained voice reflected her struggle with her overactive conscience.

"Trust me, with her playing it won't matter." Martha laughed a little, knowing she'd hit a chord.

Becky slammed the van door shut, and the sound boomed in contrast to the stillness.

Martha suddenly felt suspended in space and time. And then she felt a sense of loneliness, loss, and abandonment that was painful, almost a physical hurt.

Lillian startled her by yelling at the top of her lungs, "Group photo!" She swung her digital camera by the strap inches from Martha's face. The one she'd told everyone several times on the ride to the airport Derrick had purchased off eBay for only $99.99.

Martha seized the camera from her, doubting the picture would come out, even with a flash. "I'll take the picture, since I won't be participating in your—"

"Hijinks. Is that the word you were searching for, Martha?" Becky broke in, chuckling.

"You said it, not me."

Hijinks is right, Martha thought. *These younger women know nothing of loyalty and commitment.*

The women squeezed together, and Martha, after some difficulty finding the right button, snapped the picture.

After she returned the camera to Lillian, Becky pulled her under the streetlight. "I need to talk to you."

Martha was gripped with apprehension. She knew Becky could not read her mind, but if she could, she would be severely disappointed.

She composed herself and built a defense in her mind in case Becky was going to confront her, threatening her reputation as a leader.

"Martha."

"Yes, what is it?"

"I'm giving you a camera phone so we can send you pictures and you can text message us."

"Text message? I've never heard of it."

"But you have seen a cell phone before, right?" Becky placed the compact phone in Martha's black-gloved hand.

Martha stared at the high-tech instrument under the light, somewhat confused, somewhat relieved. She slipped it in her big plastic purse. "My niece in Chicago uses one of these."

"It's a way of communicating with us." Becky paused. "We

want you to be a part of our trip, even though you are choosing not to come."

Martha told herself again she had no intention of being a part of any of this foolishness.

Becky's frosty breath made a cloud in the cold atmosphere. "Ask Lisa at the church to show you how to use it. Here's an instruction sheet I typed up."

Martha took the paper. "Lisa?" she said gruffly.

"She has a cell phone, Martha. Cleaning women have cell phones too. Believe it or not."

"We should go now," Dawn called to the ladies as she jumped up and down as though warming up for the hundred-yard dash.

Becky gave Martha a hug and thanked her for dropping them off. The others took their turns hugging Martha and telling her how much they appreciated her hard work. Lillian's hug was tighter than the rest.

Oh, how this poor girl needs me, Martha commended herself as Lillian's hug suffocated her.

Becky literally had to pull Lillian off Martha under the pretense of offering her a breath mint.

"Does my breath stink or something?" Lillian asked as Martha continued her self-talk.

Martha felt important, even sacrificial . . . but only for a minute, until conviction overcame her like a wave. She asked God to help her to be genuinely happy for these eager women. And then an honest thought intruded and she admitted to herself that relaxing on the sunny beach under an umbrella with a good book might not be such a bad thing after all. When was the last time Harry told her to go and do something for herself? It was so long ago she couldn't even remember.

Her conflicting emotions were disturbing her mental peace.

Martha took a deep breath and pushed the bad feelings aside. *Sweep, sweep,* she said in her mind as she pictured a broom whisking away her bad thoughts.

~∽~

The ladies congregated on the sidewalk and held hands before their departure. Martha cleared her throat. Jennifer waited for the assault, but Martha's prayer was as heartfelt as any Pollyanna could aspire to.

Jennifer was amazed. It seemed to her there were no differences between them in that glorious moment. The cold air chilled their bodies, but not their spirits.

If only it could be that way forever, Jennifer thought. Never a disagreement, a harsh word, or a misunderstanding.

Dawn took Martha's arm and escorted her to the driver's side of the van.

Jennifer watched Martha's shadowy figure as she shuffled away. She listened to her boots crunch in the snow, her slow gait confirming the fact that her arthritis was worsening. "She wants to go," Jennifer told Claire as the van door slammed shut.

"No way!" Claire disagreed.

"I'm serious. She does."

Jennifer turned. She saw Lillian was already inside watching from the other side of the glass . . . and sobbing mournfully.

~∽~

Within minutes, the group had formed a line at the ticket counter as Lillian lagged behind.

"I can't believe I'm doing this. I can't leave my poor children to fend for themselves. I'm a terrible person!" Lillian wailed in her dramatic way.

"I'm sure one of the other church ladies would be happy to use your free ticket," Becky said bluntly.

"I know Ashley Welch said she would love to go," Jennifer said, knowing Lillian was bluffing. "Of course, that was after she called me a terrible sinner."

"I guess I deserve a vacation"—Lillian's transformation was immediate, much to the ladies' amusement—"plus I've been practicing up on my high school French for this trip."

Becky leaned in closer. "What an extraordinarily ambitious idea, Lil, except . . ."

Lillian's eyes widened. "Except what?"

"They don't speak French in Jamaica."

"What do they speak?"

"They have their own dialect called Patois, but they generally speak English."

That brought a round of laughter from the group.

⁓∾

After a fast shuffle through the airport security checkpoint, the ladies and their carry-on luggage settled at Gate 2. There were only three gates at the Lakeside Airport, all direct flights to Minneapolis. Theirs would be the first flight out.

The small airport was old, yet clean and cheery. Christmas tunes played softly in the background. A tired janitor sloshed his mop around in his soapy bucket; an obviously happily married elderly couple held hands in a far-off corner; and a twenty-something dreamer with a botched red mohawk snored with his nose in the air, working out his issues of social isolation.

Becky headed off to the bathroom to change into something more weather appropriate for Jamaica.

Claire leaned back in her teal linen dress, looking bored as Dawn recited another recipe. "You remove the giblets, wash the chicken inside and out with cold water . . ."

Lillian on the other side of her was as dazed as a deer blinded by a headlight, and as frightened as one, this being her first flight ever. "Do you think I'll get a window seat?" she asked Jennifer, as her teeth ripped into a piece of loose skin on her thumbnail.

Jennifer looked away and mumbled her answer. "I think all the seats on this dinky plane are window seats."

When Lillian had finished her stress-reduction ritual, Jennifer smiled tightly.

"Can I ask you a question?"—she didn't wait for Lillian's reply—"Why do you have scuba equipment on your lap?"

Lillian looked down at her lap. "Oh, you mean my fins. Walmart special, $5.99." She grinned as if it were a great accomplishment.

"I didn't ask about the price." Jennifer took another sip of her machine-brewed coffee.

"I wanted to make sure I had both of them, and now they won't fit back in my bag." Lillian's shoulder bag was chock-full of grandmotherly things like safety pins and small, magnifying mirrors.

"I believe the equipment is included when you take snorkeling lessons," Jennifer said.

"Oh." Lillian scratched her head.

⁓

"May I have your attention, please," Becky said as she swished over in her skirt and peasant blouse, an outfit she couldn't have worn three minutes outside the heated airport. She stood in front of her friends. "I want to say something before we embark on our Jamaican adventure."

Both Claire and Jennifer looked relieved.

Dawn and Lillian sat up straight as though they were in school.

Becky had their undivided attention as she quickly explained. "I have listened to you complain about your families all week, and particularly your husbands. This gives me the distinct impression you have issues. I have come to the conclusion you will not have a good time in Jamaica until you get those issues out of your system. So I'm going to try an exercise with you I practice with my nurses at the hospital in our stress workshop."

What? The ladies' heads were spinning from the speedy discourse.

Becky noted their confused expressions, reached in her big Guess bag, and pulled out four fuzzy, purple diaries, each with a different cover design. "These are journals," she said, displaying the compact bound notebooks.

The ladies looked at each other.

"Every time you have a negative thought you feel compelled to share—be it about your husband, kid, poinsettia plant, or hamster . . ."

Lillian shrank in her chair because, just this morning, she had been complaining about her son's hamster.

". . . I want you to write a letter in this journal." Becky completed her directive.

"I don't get it." Jennifer scrunched her forehead.

"I'll give you an example," Becky explained. "Let's say I'm irritated with my goldfish and am tempted to drone on about my goldfish, and bore others with my complaint about my goldfish. I write my goldfish a note." She dictated her correspondence to the air. "Dear Goldfish, it really irritates me when you leave scum on the side of the bowl. Love, Becky."

Becky handed out the journals. The heart was gifted to Dawn, the butterfly to Claire, the rainbow to Jennifer, and the tulip to Lillian.

No one quite knew what to say, except Lillian, who always had too much to say. She wanted to say that it was the job of the algae eater, not the goldfish, to clean the bowl. She also wanted to say she didn't think it was fair that she got the tulip journal. She felt Claire was more the tulip type and she was more the butterfly type, free and all that.

The other women pretended to like their journals.

Becky, satisfied for the time being, sat down, put her headphones on, and closed her eyes. Claire picked up a novel, Dawn knitted, and Jennifer closed her eyes.

Lillian, on the other hand, decided her Walmart fins were too cumbersome to carry on the plane. She got up and roamed around with her big bag swinging precariously from her shoulder, fins dangling from her fingers, until she found a chair she liked. She then laid the fins down and sat in the chair next to them.

She was back to brooding over Becky's alleged lack of sensitivity. Opening her big purse, she pulled out her fuzzy journal and happened on the page with an inscription from Becky she hadn't noticed. It said how Becky saw Lillian as a bold, colorful flower slowly blooming. Lillian was touched. Yes, the tulip journal was just perfect. If Becky were not across the room sleeping, she would have hugged her right then.

Restless again, Lillian continued to walk around the airport, picking up small scraps of litter. She suddenly worried about the fins being destroyed by an unruly child, or worse, destroyed by airport security thinking a miniature bomb was hidden in them. She scooped them up, walked over to the young man in the mohawk, and asked him if he was going someplace warm.

"Anywhere is warmer than this," he grumbled.

She did not pick up on his bad disposition. She only smiled and laid the fins down carefully on the seat next to him, assuming he was lonely and that lonely strangers appreciated gifts. "Maybe you can use these," she said and walked away, feeling she had done a good deed. She tottered over to her original seat and sat down with the others who were happily doing their own thing.

Lillian ruptured the peace.

"Da plane, da plane!" she yelled.

Their small, twin-engine aircraft had arrived.

8

Seven hours from the time they left Martha on the icy sidewalk, the weary travelers arrived at Montego Bay International Airport (the last leg of the trip out of Cincinnati).

Despite Lillian suffering minor anxiety attacks at takeoff, amid some turbulence, and during landing, the three short flights were remarkably uneventful.

When they reached the sidewalk the tropical air blasted them like a heater.

"I feel like I'm wearing a buffalo blanket," Claire said.

Jennifer pulled her Amy Irving hair up in a high ponytail.

Dawn reviewed Customs Declarations Form C.5.

Lillian flitted around like a butterfly.

Becky chose the least aggressive driver among the many vying for her attention. He was wearing jeans, a white T-shirt, and blue canvas sneakers, looking very American to her. His teeth were whiter than hers, and she spent hundreds of dollars to bleach hers. His selling point, however, was his later model white van—with three rows of backseats—which Becky presumed to be reliable transportation.

"Can you take us to the Sea View Resort in Ocho Rios?" she asked the driver.

"No problem, mon," the driver smiled. "I'll take da luggage."

"Not my luggage." Becky pulled open the double doors, and she and her mass of luggage moved straight to the back of the van.

As the driver was struggling with his stubborn trunk key, Lillian threw her two enormous suitcases by the window on the middle bench seat. Instead of sitting down next to them, she climbed out and jumped into the front passenger seat, claiming she got car sick.

The rest of the luggage was stored by the driver while the other three women climbed in. Dawn situated herself as best she could in the middle row next to Lillian's pile of bags. Claire took the window seat in the first row, and Jennifer sat next to her, directly behind Lillian.

Before they knew it, the van was rounding corners at breakneck speed down the two-lane rutted highway, the air-conditioning giving minimal comfort in the humid temperatures.

As the van careened through the streets, it barely missed chickens and goats and colorfully dressed people that seemed to pop out of nowhere.

"We're gonna die!" Lillian cried, the way she had on the plane rides.

Dawn struggled for a more comfortable position. "She may be right this time," she gasped.

Jennifer watched Lillian go on and on to the driver about every little thing, competing with the reggae on the radio. "What's wrong with that girl? She can't go thirty seconds without needing attention," she whispered in Claire's ear.

Without saying a word, Claire pulled Jennifer's rainbow

journal out of her purse and handed her a pen. "Tell it to the new complaint department."

✧

Jennifer situated her little book on her lap and penned her frustration.

Dear Lillian,

I am praying God will give me the grace to be more patient with you!!!!!

She showed her entry to Claire who smiled and tossed her blond, blunt-cut hair. "Better?" she asked.

"A little," Jennifer admitted.

And it was true. For the time being.

"Hey, maybe this journaling isn't such a bad idea. Maybe Eric and I can have our arguments by journal from now on."

She pictured big writing—I'M RIGHT, YOU'RE WRONG!

"Do you have many arguments?" Claire asked, glancing at Jennifer.

"Not as long as Eric behaves. What about you and Alex?"

"I believe one's lips need to be moving to have an argument." Claire's voice cracked as she answered.

Although Jennifer had wondered how their marriage was doing, it was the first clue of marital discord Claire had offered her. Hearing the admission confirmed her fears.

✧

"Water, water! I'm on the verge of dehydration!" Lillian's voice, shrill and desperate, carried across the lobby of the Sea View Resort in Ocho Rios an hour later.

"I told you to buy bottled water back at that little store where we stopped," Becky said.

The other ladies had been drinking all along.

Lillian grabbed a drink from a beverage tray. She was ready to guzzle it straight down when Becky pulled the Styrofoam cup from her hand and threw the contents in the big ceramic planter.

"Sorry, but I did that for your sake."

"My sake?" Lillian was completely clueless.

"I don't think Martha would approve of you drinking rum," Becky said, laughing.

"Rum?" Lillian gasped, shocked. "It's lemonade!"

Becky threw the cup in a trash can and sniffed her hands. "Can't you smell it? My hands are soaked in it." She proceeded to the washroom.

Lillian's innocent eyes widened as she explained, "I didn't smell it. I lost my sense of smell when I was eight. My grandmother packed too much Vicks in my nose when I had chest congestion."

"I figured it was something like that," Jennifer said.

"Well, not all my sense of smell," Lillian clarified. "Like fifteen percent or something."

Dawn passed Lillian one of her water bottles. "Drink slowly," she urged.

Lillian chugged it down like a greedy child, spilling half of it in her dire need of liquid.

❧

Jennifer seized Claire's hand and tugged her through the open, airy lobby. "Let's take a tour, girlfriend!"

The hotel had a tropical elegance about it. Elegant, yet contemporary and casual. They strolled through the gift shop and peeked in the boutiques, gasping at the high prices. They smelled the flowers in the florist shop, speechless with delight. They stopped at the empty disco and enjoyed the island music as they watched the rainbow strobe lights play tag on the white walls.

"'OLDIES SING-ALONG PARTY SUNDAY NITE,'" Claire read, pointing at the printed sign and laughing.

"Not on my best day!" Jennifer swallowed hard.

They dead-ended at the beauty parlor and strolled back to the front desk where Becky was registering them. An older couple, the only other guests around, had just arrived and were waiting their turn.

The baggy-kneed man was wearing white tube socks and white shoes, a Canon camera around his neck, and a golf hat with sports pins attached. He and his wife wore matching Hawaiian shirts, and their luggage was Louis Vuitton, which Jennifer (an avid magazine reader) had gleaned from a travel article was the luggage most likely to be stolen. She was glad to be dressed unassumingly in beige capris, a short-sleeved blue collared shirt, and new white Keds.

The couple started their check-in, and Becky stopped to talk with the concierge. Jennifer looked around for Claire, who'd moved to the cascading fountain. It was gorgeous and added to the ambiance. Jennifer walked over to the big picture window and stared outside at the lush garden, fascinated by the color that seemed to pulsate from the tropical flowers. Back in Lakeside her view from the kitchen window would be a one-inch covering of icy slush.

God, you're so good to me, she thought. *Better than my imagination. I would have been satisfied with an overnight trip.*

She walked over to a wicker chair next to the flowered couch Dawn and Lillian were sharing, and sat down. Dawn had Becky's cell phone in her hand and was waiting for a text message to fully appear.

"A message from Martha," Dawn stated.

"What does it say? What does it say?" Lillian hovered, attempting to see.

Dawn read it aloud. "It says TESTING, TESTING. IT'S 14 DEGREES HERE IN LAKESIDE. MARTHA."

"Let's send one back," Lillian said excitedly.

"What should I say?" Dawn wrinkled her forehead.

"Tell her Lillian's off the wagon again," Jennifer said, keeping her face expressionless. "That ought to get a rise out of Martha."

"Don't tell her that!" Lillian shouted.

"I'm kidding. You take everything so literally," Jennifer said.

Claire slipped into a chair near Jennifer and joined the conversation. "Tell her it's a hundred twenty degrees here . . . and we miss her."

"And Lisa too." Jennifer turned to Claire. "You don't think Martha is pushing those buttons, do you?"

Just as Dawn sent a message and signed off, Becky came back with the bad news that the rooms wouldn't be ready for at least another hour.

"Oh, no." Claire slumped in her chair. "I need a shower so bad."

"We can stay here in the lobby where it's air-conditioned," Dawn suggested.

"Sit in the lobby when we haven't seen the sun in months. I don't think so." Jennifer wanted the sun. "Besides, no one but us cares that we're sweating. Let's go to the beach!"

"After I change," Claire said. She looked around the lobby, and suddenly her expression changed from tired to terrified. "Where's our luggage?"

"Mine is in the corner." Becky pointed to her sturdy red luggage.

"Mine are here." Lillian patted two pieces of fake crocodile-skin luggage. "My neighbor let me borrow them. Did I ever tell you about how she was almost swallowed whole by a crocodile in a Louisiana bayou?"

Jennifer was about to say yes when her gaze landed on a pile of luggage on a cart by the door. Looking closely, though, she realized it was not their luggage.

"No way did the driver leave with our luggage." Jennifer's heart sank.

"Maybe our bags were confused with someone else's," Dawn said.

The three women were on their feet in seconds. They crossed the lobby and flew out the door to the sidewalk in front of the hotel where the van had let them off twenty minutes ago.

"Do you know where our luggage is?" Jennifer asked the smiling, semitoothless doorman, fearful for the answer.

"I can't help you with dat problem," he said.

"And we packed all our makeup in our suitcases." Claire groaned. "My face without makeup is like a wanted poster."

Jennifer's worry was much more basic. "Underwear," she said.

Dawn took a sip of her water as the three luggage-less women stood on the sidewalk, the color drained from their faces, even in the heat.

Becky and Lillian joined them.

"I'll check into the situation," Becky said, much too calmly, Jennifer thought. But then she had her luggage.

∽◈∽

"So this is where everybody is," Dawn said as the ladies reached the hundred-plus white chaise lounge chairs lined up in neat rows, all of them occupied by happy people wearing a variety of colorful outfits, and some wearing very little.

Most of the lounge chair occupants were sipping on cold, fruity drinks with tiny, bright umbrellas, chatting and listening to music under the midday sun.

"Is everybody spending Christmas in Jamaica?" Claire wondered aloud as Lillian plowed her suitcase through the sand behind them.

"With their families," Dawn added, a wistful look on her face.

A bronzed man in a Speedo flexed his toned, muscled body in their direction.

"Or not," Jennifer shuddered, finding Speedos extremely distasteful.

"Why don't we grab a towel from that cart over there and sit on the beach," Claire suggested.

It dawned on Jennifer that Lillian had been dragging one of her massive suitcases around with her. "Why didn't you leave that suitcase at the front desk with your other one so the bellhop could deliver it to the room?" she asked.

"I'm not letting this one out of my sight," Lillian replied as she readjusted her shoulder bag and shook her sore arm.

"Why, what's in there?"

Lillian hesitated before answering. "A gold mine."

"Specifically?" Jennifer was now curious.

"I have ten pairs of Spanx in here."

Jennifer felt her lips freeze in a fake smile.

"What are Spanx again?" Dawn wanted to know.

"The chic, footless pantyhose," Claire reminded her.

Lillian went on. "I have three turbo footless tights, two magic knickers, and five body-shaping tights . . . and I'm going to sell them for double the cost and make a bundle."

Jennifer stared at her in amazement. "Who are you going to sell them to? The Alaskans?"

"What?" Lillian looked confused.

"Did it ever occur to you that it *never* gets cold here?" Jennifer pointed out. "Women would sweat to death in those things in this climate."

Lillian's face scrunched before she answered. "It was Derrick's idea. You know how he's into get-rich schemes."

"Like his ATM in the Florida swamp," Jennifer said.

Lillian continued as if she hadn't heard. "He drove all the way to Neiman Marcus in Minneapolis to buy them."

"Hard to picture Derrick at the pantyhose counter in Neiman Marcus," Claire said.

9

After they applied Dawn's ultra UVA protection (that was fortunately in her handbag and not her suitcase) and were situated on beach towels on the sand— Lillian atop her crocodile bag—the gang was silent for several minutes, taking in the scenery.

"The greens seem greener and the blues bluer than the glossy pictures in the brochure," Jennifer said, awestruck by the view.

Dawn was just as impressed. "The sand is so white and the water is so turquoise."

In the distance, the water was teeming with activities— sailboating, Jet Skiing, parasailing, snorkeling.

"I'm going to do all the water sports!" Lillian insisted.

"But you didn't pass the swimming test for the deep end of the community pool where we took our children to swim last summer," Dawn warned.

"I know, I know. I don't know what was wrong with that lifeguard guy. I made it across."

"They don't consider dog-paddling swimming, I guess," Dawn said quietly.

"That is so weird," Lillian said.

Jennifer stared at her.

"Lil, I think the water activities are fairly pricey," Claire pointed out.

"But this is an all-inclusive resort." Lillian displayed the bracelet that identified her status.

Jennifer set her straight. "The brochure clearly states 'all inclusive' means some drinks, food, a shower, and a bed. Bubbles Disco and water sports are on you."

"And I only have about fifty dollars to my name." Lillian sighed. "I'll just have to sell my Spanx."

Jennifer rolled her eyes.

Claire moaned. "Where do you suppose our luggage is?"

"Did anyone see the driver put our bags in the van?" Dawn inquired.

"No," Jennifer said.

"Call me ungrateful, but my mind cannot wrap around the fact that we are vacationing in the Caribbean without our luggage," Claire said, sounding despondent.

"Ungrateful," Jennifer said and chuckled.

Her humor had no effect on Claire's disposition.

❦

It was half past three when Becky met up with the over-heated ladies on the beach. "Don't shoot the messenger, but . . ." She stopped midsentence.

"But what?" Claire asked.

Becky decided the best way to say it was to say it outright. "Your bags are on their way to Kingston."

"Kingston?" Claire shrieked.

"What are we going to wear?" Dawn questioned meekly.

"The hotel has a boutique," Lillian said.

Jennifer shook her head. "A plain T-shirt is at least thirty dollars in that boutique. Can you imagine what a whole outfit would cost?"

"And the one credit card I have with me is the one with the lousy twelve-thousand-dollar limit," Claire said, sounding defeated.

"That will work," Jennifer said.

"Not when there's eleven thousand five hundred on it already." Claire's face twisted. "I just know Alex did that on purpose."

"The cheapskate," Jennifer teased.

I'm glad I don't have to answer to a man, Becky told herself and then felt a tug on her sleeve. She turned to see Claire staring at her. "What am I, a mannequin?"

"Bec, you're what, like a size five?"

Size five! What an insult. "Don't hit me, but I'm a size one."

"There's a size one?" Claire said.

Becky shook her head apologetically.

There was a lull in the conversation as all the women stared at Becky. She felt like she was under the microscope.

Finally, to her relief, the women turned their attention toward each other.

"We're all about size eight, right?" Claire guessed.

"I'm like a size eight *almost*," Lillian claimed.

No way is she a size eight, Becky thought.

Lillian smiled. "And since I have my luggage, I have plenty of clothes you guys can borrow. It will be just like high school." She frowned. "Except that no one ever traded clothes with me in high school."

They all stared at Lillian's colorful, mismatched outfit. It looked like it should be on display in an abstract art exhibition.

I'm glad I'm not in on this clothes share plan, Becky thought.

"We'll have to get by until our stuff gets here," Dawn said quickly.

"I'm buying new underwear; I don't care how much it costs," Jennifer said again.

"We can deal with the wardrobe details later. Let's go to our room instead of sunbathing in our clothes."

Becky grimaced.

"Our rooms are ready, aren't they?" Claire asked.

Becky had nearly forgotten about the complication. "Yes, but . . . There's been a sort of mix-up with our reservation. I ordered my own private room and two rooms for you guys to share."

"And . . . ," Claire urged her on.

"I got my room and an adjoining room. They said the hotel is overbooked, and there are no more rooms available."

"Oh, no," Claire said.

"Four of us in one room?" Jennifer said.

Becky bit on her finger. "I guess . . . uh . . . someone could share my room."

Dawn jumped in. "Absolutely no way. You paid for our vacation. You're getting your private room just like you ordered."

Becky wasn't sure what to say.

Jennifer sighed. "At this point I don't care as long as it's shade." She fanned herself with her hand.

"And a shower. I need a shower," Claire said, as she raked her fingers through her limp hair.

Becky tried not to look too happy.

❧

"Tell me again how Lillian rated the first shower," Claire said fifteen minutes later. Her pale blue eyes stared at the obscured view outside their window—a cement block wall—as she recapped the past three minutes. "I started my shower, reached for a bar of soap on the counter, turned around, and there was Lillian under my showerhead soaping up."

"She has a sand flea allergy," Dawn said in Lillian's defense.

"Did you see any sand fleas?" Claire asked, still staring.

"Well, no," Dawn admitted, arranging the bottles of some generic brand of Proactiv that Lillian had dumped on the dresser.

"How could anyone cram so much in two suitcases?" Claire, a neat freak, stared at the piles.

Jennifer held up an orange and yellow outfit with ruffles and sequins. "I think this beauty belongs to Daisy Duke."

"Lillian is on a budget, you know." Dawn's pale face tensed a little.

"If I were on a budget I wouldn't buy five hundred dollars' worth of Spanx, I know that," Jennifer blurted out.

"You're not being very nice," Dawn shot back at her.

"I know I'm not being very nice." Jennifer frowned. "I haven't been nice since the holiday season started. I have a terrible attitude and I'm tired and cranky and—"

"You two are giving me a headache!" Claire said, uncharacteristically short-tempered.

"I guess I'm not the only one not being very nice," Jennifer said.

Claire gave her a look and went back to staring out the window.

☙❧

Becky opened the door separating the adjoining rooms and pranced in wearing a flowery sundress. She was shocked when she looked around at the substandard room. Although her friends had seen her elegant room, she hadn't seen theirs.

"Oh, wow, I feel bad about my room."

She expected someone to jump in the way they had at the beach with some sort of reassurance that their accommodations were fine.

Claire was looking out the window. Dawn was busy folding clothes. Jennifer smiled, but it wasn't exactly the Mona Lisa smile Becky had hoped for.

"My room has an out-of-this-world view."

"We know." Jennifer's smile was still strained.

"And with the window open I can hear the sound of the crashing waves."

Claire turned to her. "We heard." She went back to staring out the window again.

"I feel terrible about it," Becky admitted. She looked to Dawn for support, knowing she could always count on her to give a selfless response. But Dawn was still obviously preoccupied.

"What's wrong with you guys?"

"Sorry, Bec. We're just in a bad mood," Jennifer said.

"Is it the room?"

"No, of course not," Dawn said.

Claire walked over to her, looking sweaty and miserable. "My winterized body isn't used to this heat, that's all."

Finally, Dawn came to the rescue again. She smiled sweetly. "It's not your fault the hotel messed up your reservation. You deserve every bit of luxury you planned."

"If you're sure," Becky said and looked intently at Jennifer.

"Of course we're sure. We wouldn't be here if it weren't for you," Jennifer said.

"It's a blessing just to be here." Claire settled the matter.

"Okay." Becky was satisfied and sat down on the bed. It was littered with clothes. "Why all the mess?"

"This mess is our new temporary wardrobe!" Claire said.

Becky didn't understand her tone until she examined the wardrobe more closely. "Oh."

Lillian came out of the shower just then in the only hotel robe, a towel loosely fitted over her hair. "Claire, did I hear you say you wanted to take a shower?"

Claire dashed into the bathroom.

Lillian did a double take. "Guess so."

❧

"Lil, how was your shower?" Becky asked.

"Wet," Lillian replied.

"I can see that. You're dripping water all over the carpet."

"Sorry." She towel-dried her shoulder-length, frizzy brown hair.

Dawn finished straightening up and gave a lingering sigh. "I'm so full from those snacks on the plane."

"Me too," Jennifer said and pushed the gift basket aside.

Lillian went over to the table and picked up her half sandwich and stuck it in Jennifer's face. "Want a bite?"

"No. I just said I was full."

Lillian offered the sandwich to Dawn, and she shook her head no.

"Bec?"

"No thanks."

Lillian sat down next to Becky, bit into the sandwich, chewed, and swallowed. "I'll bet you didn't know that the sandwich was invented by the Fourth Earl of Sandwich."

"Not in that specific detail. No," Becky said, looking away disinterested.

Lillian, unattuned to body language, continued. "See, he was playing this card game, you know, and—"

"Lil, can you save that story for later? I'm going to get a massage and then hit the beauty parlor for a manicure and a pedicure. Anybody up for it?" Becky addressed all the ladies.

"Me!" Lillian screamed.

Becky winced and rubbed her ear. "On your own dime, of course."

"How much of a dime?"

"Three hundred and fifty or so American dollars," Becky answered.

Lillian frowned.

"Anybody?" Becky gave one last chance.

They all shook their heads.

Becky stood up, stepped through the sliding door dividing the rooms, and then looked back. "I think I may get the seaweed facial and aromatherapy too. In fact, the full spa treatment. Better not wait up for me."

As soon as the door was shut, Lillian bounced on the bed. "I get dibs on this one since I like to be closest to the bathroom. Who wants to sleep with me?"

Jennifer leapt on the other bed like a flash. "I'm fast. I was on the track team."

"So was I," Dawn said and gave her the eye.

"So will you sleep with me, Dawn?" Lillian's optimistic eyes held out hope.

"Well, okay," Dawn smiled, and sat on the end of her new bed.

❧

Just as the ladies of Room 202 were all set to go on a shopping excursion, a torrential rain started up, changing their plans.

Dawn pressed her forehead against the window. "Our first day here and it's pouring."

"What do you do in paradise when you can't go outside?" Claire joined her at the window.

"We could stare at the amazing view of our brick wall," Jennifer suggested.

Lillian leapt from the bed and grabbed a flyer. "There's a circus workshop starting at seven o'clock. It says here it improves your general fitness, strength, and flexibility."

"I didn't fly all the way to Jamaica to take up the flying trapeze," Jennifer said.

"They have other stuff too. Like juggling and the trampoline. It's the only other free indoor activity they have this evening, except an aerobics class."

"Anything but aerobics or the circus," Claire said.

"I know, we could play charades then," Lillian suggested.

"Anything but aerobics, the circus, and charades."

"Oh, come on, Claire. Charades are a blast. Remember the time I was supposed to be Paul and you thought I was Noah." She chuckled.

"All too well."

"Okay then. Travel games. I have Bingo, Scrabble . . ."

"What's the featured movie?" Dawn asked.

"*Cool Runnings*," Jennifer said, having read the TV guide cover to cover. "I've seen it a million times."

"I haven't seen it," Lillian said.

Claire shook her head. "All I can say is the sun better be shining tomorrow morning."

10

hen Lillian turned the channel to the *Dukes of Hazzard* marathon at half past nine, Jennifer noticed the light coming from under Becky's door. She told the gang she was going in her room to keep her company for a while.

When their rousing game of Crazy Eights was over, Jennifer tiptoed back into her room and got into bed, being careful not to stub her toe in the dark or wake her sleeping friends.

"Good night, Jen." Lillian's voice boomed in the stillness.

"Good night, Lil," Jennifer whispered.

She settled into the saggy, lumpy mattress, wishing it were firmer. As tired as she was, she expected she would fall asleep anyway.

In the middle of Jennifer's prayer of thanksgiving, Lillian started up in a blast of loud snores.

"Ohmigosh"—she popped upright in bed—"call Homeland Security, people. We're under attack!"

No one was awake to hear her.

Unable to fall asleep, Jennifer prayed again. She exhausted memory verses she knew by heart, counted sheep, and when that didn't work, thought of some of the off-the-wall events in her life, hoping those thoughts would entertain her to sleep.

Her mind traveled around like a spaceship. The only place she would not let her mind go was to home. If she thought about Eric and Trevor, she might believe she'd made a big mistake by coming to Jamaica.

At one point she almost fell asleep, but then Lillian's snoring kicked up another notch.

For Claire's sake, she had been trying not to move, but now her body was uncontrollably wriggling, like a freshly caught fish on the bottom of a boat. She felt itchy and sweaty, and more stressed than ever.

Jennifer shook Claire awake and then asked her if she was.

"Do I look like it?" Claire asked sleepily.

"I don't know. I can't see you in the dark. But you sound awake." Jennifer sighed. "Listen to Lillian snoring like a jet plane."

"That is loud!"

"Do you recall her mentioning she was planning to torture us all night?"

Claire turned over and pulled her sheets up to her neck. "She and Martha always room together."

"I feel like I'm back at the airport." Jennifer held her head.

"I feel like I'm on the planet Venus," Claire said.

"Why, is that a noisy planet?"

"It's a HOT planet. Turn up the air conditioner," Claire moaned.

"We can't," Dawn's small voice piped in from her side of the room. "Lillian will get a chest cold."

"So, you're awake too, Dawn?" Claire asked.

Dawn stumbled over to the curtain and opened it partially

so some light from the walkway shone in the room. She sat down on the end of Jennifer and Claire's bed and sighed. "It'd be pretty hard to sleep through this."

"Kick her," Jennifer demanded.

"I can't kick someone just because she suffers from sleep apnea," Dawn said firmly.

"Let's get her her own room," Jennifer griped. "I'll even rob a bank if I have to."

"All the rooms are booked in this hotel. Remember?" Claire said.

"Besides it would hurt Lillian's feelings," Dawn whispered.

"We'd hurt her feelings?" Jennifer said sarcastically.

"Let's buy her some Breathe Right Strips tomorrow. They have them in the gift shop," Claire suggested.

"They don't work for snoring," Dawn said.

"Earplugs then." Claire wasn't giving up.

"I promise you I have tried every earplug known to man. In fact, every trick known to man. Sleeping with my iPod blaring, a thunderstorm soundtrack. None of it works except chopping off the head. And murder is strictly against my religion."

"How do you know so much about sleep apnea?" Claire asked.

Dawn leaned in closer. "Tommy snores when he's exhausted. And when he does, I sleep on the couch."

The noise pollution continued.

Claire suddenly sounded cranky. "Why did you get us up, Jen? Why?"

"You know I have trouble suffering silently."

"That's the understatement of the year. When Jennifer suffers, everyone suffers."

"Sounds completely fair to me," Jennifer said.

"Not to me." Claire rubbed her temples.

"You two are just like sisters," Dawn observed.

"People have been telling us that since grade school," Jennifer said.

Claire sighed. "And I've been denying it since grade school."

⌖

At 7:30 a.m., after less than five hours' sleep at best, Jennifer felt movement at the end of her bed and peeled her tired eyes open to witness Lillian jumping up and down on the saggy mattress.

"Were you thinking this is a trampoline?" she asked groggily. She sat up and noted a clear patch of sunlit sky out the dull linen curtains.

Lillian looked at her wide-eyed and eager. Her bright orange hand-sewn pants and matching sleeveless shirt reminded Jennifer of the outfits she saw on prisoners picking up trash on the side of the road. Only those were jumpsuits.

"No rain today. Maybe we can hit the Bouncy Boxing Ring," Lillian said enthusiastically as she examined the flyer that had come with the newspaper that was delivered earlier.

"Bouncy Boxing Ring?" Jennifer said. "Is this a resort or carnival?"

Lillian laughed heartily and went back to reading the flyer.

Jennifer slowly rolled out of bed.

Lillian ran over to the window and opened the curtain all the way. "It's so unearthly beautiful here! Like a picture postcard."

"I haven't seen many picture postcards of block walls," Jennifer said, raising her eyebrows.

Lillian jumped and landed and jumped and landed. "If you jump and crane your neck, you can see a patch of sky and sand and ocean."

"That's a little too much effort for me this morning." Jen-

89

nifer looked down at Claire who was beginning to stir. One look at her strained, sweaty face and Jennifer could see how uncomfortable she was.

"Lil, it's a hundred ten degrees in here. I beg you to turn the air conditioner on full speed!"

Lillian smiled. "Okay, but only during the day. If I get a chest cold I will be hacking all night and keep you guys awake. And I wouldn't want to do that."

"No, you wouldn't want to do that, would you?" Jennifer said, sharing a look with Claire who was fanning herself with one of Jennifer's magazines.

Lillian fiddled with the air conditioner.

"Good morning!" Dawn came out of the bathroom, sounding upbeat.

The usual morning greetings went back and forth.

Claire took her turn in the bathroom, and while Jennifer awaited her turn, the three roommates watched CNN.

After a few minutes, Lillian got restless. "Who wants to go wading in the surf with me after breakfast?"

"We have no bathing suits," Dawn reminded her.

"I just remembered I have an extra one-piece. It has little hearts on it," she said as incentive.

"Can I have a cup of coffee before I let you know, Lil?" Dawn said.

"Sure, I can't wait to try the Blue Mountain coffee myself." Lillian twirled, reminding Jennifer of a spinning top, and then continued her energetic dialogue. "I hear it's real strong and has an unmistakable aroma. Do you think the mountains are actually blue around here?" She took a shallow breath. "I mean, is that possible, or is it like some kind of reflection of the sun, or maybe the way the light plays or something. I can't imagine dirt being blue. Can you?"

Jennifer simply said, "No," not wanting to promote more monologue.

Lillian was blessedly quiet for several minutes as Jennifer and Dawn dressed in Lillian's saggy, baggy, outdated wardrobe. Then after a round of jumping jacks and toe touches, Lillian was visibly restless again. She took two oranges out of the fruit basket and threw them in the air. "Hey, I should join the circus," she crowed, as she performed her amateur juggling act.

Dawn was brushing her long hair. "You're good at it, Lil."

Lillian then took an apple and upped the ante to three pieces of fruit.

Jennifer looked over just as one of Lillian's oranges flew out of her grasp, sailed through the air toward Jennifer, and hit her right in the eye. Whereupon she promptly forgot about the Christian virtues she was aspiring to. "Thanks for the black eye!"

"Sorry—"

"You're not going to have a black eye, Jen," Dawn assured her, checking for certain.

"I'm sorry, I'm sorry, I'm sorry," Lillian cried. "Want me to get you some ice?"

Jennifer shook her head. "No, I'm the one who's sorry." She touched Lillian's shoulder. "It doesn't even hurt. Honestly. You just caught me off guard, and I'm tired."

"Jet lag," Lillian said, and Jennifer nodded as though she were in agreement.

"How about if I read a devotion?" Dawn, the peacemaker, took out her *Utmost for His Highest* devotional and turned to the date for some Oswald Chambers inspiration.

"That's a magnificent idea," Claire said as she came out of the bathroom.

Dawn began. "'And we know that all things work together

for good to those who love God . . .'" The verse seemed appropriate. "'It is only a faithful person who truly believes that God's sovereignty controls his circumstances . . .'"

An instant calm came over the group as Dawn read. Even Lillian settled down—for the time being.

11

E arly morning sunshine graced the terrace of the Seaside Restaurant affording its diners a clear view of the white sand beach. But the three women at the breakfast table were not watching the view. They were staring at Becky. She looked positively radiant after her full spa treatment. Her makeup was a warmer shade that brought out her golden skin tones, and her hair was cut short and layered. She looked at least five years younger. She felt great too.

"You couldn't look any better," Jennifer said.

Becky pulled out her compact mirror for a look. "Thanks, I think."

"You know what I mean."

She smiled. "Yes, I know what you mean."

"Seriously, you do look great, Bec," Dawn said.

Claire yawned. "Fantastic actually."

Becky, uncomfortable with the attention, turned the conversation around to her friends. "So how did you sleep in your cozy quarters?"

When no one answered, Becky looked to Jennifer. Her head was turned, and she was obviously looking for someone.

"If you're looking for Lillian, she's in line to order a custom omelet."

Jennifer eased into her cushioned chair. "So, did you hear her last night?"

"Hear her what? I was out like a light." Becky took a swallow of her juice. "So you guys didn't answer me. How did you sleep?"

"Like a log," Claire said.

"A log rolling down a mountain," Jennifer mumbled.

Becky looked skeptical. "I'm not sure I heard you right. Did you say—"

"Ignore her. We slept fine," Dawn declared.

"Good." Inwardly, Becky heaved a grateful sigh. She loved her room.

She turned her attention to her high-caloric feast and spread butter on her waffle, swirling on the maple syrup and loading on the whipped cream. One humongous bite followed another, and then she added more whipped cream.

Jennifer was smiling at her when she put her fork down. "Bec, your metabolism is a wonder."

She swallowed her mouthful. "I'd tell you it wasn't true if it would make you feel better."

"It wouldn't." Jennifer examined her own body. "I think I've expanded since Thanksgiving. Lillian's cowgirl outfit here almost fits me."

"So you're not going to eat that éclair on your plate then?" Becky said.

Jennifer picked up the breakfast dessert, bit into it, and rolled her eyes in pleasure.

Becky stared at the gang. Her eyes stopped on Claire. "There's something different about you besides those circus outfits you're wearing."

"Could it be that I look like I belong in the hospital with no makeup?" Claire raised one undrawn eyebrow.

"I'd offer you some of my makeup, but I have this thing about sharing makeup."

"One too many conjunctivitis videos?"

"Something like that."

"You can borrow some of Lillian's makeup," Dawn suggested, looking an even paler version of herself in Lillian's powder.

"What brand?" Claire asked.

"Most of the names are worn off," Dawn said.

"No thank you. I like to know what I'm putting on my face." Claire picked up Becky's compact from the table and examined her face. "If makeup didn't exist, I would never leave the house," she stated adamantly.

"Me either," Jennifer agreed.

"Does that make us shallow?" Claire asked.

"It makes us sallow." Jennifer laughed at her joke.

"I called the guys shallow."

"We are shallow. We left our families alone at Christmas to party in Jamaica," Jennifer said, matching the tone of her joke.

Becky found the conversation depressing. "You're not shallow. You're smart," she said, hoping they'd move on to another subject.

A middle-aged man decked out for the Love Boat walked by just then.

"That guy with the greasy blond hair who just slithered by was definitely giving you the eye, Bec," Jennifer said, wrinkling her face in palpable disgust.

Becky looked down at her plate.

"He has a button-down shirt and wiry chest hair," she added.

"Yuk," Claire said, stirring in her seat.

Becky was as disgusted as anyone. *I can't stand hairy men.*

"Can we cut the high-testosterone talk? I'm trying to eat here." Dawn dabbed her face with her napkin.

"What is it with men? How do they always know that I'm the single one of the group?" Becky asked.

"It's called a ringless finger," Jennifer said. "And men can spot it a mile away."

"Oh."

"If you found the right man, would you consider marriage?" Dawn asked.

It was a question Becky had heard countless times. "I've been waiting for the day when one of you was going to ask me that," she said.

"Well, you knew someone had to bring it up sometime. We want you to be happy," Claire said.

"I know."

Becky sighed heavily and was silent for a minute, weighing her thoughts. Knowing she was among friends, she decided to be honest with both herself and them. "If I found the right man, maybe."

After no one said anything, she started in again, this time with the list of specifications she had outlined in her head. "No dirt under the fingernails, must take the garbage out on a daily basis, have a sense of humor, and pray at meals."

"Oh, no, we forgot to say grace," Dawn interrupted and immediately said a prayer for the group.

When a respectful time had passed, Becky went on. "He has to be at least six feet tall. And a witty conversationalist. Have rock-hard abs." She thought and smiled. "And let me watch the Hallmark Channel anytime I want."

As long as she was being candid, she thought she might as well finish. "Oh, and most importantly, he must not wear a checkered sweater-vest." She made a face. "I hate checkered sweater-vests."

"Eric wears checkered sweater-vests when he dresses himself," Jennifer confessed.

"Dressing a man is precisely what I'm trying to avoid."

"Wow, you sure know what you want," Claire said.

Becky found herself nodding in agreement.

Dawn squinted at her. "I'm wondering if any man can meet your standard."

"All this talk is nonsense, regardless," Jennifer said. "It is highly unlikely Becky will meet someone of her strong faith and moral conviction here."

"True," Becky agreed.

"When we get back I'll introduce you to my butcher," Dawn offered.

"Is he the one with the overbite?"

"When he gets his braces off, he'll be really handsome."

Becky grimaced. "Someone else tried to fix me up with him." She was feeling more uncomfortable by the minute. "Did I say I'm interested in love? The last thing I want right now is to have a man messing up my near perfect life."

Her friends grew quiet, suddenly interested in their food.

⁂

Lillian joined the group with her plate of food, dropping loose grapes all over the place. She shook the table with her lumbering movements as she sat next to Becky.

She received a "watch what you're doing" look from Jennifer (half her cappuccino was now a stain on the white linen tablecloth).

By now Claire had dozed off.

Becky was eating again.

Lillian stuck her fork into the melted cheese and wound it

like spaghetti. She held it in midair and stared at it. "Gross. This is sharp cheddar or pravalani or something. I like Velveeta."

"Velveeta?" Dawn said, and sucked in her cheeks.

Lillian stared down at her omelet spilling out mushrooms, cheese, bacon, and bell peppers. "Besides, I can't eat this. I'm full." She set her fork down abruptly.

"You shouldn't waste food when people are starving in China," Jennifer said before grabbing a muffin out of the bread basket and buttering it.

"I don't think people are still starving in China. Or they wouldn't be having the next Olympics there." Lillian set the full plate on top of her other empty plate.

After a minute of silence Lillian prodded, "So what were you guys talking about while I was gone?"

"Uh . . . recipes?" Becky didn't feel like going into her love life again.

"Speaking of recipes, I think I'm going to go splurge on the cookbook I saw in the gift shop," Dawn said.

"I'll go with you if you promise not to discuss the male species." Becky took one last bite.

"I promise."

Dawn and Becky grabbed their purses and left the table.

"See ya," Lillian and Jennifer called together.

⌖

Claire was sound asleep with her mouth unattractively hanging open. If Jennifer had possessed the energy, she would have taken a picture with the camera phone Becky had left on the table. But she was so exhausted she didn't feel like moving or talking.

Lillian fidgeted. She picked up Dawn's pen and flicked it a few times and then poured water from one glass to another.

And then she tapped her fingers on the table. "I can't stand long pauses," she finally said.

"I'm fine with long pauses." Jennifer leaned back and crossed her arms, trying to give the impression of a fortress.

It looked like Lillian wanted to say something. And so Jennifer added a heavy sigh to her closed body posture to make the obvious even more obvious. "I'm just enjoying the salty air and the vitamin D my body has been craving," she finished, and closed her eyes.

"That reminds me of a funny story," Lillian said, and started in with a detailed account of how a three-legged dog named Blue—who was actually black—came to live with her one stormy November.

By the time her story was over, Dawn was back. She sat down and opened the plastic cover of her new cookbook.

"The End," Lillian announced proudly.

Jennifer's eyes snapped open. "That's a remarkable tale of courage, survival, and friendship," she said.

"What is?" Dawn asked, her blond head going back and forth.

"I can tell it again," Lillian offered.

Jennifer gave some obvious *I'll-kill-you-if-you-ask-her-to-tell-it-again* body language.

"That's okay," Dawn said and looked down again.

Jennifer glanced in the direction of the hotel lobby. "Where's Becky?"

"She's talking to the concierge about what she's going to do today."

Lillian pulled a bell pepper out of her omelet and ate it. "I talk to the *sea air* sometimes myself."

To keep from laughing Jennifer changed the subject. "There's so much to do on this island, isn't there?"

"If you have money," Lillian whined.

Dawn pursed her lips. "Becky needs to find a companion so she can do some of this stuff we can't afford to do with her."

Jennifer looked as though she had just smelled a foul odor. "Please don't encourage that, Dawn. This is the last place we want her to meet someone."

"What's wrong with her meeting someone here?"

"I subscribe to the Ten Star Women's Magazine Club. And let me tell you about these tall, dark, handsome strangers you meet on exotic vacations who turn out to be weasels."

"Tell us," Lillian encouraged.

"They take your money."

Lillian looked around the dining area. "And Becky has lots of that."

"Her finances are none of our business," Dawn said.

Jennifer agreed with a nod.

"So, I think I'll go swimming in the ocean . . . by myself . . . all alone." Lillian was bored and obviously hoped someone would join her.

Jennifer wasn't sure what she wanted to do, but she knew swimming wasn't it. Even if she had her bathing suit she wasn't that brave.

"I have my bathing suit under this." Lillian flipped her shirt up, exposing the top half of her gaudy fashion violation.

"You should go swimming," Dawn said, and looked down at her cookbook.

Jennifer tried to sound nice. "I don't know how you do it, Lil. I'd be lucky to make it to the sand. I am utterly exhausted."

"Jet lag," Lillian said.

Jennifer coughed. *The woman has no idea she is wholly responsible for my sleep deprivation,* she thought.

"I'm going then," Lillian said.

"Remember, it's not like the lake. There are waves," Dawn said.

"I know. I know." She stood up, her beach towel draped on her shoulder. "You guys watch my stuff, okay? And watch me in the water too."

"We'll wave every time the carousel goes around," Jennifer said and grinned.

"Jennifer, you are so funny. You must be related to Chonda Pierce," Lillian said as she shook her head back and forth.

"Nah, we just have the same mother."

Lillian's eyes got big. "Really?"

"No, not really."

Lillian chuckled, and off she went, bounding for the ocean.

Becky sat alone on the bench at the gazebo. She examined her new designer watch she'd bought in the gift shop a few minutes prior. She didn't need it or even particularly like it. It was too sporty for her.

She stuffed it back in the box. She'd give it to Clarissa, one of the candy stripers at the hospital. She would appreciate it.

Shifting her gaze to the beach, she spied a happy young couple in the crowd, playing in the ocean surf. They seemed so carefree.

Everyone seems to have someone. She sighed. *What did I expect? This isn't a singles resort.*

She watched a couple sail by on a catamaran, obviously enjoying themselves. *Most people have absolutely no clue how hard it is to meet Mr. Right. You get all gussied up for a night on the town, put on your best high heels, and let your expectations soar, only to be disappointed when you find out he's not your type—at all.*

Her last date had the audacity to tell her—after the salad arrived—that he would pay for her dinner if she paid for his dessert.

If a man asks you on a date he should pay the bill, she'd told Greta, the front desk registrar at the hospital.

Her response was that she was too picky.

I'm not picky. And if I am, I have a right to be. I'll know when he comes along. I don't need to settle for less.

A stray dog appeared at her feet. Skinny, malnourished, and with one ear. "I know, I know. I'm thirty-nine and no spring chicken anymore."

She fed him a piece of beef jerky.

"But, hey, I look pretty good for my age. Darn good, in fact."

12

Jennifer wondered where Becky had been off to for so long as she sat down in her same chair, glanced round the crowded table, and gave her friends a nervous smile. "We're on a holiday!" she said.

Jennifer picked up on the artificial tone immediately.

"Yes, we are," Dawn said, glancing up from her book momentarily.

Claire was now fully awake and overheated. "We must be on holiday, because we're not in Minnesota. That's for sure." She took a sip of water.

It seemed to Jennifer that Becky had something on her mind. "Everything all right, Bec?"

"Of course."

Jennifer didn't believe it. She was suddenly worried about Becky. She was the woman she most admired after Claire. She was independent and dedicated to her calling. Mature, stable, and responsible. The list went on.

A deep American-sounding voice came from behind. "Good morning, ladies."

The group responded instinctively, "Good morning."

Jennifer was taken aback. *Who does he think he is, barging in like this?*

As the stranger came around in front of them, Jennifer noticed Becky's eyes widen and remain glued to the tall, dark, and handsome stranger. This was the thrill of a woman meeting a man. Becky met lots of men on a regular basis, but never with this obvious a reaction.

"Have you seen my pet jellyfish milling about?" the visitor quipped.

"Now that's a classic line," Claire said, amused.

Everyone laughed but Jennifer. "We're married!" she said forcefully.

"I'm not married." Becky fluttered her eyelashes and sighed.

"I'm sorry, ladies, if I gave you the wrong impression. I'm not interested," he said, apparently confused by the mixed reactions.

"You're not?" Becky sounded disappointed.

He smiled. "Well, I didn't mean that either," he said.

Becky gave her biggest smile.

Jennifer's antenna went up. *Don't fall for it, Bec,* she cautioned her in her mind.

"I'm simply looking for a table, and you seem like a friendly group. I assure you I am perfectly harmless," the man said.

"And married?" Becky asked, keeping her voice even.

"As a matter of fact . . . no."

"How old are you?" Jennifer boldly asked.

"Forty-two."

"That's a perfect age," Becky said.

"There is no perfect age." Jennifer's radar was on high alert.

His emerald green eyes twinkled in the sunlight. "Now if you find me to be a suitable companion, perhaps you'd allow me to sit down. This plate is getting rather heavy."

"Oh, sure," Becky said and scooted over an inch. He took Lillian's empty seat and set his bulging plate down.

"So, are you staying here?" Claire asked.

"I volunteer at the mobile health unit," he said.

"I believe in volunteer work. Absolutely," Becky smiled.

"You look the type to do volunteer work," Jennifer said. "I'll bet you were a Boy Scout and a junior lifeguard."

"You joker, you." Claire kicked her under the table.

"Actually, yes," he said, seemingly unaffected by Jennifer's caustic manner. He looked directly at Becky. "What's your name?"

Becky gave him a blank look.

He rescued her by giving his name instead. "My name is Jonah Beach."

Nobody is named Jonah Beach, Jennifer thought. *He's making that up.*

"Oh . . . mine is Becky Holden." Becky had found her voice and her manners. She stretched out her dainty hand. He took it.

After several long seconds had passed and it was apparent neither infatuated party had any intention of letting go of the other's hand, Dawn made an unsolicited introduction. "And we're Dawn, Claire, and Jennifer," she said. "We're taking a vacation from Christmas."

Jonah finally let go of Becky's hand. "It's nice to meet you lovely ladies," he said, and smiled again at Becky.

Becky smiled wider than Jennifer had ever seen her smile.

Suddenly Jonah stood up. "Excuse me while I get myself a cup of coffee." He looked expectantly at Becky. "Can I get you ladies anything while I'm up?"

"No, thank you," Claire said. Everyone else was fine.

Becky displayed her empty coffee cup. "I'll come too, Jonah." She quickly stood up and they strolled off together.

When they were out of earshot, Jennifer sighed. "I can't believe she's even talking to that phony. 'Have you seen my jellyfish?'" she mimicked.

"I thought it was cute. In fact, it's just like Becky ordered him out of a catalog. He meets all her specifications."

Jennifer gulped the last of her cold cappuccino. "He doesn't look like the type to take out the trash."

"He's wearing a cross," Dawn said.

"Oh, well, a cross," Jennifer said, rolling her eyes. "Then he must have A-plus morals."

"You don't have to worry about Becky. She's not easily smitten," Claire said.

"Do you wanna bet? Look at her over there, practically falling over him at the beverage table." Jennifer inclined her head in their direction as Dawn and Claire turned to look.

"I think she tripped," Dawn said.

"If she did, it was on purpose," Jennifer said.

"I wouldn't blame her a bit. The man is just about perfect." Claire turned back toward her friends.

"I think he's way too formal with his 'rather' this and 'perhaps' that," Jennifer said. "Who talks like that unless you're from England?"

"He's classy," Dawn said, ending the conversation.

❧

Jonah picked at his food. Becky watched Jonah pick at his food. The ladies watched Becky watch Jonah pick at his food.

It was five past noon, and the outside dining area was getting as crowded as Lester's Diner in Lakeside when pot roast was the Early Bird Special.

Two middle-aged women with trays of pastries and coffee

planted their feet on the cement a couple of feet away from the group, obviously intent on taking their table.

Dawn suggested that maybe they should move along.

"Oh, have we been here long?" Becky asked and smiled her new perpetual smile. And then she asked herself how it was possible that she could have such feelings for a stranger.

≈

Jonah rented some umbrellas for the ladies and situated them in the sand a few yards from where Lillian was happily dog-paddling in the surf. He stood back and eyed his colorful arrangement.

"How's that?"

"It's wonderful. Thank you, Jonah," Becky said from under her shady shelter.

Jonah sat down at the end of her favorite extra-long towel.

"So what are you doing today?" Jonah addressed the group, not seeming to notice they were dressed in Lillian's vibrant array of colors.

"Watching our friend out there swim," Dawn said, applying another layer of Banana Boat.

"Which one is your friend?" Jonah asked.

"The one in orange," Becky said.

They watched a wave bulge and then recede.

"She looks like a buoy out there," Jennifer said.

"A boy?" Claire asked.

"No, not a boy. A buoy."

Jonah looked concerned. "The waves look swelled."

Lillian's arm gestured as the ocean surged. Jennifer took it as a wave and waved back.

"She looks like she's drifting out there. Is she a strong swimmer?" Jonah asked.

Dawn shook her head. "Definitely not."

Becky tore her sunglasses off. "She's dangerously close to the Jet Ski zipping around."

"She's definitely in some sort of trouble." Jonah stood up for a better look, his face alight with concern.

"She's just being friendly," Jennifer assured him.

Two seconds later, Lillian's scream contradicted her belief.

"Help! . . . Help!"

"Save our drowning friend!" Dawn looked frantic.

Jonah was already on his feet. In a few short, quick steps, he waded into the ocean, swam several powerful strokes, and grabbed the drowning victim.

"Ohmigosh, he probably was a lifeguard," Jennifer said, humbled for the moment.

*

Lillian lay prone on the sand. Jonah slipped his arm underneath her neck and prepared to perform CPR. Lillian choked and gasped, and then her eyes bugged out like a lemur's. Jonah assessed the situation and deemed her shaken but unharmed. "Your husband is a lucky man," he said.

Her pupils darted around as she lay in his muscular arms.

"I think he means because you're alive," Becky said.

Lillian looked up at him. "Who are you, some kind of superhero?" Her words were slurred.

"I'm afraid I can't disclose that," Jonah teased.

After coming to her senses, Lillian sat up. "The wave was holding me down. I thought I wasn't going to come back up."

Dawn wrapped a towel around Lillian's dripping body as Jennifer and Claire looked on.

"This is Jonah." Becky made the introduction.

"You saved my life, Jonah," she said gratefully. "May I take a picture of you for my memory book?"

"Uh," was all Jonah could say.

"Why don't you write it down in your journal," Jennifer said.

"Okay, I'll go get it."

"Not now, Lil."

"Let me check you over first," Becky said. She turned to Jonah. "You go dry off."

"I have a change of clothes in the mobile lab. I'll be back shortly," he said and trotted off in his wet cargo beach shorts and Ocean Pacific shirt.

After a thorough going over, Becky, too, deemed Lillian healthy. "You'll be fine. You just swallowed some salt water."

"I think you like that guy, don't you?"

Jennifer answered for Becky. "Of course not, Lil. He could be an ax murderer for all we know."

"Never mind," Becky said, giving Jennifer a look and Lillian a hug. Then she moved into supervisory mode. "Dawn, take Lil back to the room, get her in the shower, and then down for a nap."

"Ah, do I have to?" Lillian looked like a child who'd just gotten grounded.

"Yes," Becky said authoritatively.

"C'mon," Dawn urged, and the two headed down the beach.

13

Jennifer watched from a distance as Becky paced the length of her extra-long towel, attempting to regain her composure. She was about to go talk to her when Jonah returned. He was wearing a blue T-shirt and white beach shorts, and his dark, wet hair was slicked back.

They began talking.

The way the stranger was leaning too close for Jennifer's comfort made her decide to inch closer to the pair.

He glanced briefly in Jennifer's direction and then back to Becky, who smiled extraordinarily wide.

Jennifer pretended to pick up seashells as she searched his attractive form, trying unsuccessfully to find one single physical imperfection.

Three more big steps and she planted her feet in the sand and not so subtly eavesdropped on their conversation. She caught the last sentence. "Are you a nurse then?"

"Yes, I am," Becky said. "But now that I'm a supervising nurse, I don't handle many trauma cases." She hesitated. "Are you a doctor?"

"I'm a retired doctor," Jonah said.

Jennifer's past had tainted her view of doctors, and therefore, she did not trust them. She also doubted Jonah was telling the truth. She interrupted the private moment. "Are you a certified doctor?"

Jonah ran his fingers over his freshly shaven chin, obviously perplexed by the question. "Are there other kinds?"

"Well, you can get a certificate on the Internet pretending you're a doctor." Jennifer narrowed her eyes.

"Yes, you can. But that would be illegal," he said.

"What hospital do you work at?" Jennifer asked.

"I don't work at a hospital. I'm retired," Jonah replied. He seemed interested only in Becky, not in the awkward questions.

"I see." Jennifer's tone was peevish. She knew Becky wasn't happy with her, but she couldn't help it.

Becky looked squarely into Jennifer's earnest brown eyes. "I don't think you do!" she said.

Claire called Jennifer over.

"My friend wants me," Jennifer said.

"Good," Becky snapped, and then recaptured the moment with Jonah with a flirty smile.

Jennifer jogged over to Claire and plunked down on her towel. "What do you want?"

"Well, that was about as subtle as onion rings!" Claire said in a perturbed tone. "Especially after the man just saved Lillian's life."

"Oh, that." Jennifer laughed it off with random humor. "I'm trying not to mask my feelings. My therapist thought it would help."

"You don't have a therapist."

"I forgot I fired my therapist. She was driving me crazy. Ha."

"What's wrong with you?"

Claire crossed her arms and Jennifer crossed her eyes.

"Okay, okay, so I don't trust him for some reason."

"What reason?"

"He's got con artist written all over him."

Claire had the look of a strict teacher. "You're sounding ridiculously paranoid. Maybe you shouldn't have fired your therapist."

Jennifer gave her a blank expression and kicked the sand. For once, she had no comeback.

⮑⮐

Claire and Jennifer had a foot race to their hotel room, the way they used to race in grade school.

When they got near their room Claire made shushing noises. "Lil is probably asleep."

But Lillian was wide awake and writing in her journal.

"More to follow. Love, Lillian," she said aloud as she finished her entry.

Claire smiled. "I'm glad somebody's writing in their journal. I'm certainly not planning to write in mine."

Jennifer reached out and touched Lillian's knee. "Becky told you to rest."

"I feel all better now."

Dawn shrugged helplessly.

Lillian closed her journal with a snap and put it in the lampstand drawer. She pulled out a brochure and handed it to Jennifer. "I'm ready to go climb Dunn's River Falls!"

Jennifer scanned the brochure. "I don't know, Lil. Thirty minutes after your near-death experience, you want to climb a massive waterfall?" She looked at her and shook her head.

"Well, you know the old saying." Lillian winked.

"Which one?" Jennifer asked.

"When you fall off a horse you have to put your foot back in the stirrup and ride again." She tossed her head.

"Not to get technical, but I thought it was simply if you fall off a horse you have to get back on," Dawn said.

"That's what I said," Lillian claimed.

"I'm not sure what that had to do with anything," Claire said.

Lillian scrunched her forehead. "Besides, I've just faced my worst fear. Well, maybe not my worst fear. My worst fear would be tripping at the Mrs. American pageant. My second-worst fear is drowning. But I feel abominable." She grinned in triumph.

"Abominable like the Abominable Snowman?" Dawn asked.

Jennifer tilted her head. "I think you mean *invincible*."

"That's what I said. Invincible."

"My worst fear is vacationing without my luggage," Claire said.

◈

Persuaded by Lillian's enthusiasm, the four adventurers situated themselves in the shuttle bus an hour later with their backpacks.

"Have fun at the waterfall!" Becky called into their open window as she stood smiling with Jonah.

"We will," the group assured her.

"We'll see you later," Jonah said.

As the bus whisked them away, Jennifer began thinking about herself—again.

Originally, she had blamed her shifting moods all on Christmas. But here she was away from all holiday reminders, from the stress of shopping and pleasing people, away from the snow and cold and winter and bleakness and gray. And she still had the same empty feeling eating away at her.

She was sure now that it had little to do with her family.

Yes, Eric was a workaholic these days, and they could use a little more adventure. (Here she was, having hers.) And, yes, it was also true that Trevor was growing up and didn't need her as much.

Still, that wasn't it.

She pushed the thoughts aside as the bus pulled into a parking lot. The group exited the bus and stood in the potholed parking lot in the exhaust of the tour buses.

Jennifer watched Lillian struggle with her backpack.

"What's wrong?" she asked, though it was rather obvious.

"It's heavy." Lillian sighed in her dramatic way.

Jennifer was sure she was exaggerating. She had the same backpack the hotel had provided, and it wasn't that heavy.

Lillian sighed, another long and lingering sigh.

Jennifer waited a moment before she offered to carry her backpack.

"Well, okay." Lillian gave in easily.

"Wow, this is heavy," Jennifer said as she seized the bag.

"I told you."

"What's in here?"

"A towel and change of clothes."

"I have a towel and change of clothes, and it's not this heavy." Jennifer compared the two bags, one in each hand.

Lillian folded her arms. "Oh, and three pairs of Spanx."

"At fifty pounds each?"

"Oh, and my *Encyclopedia of Birds of the Caribbean* is in there too." She pulled the hardcover book from the backpack. "Becky sold a pair of my Spanx to a tourist from Canada, and I bought this bird book with the money."

"That's nice."

"I love birds, don't you?"

"Love 'em." Jennifer smiled, trying to be nicer than she felt. She slung the backpack on her other shoulder.

114

14

It was fifteen minutes later. Jennifer's feigned niceness was wearing off. Particularly since Lillian had refused to leave her backpack in the lockers with the other packs.

She was considering ripping it off her own back and dropping it at Lillian's feet to work it out herself when the tour guide stepped up. He was barefoot and his dreadlocks touched the collar of his official blue polo shirt.

"I welcome you to Jamaica," he said as he collected the cameras from his group to store in his waterproof plastic bag, and then continued. "Dunn's River Falls is da most famous and visited attraction in Jamaica. Da falls overflow right into da deep blue waters of the Caribbean—"

"Excuse me, Mr. Tour Guide." Lillian shot up her hand.

Jennifer cringed.

"You don't have to call me Mr. Tour Guide, ladee. You can call me Pete," he said.

"Okay, Pete."

"It's not my name, but you can call me dat," he said, expressionless.

"Is there a restroom?"

"You can use da bathroom when we finish our six-hundred-foot vertical climb." He laughed a reverberating laugh. "So try to hold it." He flung his dreadlocks back and continued.

Jennifer decided now wasn't the time to cause a scene about her being Lillian's personal attendant. She frowned at Lillian, who was now looking up at the falls, clutching her prized bird book. She seemed unaffected by anything going on around her. Jennifer sighed.

The tour guide continued, "Now, as I was saying . . . da falls overflow right into da deep blue waters of the Caribbean . . ."

The friends managed to be the first four links of the human chain. They held hands as they began the ascent up the cliff, single file in their rented rubber water shoes.

The rocks were slippery and hard to climb. Some older women Dawn had befriended gave up after a few steps and took the stairs instead. Jennifer thought about giving up too. She hadn't counted on getting wet.

Lillian stopped suddenly. The ten people behind her bumped up against each other. The mumble of complaint it drew went unnoticed by Lillian.

"Pete"—she opened her book—"is that bird over there a Jamaican vireo or a saffron finch?" She tried to match the full-color pictures with the bird perched on the branch.

The guide turned around. "Neither. It's a woodpecker. So watch your head." He cackled like Woody Woodpecker.

Lillian stood in the current, staring at her open book.

"C'mon," someone yelled at the back of the cattle drive.

Someone else joined the scolding. "You can take a tour of the enchanted gardens later. They have over three hundred species of birds."

"Can you draw me a map?" Lillian asked the tourist.

"Ladee, put dat book away and let's start moving," the tour guide ordered.

"You are ruining your book, Lil," Claire said.

Lillian closed it and handed it to Jennifer as though it were her responsibility.

"Why not just throw it in the waterfall, Lil. It's dripping wet already."

"I'll dry it in the sun later."

"After it breaks my back?"

"You're so funny."

"Hilarious."

Jennifer stuffed the damp book in the damp backpack and slung it on her shoulder. She struggled with the weight.

I'll think of this as an object lesson. The weight is like my personal baggage, she thought.

The same person in the back yelled again. "C'mon."

Jennifer labored up the trail.

They'd gone a few more feet when Lillian yelled, "Stop!"

Again, the domino effect.

"Is dare another problem?" the guide asked as patiently as he could.

"I want to take a picture and you have my camera."

He wiped his brow. "You want your camera to get soaked, ladee, you got it!"

He passed it over.

"Thank you," Lillian said, and called for a group photo.

After the crammed photo session with her irritated friends' strained smiles, Lillian returned the camera to the tour guide.

His thick brows met in the middle of his forehead. "All done?"

"Yes, sir."

He wiped the water off her camera with his shirt and returned it to the waterproof bag, shaking his head. "Shamu the whale couldn't have done a better job of getting your camera wet."

"How do you know Shamu?" Lillian asked.

He glared slightly. "Can we continue, now?"

Lillian smiled. "Of course."

"I'm so embarrassed I'm ready to jump in the waterfall," Jennifer mumbled under her breath, fed up with Lillian. She decided it was time to give Lillian her backpack back and handed it to her as the line started moving again.

Lillian accepted it reluctantly. "My ankle is hurting," she complained in Jennifer's ear.

"And my back is hurting," Jennifer said over her shoulder.

Things moved along well for a few minutes as they continued up the cascading waterfall, enjoying the spectacular beauty.

And then Lillian said she spotted a Doctor Bird and wanted to go after it.

"Ladee, if you promise not to chase da birds, I'll pull you a feather from a Least Pauraque," the guide said with a sarcastic edge to his voice.

"Sor-ry!" Lillian said and then whispered to Jennifer, "I wonder what a Least Pauraque is. I can't wait to look it up in my encyclopedia."

When Lillian stepped on Jennifer's heels for the fourth time and didn't notice, she shrieked, "Ouch!" in hopes that Lillian would be more careful.

"I know. There are lots of bities around here," Lillian said. "That means bugs in Australian, in case you didn't know."

Jennifer couldn't believe how clueless Lillian was. "Thank you for that fascinating fact."

❧

The guide was hanging around with his outstretched hand fixed in position after the tour.

Lillian tried to make a joke. "I'll take my feather from that bird you mentioned."

"Sorry, ladee, but da Least Pauraque has been extinct for over one hundred fifty years," he informed her. "But I'll take my tip," he said, pushy, but smiling. He gave them a mock bow.

Lillian dropped a couple of coins in his hand. As he looked up, his expression made it clear he was livid at the inadequate tip.

"Lillian did cause him a lot of trouble," Jennifer whispered in Claire's ear, fumbling in her purse for change.

Claire took out a couple of bills, and the tour guide grabbed them. In exchange, he gave her Lillian's camera.

Off he went.

"Where did he go?" Lillian asked when she looked up. "I was going to give him a Christian tract."

Claire returned Lillian's digital with no explanation.

Lillian's face contorted when she saw how wet it was.

"I think your camera is ruined," Dawn said. "You should have bought a waterproof camera."

Claire, drenched in Lillian's vintage, funky, red-rose shorts set, didn't seem all that unhappy about it. "No more pictures, oh well."

"We'll have to go with the pictures Becky is taking on her camera phone," Jennifer said.

Lillian stared at the piece of wet equipment, made a funny laugh, and said with conviction, "I'll pray over it and it will be fine."

"Let's change our clothes in the bathroom." Dawn steered her toward the dressing rooms.

"Oh, yeah. I forgot I had to go to the bathroom, like, twenty minutes ago."

When the gang returned to the hotel room around four, they found a note from Becky that read MEET US ON THE BEACH.

"What's with the 'us'?" Jennifer said. "A few hours together and now they're an 'us.'" She picked up the note, crumpled it, and threw it in the trash.

"I suppose she could have said, 'Meet me and the good-looking stranger on the beach'?" Claire said.

"He is good looking," Lillian remarked with a wistful smile. "Almost as good looking as Brad Pitt. He's the one with lots of muscles, right?"

"No, the one with lots of muscles is Arnold Schwarzenegger," Jennifer said with a wry smile.

"The fashion designer?"

"Goodness, I hope not."

The gang met up with Jonah and Becky on the beach a few minutes later, all wearing a fresh assortment of Lillian's clothes. Jonah had his arm wrapped around Becky's shoulder, and they stood a few feet away from a raging bonfire that he, no doubt, had started to create a special mood (since it was nearly ninety degrees and ridiculously humid). He was singing her a sentimental song.

They looked alarmingly like a couple, and this disturbed Jennifer. She was even more disturbed when Becky announced she had some good news to share.

Oh, no, not already! Jennifer's mind flashed back to the article she had just read about a man who met a woman, saved her life, and proposed to her all in the same day. *I can't let this happen!* She could feel the panic rising.

Becky's next words put an end to her temporary insanity.

"Your luggage will be here tomorrow," she said, throwing her arms wide in a generous arc.

Jennifer heaved a sigh of relief.

Dawn danced around.

Claire was the happiest, as she broke out in song. "Tomorrow, tomorrow, I love you, tomorrow!"

Only Lillian looked disappointed. Her shoulders slumped.

Jennifer touched her arm. "Lil, you look like you've lost your best friend."

"I liked sharing clothes. It was fun to be one of the girls."

"You're one of the girls," Jennifer said and tried to mean it.

Dawn danced over to Lillian.

She's so much better than me at being nice, Jennifer thought.

"C'mon, Lil! Let's try playing Giant Chess in the garden area."

"The one with the huge black-and-white checkerboard straight out of Alice in Wonderland?"

"Why not. It's free."

Lillian's mood improved in a nanosecond, and she went off smiling with Dawn.

Jennifer's mood worsened just as rapidly as Lillian's had improved. Her eyes were fixed on Jonah as he impulsively grabbed Becky's hand. They started running down the beach together, looking like a happily married couple.

Jennifer's lips spread into a pout.

"That is so cute," Claire exclaimed.

"Until he breaks her heart." Jennifer crossed her eyes and her arms. So much had happened since this morning. She was feeling such a wide range of emotions it was hard to put her finger on one in particular.

"Let's put Becky's love life on hold for the time being, Jen. Wouldn't you rather watch the orange Caribbean sun sink into the ocean?" Claire started toward the water, then turned and motioned for her to follow.

"Yes, I would," Jennifer said, but she didn't move. It was obvious she was in la-la land.

Claire stopped and faced Jennifer. "What's wrong? Is it Becky?"

"Yeah."

"I think there's more to it than Becky."

"Like what?"

"I don't mean to hurt your feelings, but you get moody every Christmas."

Whether or not it was true, Jennifer did not like the sound of that. "No, I don't." She started walking past Claire toward the water.

"I don't mean it as an accusation. I'm just concerned," Claire called after her.

Whatever, Jennifer thought. She turned around. "Be concerned about Becky," she said, and went on walking.

"Becky is having the time of her life."

Knowing she was being a brat, she slowed and stopped until Claire caught up to her. "Sorry for being defensive. I know I get weird at Christmas."

Claire nodded to indicate she was listening.

"But I don't know why."

Claire looked out toward the sunset. "I think you probably do."

Jennifer's brown eyes glanced in the same direction. She was right. They ended up talking about it every holiday season. They'd talked it to death. And she wasn't going to talk about it anymore.

"One word, ten letters," Claire said, her blue eyes still looking ahead.

Jennifer sighed. Obviously Claire was not going to let it

go. She decided to play along. "It can't be the Grinch, that's only six letters."

Claire laughed.

Jennifer tried to.

Their eyes met. The way Claire was looking back at her made her feel as though the whole world was standing still, waiting for her to reveal the real answer.

"Stepfather," she uttered.

Claire stared at her expecting something more.

"Please, let's not go there," Jennifer said.

Claire smiled compassionately.

There was silence.

"I think that's the most beautiful sunset I've ever seen," Jennifer said after she could stand the silence no more. "I wish Eric was here to see it." She meant it.

Jennifer waited for Claire to say she wished Alex were here too.

Instead, Claire's face was now etched in pain.

What a pair we are, Jennifer thought.

Another moment of silence passed as both women pretended to be spellbound by the sunset. Finally, Jennifer was so uncomfortable with the whole situation that she brought up the subject of the Jamaican croaking lizard, a reptile she knew very little about.

၈၄၃

After dinner, Jennifer stood alone on the beach in the dark, mindlessly listening to the restless water lapping against the shore.

A tall figure approached her. By the smell of her sweet perfume, she could tell it was a woman.

"Stuff goes on after dark you don't want to know about.

You should go to da hotel lobby if you want some privacy."
She sounded genuinely concerned.

"Thank you. I'm sure you're right."

Although she hadn't come across them personally, Jennifer had heard about the "hustlers" who harassed you on the beach or anywhere away from the resort.

"My name is Felicia."

She thought the voice sounded familiar. "You're our maid, right?"

"Dat's right."

Jennifer couldn't see her face. "Thank you for the extra towels," she said.

"I take good care of you." And with that comment, she was gone.

Jennifer heeded the maid's advice and moved to the hotel lobby—the only place at the resort this time of night that wasn't noisy. She sat in a comfortable chair near the fountain and situated her red-and-white-checkered handbag at her feet.

Immediately she started thinking about the past. Suffering from memories she couldn't forget.

She tried to distract herself by people watching, which she always found entertaining. And yet, unwillingly, her mind bounced right back to where it started. Now the memories were becoming overwhelming, a boulder in her path to peace. They all had to do with that powerful, ten-letter word Claire just had to bring up. STEPFATHER.

The last time she had seen the "cold-blooded reptile" (as Eric called him on her behalf) had been Christmas Day when she was nineteen. Jennifer was in her first year at college, an English major happily living in the dorm, and so sure of herself. Brave and hopeful, she decided she could no longer stand by helplessly and watch her mother be caught in her stepfather's web of deceit. Every word he uttered was a bald-faced lie.

Not that her mother wasn't aware. When they were dating she'd found out he was lying about being a doctor, and still she had forgiven him.

Shakespeare was right in her case. Love was blind.

On that unforgettable Christmas morning Jennifer had the evidence in hand. She knocked on the door, and the second her mother answered she presented the bank statements she had managed to talk a bank teller into copying for her. "Where did all of Daddy's money go?" she said directly. "There's less than a thousand dollars in all three joint accounts."

Ron Martin suddenly appeared, and her mother confronted her husband. An argument ensued.

Ron left—for good. But not without taking all the Christmas presents from under the tree, the ones that he had bought with her mother's money. None bought out of love, only to appease.

From that day on, her mother was a different person. Soon after, she had a nervous breakdown. Because she couldn't support herself, Jennifer quit school. Entrenched in sorrow, she willingly buried her dreams for the future with her mother's illusions of the past.

Jennifer struggled financially until she met and married Eric at twenty-two. And then they struggled together to care for her mother. Eventually the state took over her mother's care. Before Trevor had been born, she was placed in a group home run by a caring couple who now attended her church.

Long ago Jennifer had forgiven her and accepted the fact that her mother was incapable of maintaining a normal relationship with her.

The last time she had visited her mother she didn't even acknowledge that Jennifer was there. She only stared out the window and talked about Ron as though he had been her savior.

Jennifer tried to remind her of the happy, happy times they had when her father was alive.

"Ron, I miss Ron," her mother said, even louder.

"Do you want me to come back?" she asked as she was leaving.

"Only if you bring Ron with you."

Some rowdy guests passed by on their way out, jolting Jennifer back to the present.

No wonder I don't want to think about my past. Jennifer sighed. *How depressing.*

Frustrated, she grabbed the journal and pen out of her purse in one swift motion. She turned to a random page and scribbled.

EVICTION NOTICE

Ron Martin, you are hereby evicted! You are no longer permitted to rent space in my brain. Cease and desist messing with my head.

She lifted the rainbow journal and held it to her chest, took a long deep breath, and dumped it in the nearest trash receptacle.

"Sorry, Bec, but it's served its purpose," she said aloud.

Clicking her pen furiously she told herself, *No tears, no fuss, no problem, mon.*

Claire tugged at her shirt, startling her. "Where have you been? I've been worried sick about you!"

Jennifer smiled wide. "Nothing, just people watching."

"What people? There's no one in here right now."

"Okay, hotel lobby watching." She shrugged.

"Well, don't scare me like that again."

"Yes, mother," Jennifer said.

Just after ten o'clock, the hotel room's adjoining door slid open and the ladies watched Becky glide in. Her glowing face complimented the stunning calf-length red dress she wore.

"How was your romantic dinner under the stars?" Claire asked.

"Wonderful. Jonah Beach is the most perfect man I've ever known." Becky sighed, floated back in her room, and slid the door closed before anyone could get a word out.

"Isn't that sweet," Dawn said.

Claire agreed. "Becky and Jonah are adorable together." She and Dawn smiled at each other.

"Aren't you guys going a little overboard?"

"Do you think if they get married, Becky would choose me for her saint of honor?" Lillian asked out of the blue.

Jennifer exhaled slowly. "You mean matron of honor?"

"I always thought it was 'saint.'"

"Well, it ain't."

"Really?"

"Yes, really."

A mental fashion show of Lillian's possible picks of ugly bridesmaid dresses paraded through Jennifer's mind. It was quite funny.

Dawn sighed. "Just think, Becky finding the man of her dreams in such a place."

That was not at all funny to Jennifer. "I believe we had this discussion earlier today," she said, eyes narrowing.

Claire looked at Jennifer. "What discussion?"

"I think you were asleep."

"What discussion?" Lillian asked.

Dawn answered for Jennifer. "You remember, Lil. The 'men who you meet on exotic vacations turn out to be weasels' talk."

127

Claire crossed her arms. "If he's a weasel, I'd like my sister to meet his brother. If that makes sense?"

"It doesn't," Jennifer said.

"Oh, yeah, he doesn't have any family."

"So he says."

"What is a weasel anyway?" Lillian asked.

"Something like a wolverine," Dawn said.

"What is a wolverine?" Lillian asked.

"We studied wolverines last month in our home school unit," Dawn said.

Jennifer couldn't help herself. "Trevor did a report for school last year. They're extremely aggressive and nasty tempered."

Claire was giving her a look. Jennifer knew she wanted her to keep quiet. But she couldn't.

"Did I mention they're terribly clumsy?"

Claire glared this time. "Jennifer, please stop with the Jonah bashing."

Jennifer knew she was behaving badly. Her mind had cemented off all thoughts of her stepfather, refusing to see any relation between her feelings toward Jonah and her own experiences. She was convinced her concerns came from what the magazines said. "I can't help but have a niggling feeling about him that won't go away."

"Pray it away."

"I'm trying."

"You're not."

When the head wagging ceased, Lillian asked the predictable question. "What does niggling mean?"

Jennifer laughed and felt her sense of humor return. "Lil, I'm going to buy you a brand-new set of encyclopedias on your next birthday so you can look your questions up yourself."

"Really?"

Jennifer shook her head. "No, not really."

15

Lillian had acquired a slight head cold. Her snoring was worse than the previous night—louder and more obnoxious.

She was sprawled out on the bed comfortably while poor Dawn hung precariously off the edge.

Suddenly, Dawn dropped on the floor with a loud plunk.

"Are you alive down there?" Jennifer called to her, jolting Claire awake.

"Yeah." She moaned. "This is worse than sleeping with a toddler. I've got an inch of space, if that. Can I get in bed with you guys?"

"Sure," Jennifer said and squished in closer to Claire.

Dawn found her way to the bed in the pitch black and secured her position. The threesome tried to settle in.

Claire broke the silence. "This bed has to be a double."

"I don't even know if you could call it a double," Dawn said.

Jennifer, in the middle, felt claustrophobic. This was not going to work. "No offense, Dawn, but three people in one bed? This is nuts."

"I have a friend who's into this family bed concept," Dawn said.

"Well, your friend is certifiably insane," Jennifer said.

"My friend is a family therapist."

"Take her number down, Jen," Claire teased.

"Maybe tomorrow. I'm too exhausted."

They lay flat on their backs in silence—three in a row, like sardines, with no room to move whatsoever.

"I know this is uncomfortable, but let's try to fall asleep," Dawn urged.

After a few excruciating minutes of unrest, Jennifer said, "Becky's bed is twice this size, you know."

"I know," Claire said.

"But it's her bed, not ours," Dawn said, selfless as ever.

Lillian's noise level increased.

"I wonder what that girl is dreaming about," Claire said.

"Probably running through a field of daisies. I'm jealous," Jennifer said. "If I were asleep, I'd be dreaming about being entombed between two massive stone blocks."

"Thanks for the *huge* compliment. Good night," Claire said and rolled onto her side.

"Good night," Dawn said.

"Good night, Mary Ellen." Jennifer ended the exchange.

The next several minutes the ladies gave it another good try.

And then Jennifer had enough. She sat up, grabbed her pillow, and threw it at Lillian, which had no effect on her target except to make her turn over and snore even louder.

"That wasn't smart. Now you have no pillow," Dawn said.

"Don't you think I know that?" Jennifer clenched her fists and sighed. "I'm going to tear my hair out by the roots if she doesn't stop snoring. I tell you, she is intent on making my life miserable."

"Calm down, Jen. She's asleep. How can she be intent on making your life miserable when she's asleep?" Claire said. But after listening for another moment, she retracted her statement. "On second thought you may be right. Lillian and her aversion to air-conditioning. It's as hot as Haiti in here."

"Or Jamaica," Dawn said.

Again, they were silent as they listened to Lillian's annoying concert.

Jennifer spoke forcefully. "I can't take a second more of this. I say we go sleep in Becky's room. She won't even notice."

She pushed Dawn to her feet and fumbled for the lamp to turn it on low. She headed toward the door. "Come on, Claire. Leave the light on. Lil won't wake up anyway."

Jennifer inched the door to Becky's room open like a sleuth. Dawn followed close behind her, and Claire carefully closed the door.

The room was lit by the glow of a night-light across the room.

"A scented night-light. She gets all the perks," Jennifer whispered.

"Apple Cinnamon," Dawn's nose determined.

"Or is it Cinnamon Apple." Jennifer sniffed.

Becky was on her side near the far edge of the bed, facing the wall with headphones on.

The three intruders stood for a moment listening to Lillian's snoring, now a distant battering. They looked for any movement from Becky to be sure they were undetected. She appeared to be deep in dreamland.

Without speaking, each knew instinctively which spot to take on the humongous, circular bed.

Claire slid onto the end near Becky's feet, Dawn took the middle, and Jennifer the edge.

"Ah, this is one of those foam memory mattresses that molds to your body," Claire whispered as she settled in comfortably, enjoying the cool breeze from the ocean. "You can practically jump on it and it doesn't move."

"'Do you find yourself tossing and turning at night? Our viscoelastic mattress—'"

"Jen! You read too many magazines."

"And that's why I'm so smart."

"You guys, we should stop talking before we wake Becky up," Dawn whispered.

That thought, along with the lull of the waves, quieted them.

Within minutes the parties were enjoying the sleep of the sleep deprived.

⚬↶↷⚬

Two hours later, Dawn was awakened by a rattling in the corner. Rattling she suspected was a mouse.

Last year, in her old Victorian house in Lakeside, a mouse appeared, so loud and pesky they named him Templeton (even though Templeton was actually a rat). Dawn talked Tommy into a cat whom they named Cheshire, and Templeton became his prize. Problem solved. That was until her mother-in-law, Edna, moved in and claimed she was allergic to cats (though oddly she had no symptoms), and Cheshire went to live in Dawn's mother's house to take care of her mice.

Dawn despised the inhumanity of mouse traps, so now she lived in fear of mouse invasion. Thus, her paranoia of mice had recently intensified.

She sat up with a start, drew her knees under her gown, and hugged herself, too afraid to look at the source.

132

After a few tense minutes of listening, she shook Jennifer awake. "Jen. Jen."

"What!"

"I'm sorry to wake you up, but there's a rodent of unusual size in the corner nibbling."

Jennifer rubbed her eyes. "Jamaica is an island. How would mice get on an island?"

"There are cruise ships."

"You have a point there."

Jennifer then heard the noise. It came from the corner not far from the bed. She noted the silhouette of the creature perfectly lit by the glow of the night-light. "It's a mouse, alright."

Dawn tried not to squeal.

"But who cares. It's better than roaches."

Dawn shuddered as Jennifer went on, "Let the poor little guy satisfy his munchies. He's quieter than Lillian's snorefest. I'm going back to sleep before Becky wakes up."

A minute later Dawn whispered in Jennifer's ear. "Can mice climb, Jen?"

"Go to sleep, you paranoid rodent freak!" she muttered under her breath.

Dawn tapped her shoulder. "What did you call me?"

Jennifer turned toward her. "Nothing, Dawn. I just need to get some sleep."

"I'm sorry, but I can't stand it. I'm going back in the other room. Will you come with me?"

Jennifer sighed noisily.

"Before you wake up Becky . . . yes, I'll come with you."

"Me too," Claire whispered. "And, yes, mice can climb."

Dawn's eyes grew wide with disgust. "What if it runs this way?"

"Someone has to turn on the light or we might step on the thing," Jennifer said.

"When I count to three, we'll all get up at the same time and Dawn will turn on the light." Claire pointed to the nearby lamp.

"Okay," Dawn agreed.

They prepared themselves for the simple plan.

"One, two, three." Jennifer was the first to hop off the bed.

They scrambled for the light switch. Dawn forgot she was supposed to turn on the light. Claire managed to turn it on as they all danced around, peering toward the corner.

Dawn watched the mouse scurry away. It wasn't a large mouse at all; in fact, it was harmless looking. She felt bad for all the fuss she had caused.

The ruckus woke Becky up with a start. She pulled up her eye mask and ripped her headphones off. "What are you guys doing in my room?"

Everyone froze.

Claire did a tap dance. "Would you believe we're training for a career as Irish clog dancers?"

"No."

"Would you believe I'm looking for chocolate?" Jennifer smiled, and Dawn elbowed her.

"From anybody else, no. From you, Jen . . . yes."

Becky gathered the sheet and wrapped it around herself. "You'll find a chocolate bar on top of my dresser. Now turn off the lights and go away! You're interrupting my beautiful dream."

"Dr. Jonah Beach Livingston, I presume," Claire said.

"Just go away so I can reconnect with my dream," she said, replacing her headphones and eye mask.

Jennifer grabbed the chocolate, Dawn turned off the light, and the ladies darted into their adjacent room.

Claire slid the door closed.

16

Jennifer sat next to the light in their room and tried to read the chocolate bar to see what brand it was.

"Did we just tell Becky a white lie?" Dawn said.

"It was omission. It doesn't count." Jennifer squinted at the chocolate bar.

"Yes, it does count."

"You're right. Does that mean I have to give the chocolate back?"

"I don't think so. But we should've told her about the mouse."

Jennifer thought about it. "No sense in freaking her out. We'll call maintenance tomorrow." She paused. "Besides, I don't think even a mouse could disturb her right now."

"I want the fresh air in Becky's room," Claire moaned.

Lillian's shrill voice startled them. "Are you guys having a party without me?"

Dawn was caught off guard. "A party?"

Lillian spotted the chocolate Jennifer was clutching like a treasured possession. "Goodie. Can we make s'mores?" she cried.

Dawn scratched her head. "I do have graham crackers."

"We'll have a slumber party!" Lillian exclaimed.

"I think Becky has some marshmallows left over from our roast on the beach." Claire shook her head. "Did I just say that?"

"I'm not going back in there," Dawn said.

"Going back in where?" Lillian asked.

Jennifer sat on the bed next to Lillian still clutching the chocolate bar.

"I'm not sure about that chocolate, Jen. We don't know where it's been," Dawn said.

"In the wrapper, duh." Lillian squinted.

Dawn unfettered the bar from Jennifer's tight fingers and checked it under the lightbulb for teeth marks.

"Oh, c'mon, Dawn. Don't be ridiculous."

Jennifer watched Dawn dump her treat in the trash can.

"Sorry, we can't be sure."

"I was absolutely craving that chocolate."

"I know, but we can't chance it."

"Okay," Jennifer said.

Lillian was trying to piece it all together. "You guys are really weird in the middle of the night," she observed.

"I have a very good reason to be weird." Jennifer raised her eyebrows.

They sighed collectively.

Dawn got into bed.

Claire prepared to do the same.

Jennifer was ready to turn off the light when Lillian yelled, "Wait, Jen!"

She froze.

"I want to have a pillow fight. Oh, please, can we have a pillow fight?" Lillian made a puppy dog face. "I've never had a pillow fight in my whole life."

Jennifer looked at the digital clock that read 1:54 a.m. "Would that be fun?"

Lillian scratched the top of her head. "Of course."

"Sorry, Lil, I love you, but I'm not engaging in a pillow fight in the middle of the night." Dawn positioned her pillow over her head.

Claire fanned herself and grimaced. "I'll make you a deal. If I can turn up the air-conditioning we'll have a pillow fight."

"Well . . . okay," Lillian agreed, and Claire dove for the thermostat.

Jennifer plowed Lillian with the pillow she had thrown at her earlier.

Lillian giggled as though it were a treat.

Jennifer plowed her again.

Lillian giggled again.

"You're not getting the concept, Lil," Claire noted from the sidelines. "You're supposed to hit her back."

Jennifer plowed her with the same pillow four more times.

"Close your mouth, Lil"—Claire picked up her pillow— "don't want you to bite your tongue." She hit her smack in the face with the pillow.

Lillian staggered, a dazed look on her face. She shook her head and giggled again.

"Let's go to sleep now, please," Jennifer said as she and Claire hopped into bed.

"You know, I'm so rested I feel like it's already morning," Lillian said.

Jennifer kicked Claire under the sheets.

"Ouch!"

❧

Jennifer was sitting on the edge of the bed feeling the effects of another night of lost sleep when Lillian tapped her on the shoulder. She was too tired to be startled. Lillian had been the last thing she had seen last night, and here she was again, with that same zany expression she'd had on her face at 2:00 a.m.

"So how are you feeling this morning?"

Jennifer looked at her and shrugged.

"Cranky?"

"Way cranky."

"I'll bet it's the spicy goat curry you had yesterday. Is your stomach doing flip-flops?"

Jennifer moaned. "Now that you mention it . . . yes."

Dawn came out of the bathroom. "I'm ready."

Lillian picked her orange, flowered beach bag up off the floor.

"We'll meet you guys at The Church on the Beach our nice maid recommended," Dawn called over her shoulder as they left.

"I almost forgot it was Sunday," Jennifer said, as her eyes rested on the same stale outfit she'd be wearing again this morning, draped over the crooked hanger in the wardrobe.

Claire emerged from the bathroom showing her pearly whites. "I can't wait to use my Oral-B Professional Care tooth-brush again," she said.

"I can't wait to get my special grip tweezers back so I can rip this stubby hair out of my chin."

"If a stubby chin hair is the extent of your problems, that's something to be thankful for."

"Well, it's not. My mouth is my problem."

Claire's expression was blank. After a long pause, she said, "I know. You have a persistent rebellious streak these days."

Jennifer didn't feel as repentant as she wanted to.

"So you noticed I've been . . . a little off?"

"Noticed? Like the Leaning Tower of Pisa is a little off, I noticed."

There was a pause.

"Claire, I want to apologize."

"You want to or you are?"

"Okay, I am apologizing."

"Then I forgive you."

"For what?"

Claire threw her hands up in the air. "Jennifer, sometimes you are completely maddening."

"But you love me anyway."

"True."

17

Claire and Jennifer walked up to Lillian and Dawn standing under the thatch roof on the beach, under the sign that said CHURCH SERVICE TODAY AT 10:00.

"We're running on Jamaican time, I guess," Jennifer said.

"I guess," Dawn said.

"Where's Becky?"

"Remember, she's having breakfast with Jonah. He goes to this church, but he has to work in the mobile lab today."

"So he's a churchgoing retired doctor?" Jennifer said with a sideways look at Claire.

"And rich too, I heard," Claire added with a grin.

So he says, Jennifer thought.

They sat in tired silence for a few minutes.

Lillian did some push-ups. She kicked off her sandals and burrowed her toes in the sand and started laughing hysterically as her friends stared.

"I'm laughing because this is the first time in my life I haven't been knee deep in snow in December."

"I don't know. I sort of miss sitting by a roaring fire with a cup of hot chocolate," Dawn said.

Jennifer wrinkled her nose at the thought. The last thing she was interested in was the cold. "And having to scrape the snow off your car . . . and skate to the mailbox," Jennifer added, as she made a mound of sand around Lillian's toes.

"Dawn, isn't that the point of all this?" Claire gave her a compassionate smile. "Getting away from Christmas?"

"I think for me it's more about getting away from my mother-in-law." Dawn drew a long breath. "I'm not the same person when she's around."

Claire and Dawn went off, arm in arm, to talk privately.

"So just walk off without saying good-bye," Jennifer yelled. When she caught Lillian's baffled look she apologized. "I'm not usually this callous, Lil. It's my lack of sleep."

Lillian looked up at Jennifer. "I know. Our mattress is sort of lumpy too."

"It's not the mattress. Trust me," Jennifer said, as she plopped on the sand, disregarding the cotton dress she was wearing.

"Hey, maybe you're pregnant. I'm always bushed in my first trimester."

Jennifer almost choked at the thought.

Lillian somehow took her reaction as confirmation. "This is so perfect. I always felt sorry for you, Jen. And poor little Trevor, a lonely only."

"Trevor doesn't feel sorry for Trevor, so why should you?"

"So you're not pregnant then."

"Nope."

"That's too bad."

"It's not too bad; it's impossible. Eric's fifteenth anniversary present to me was . . . ," she hesitated and made a face, ". . . snip, snip."

"Gold-plated scissors?"

"Forget it. Let's change the subject."

Lillian picked up a squeaky hammer toy left by some child and pounded the sand, her brow furrowed in thought. "So, Dawn and I were having this discussion," she said.

"Is that so?"

"And I want to get your wise opinion on the matter."

"My wise opinion, huh." Jennifer posed in contemplation with her finger in the air, waiting for some deep spiritual question. Maybe the kind of question that Trevor asked. Like, what does God think about?

"Dawn and I were disagreeing about what the greatest superhero power is."

That's what we're talking about? Oh, pleeease!

"She and her daughters think it's breathing underwater. I mean, don't you think X-ray vision or climbing and sticking to walls is better than breathing underwater?"

"That's a toughie, Lil."

"I know."

Jennifer suddenly remembered having this same discussion with Trevor last year. It seemed silly, but she said what came to mind anyway. "If I had to say . . . I'd go with flying . . . No, being invisible."

"Of course. That way you are completely undetected." Lillian beamed.

"But super strength is pretty important too. Especially if you're rescuing people," Jennifer said with a half smile.

"I've considered putting all this in a Sunday school lesson format, you know."

Jennifer made a trail in the sand with a sea shell. "What about a female superhero who wears Spanx?"

"I never thought of that before." *Perhaps for good reason,* Jennifer thought and laughed to herself.

☙❧

Jennifer caught up with Becky after the church service. "Want to go for a walk?"

Becky gave an impatient shake of her head. "I've already heard one sermon today."

In spite of her objection, Jennifer dragged her a few yards down a private section of beach and then stopped. She matched her bare foot in a larger footprint. "People are more irresistible on vacation than in real life, Bec," she said.

"What do you have against Jonah Beach, besides his name?"

"I think he's perfect. And guys who are too perfect never are . . . as perfect as they seem."

Becky just looked at her. "Jen, he's the kind of man I've always wanted. I realize that now. You should see his fingernails. They gleam they're so clean."

Jennifer twisted her wedding ring. "Bob has clean fingernails. I checked for you."

"Bob who?"

"Bob the preacher, of course."

"The preacher who spoke this morning . . . with the yellow straw hair?" She made a face.

"I thought of it as more of a fashionable tangled look."
Becky gritted her teeth.

"He'd be a good catch," Jennifer said.

"He's not my type. And he looks like he's twenty-one."

"He's thirty-five. And a half. I checked. And he preaches a good sermon."

"I don't think it was all that deep. I mean, love the unlovable, help those who cannot help themselves. Isn't that pretty obvious?"

"Sometimes you need to hear the basics again. And preachers are a safe bet."

"Preachers are people too."

Jennifer did not want Becky getting serious with Jonah. "But he's tall, and a witty conversationalist. And he definitely prays before meals."

"Jennifer, Jennifer, Jennifer. What are planning to say next? That Bob has rock-hard abs?" Becky exhaled. "Now that would be a tremendous stretch."

"Well, he surfs."

Becky exhaled again.

"I just want you to check out some other fish in the sea."

"The only fish in the sea that I plan to check out in the near future are going to be under a glass bottom boat."

Becky laughed.

Jennifer knew she wasn't taking this conversation seriously. She lifted a hand to shade the sun, and Becky's diamond earrings sparkled.

"Those are beautiful, by the way."

Becky paused before responding. "In case you're thinking they were a gift from some tragic lost love, I'll clarify it for you. They were a gift from my father on my thirty-fifth birthday. They belonged to my mother."

The mention of her father struck a nerve with Jennifer. Her lips curved into a sorrowful grimace. "I just don't want Dr. Livingston to get the idea he can charm you and steal all that money you won't admit you have."

"Why are you so cynical all of a sudden?"

Jennifer's mind raced. She looked away. "It was my ex-stepfather doctor who wasn't really a doctor. He charmed my mother right out of my father's life insurance money."

Jennifer wrung her hands nervously and hoped she wouldn't ask her to elaborate.

Becky took off her Gucci sunglasses and tilted her head. "That's harsh about your stepfather, Jen. But I don't think pretending to be a doctor is high on the list of most men in America, Jamaica, or anywhere else in the world."

Jennifer tried a different approach. "Don't you think he's too young to be retired? What is he running away from? The trappings of modern civilization?"

"You saw that Cary Grant movie too?" Becky laughed.

Jennifer grew even more serious.

"Jen, he probably wanted a change. It's not against the law."

Jennifer smiled a lopsided smile. "So you wouldn't mind if I checked him out, then. His background, I mean."

"There's an Internet café down the street, Sherlock." Becky threw her head back and laughed, irritating Jennifer.

∽✾∼

An hour and a half later, back in the hotel room, Claire was lying on her stomach on the flowered comforter, her legs moving back and forth in windshield wiper motion. She was intent on a novel with the air-conditioning blasting. Jennifer sat down on the bed next to her.

Claire read one more line and then raised her eyes. "Where did you go off to? You missed some good fellowship."

"I was doing some investigative work on Doctor Jonah Beach."

"You hired a private detective?"

"No, I gave my cousin Rupert Jonah's name and age to look him up in his database."

"Does he work for the CIA?"

"He wanted to. The DMV was his second choice."

Claire sat up. "The DMV. Oh, wow, what an intriguing place to work."

"He can tell me if Jonah Beach is who he says he is."

Becky popped her head in just then. "I heard that last sentence. Poor girl needs a hobby," she said, laughing.

"Never mind," Jennifer said. "You'll thank me for it later."

"I doubt it."

Claire interrupted the flow. "You look very island-like in a beautiful dress I wish I were wearing."

A smile overtook Becky's freshly tanned face. "Your luggage is here!"

Claire jumped to her feet and looked at Lillian's funny outfit one last time.

"And more good news," Becky announced. "We're all going on a sunset cruise this evening. Jonah's treat!"

"That's great!" Claire said.

"I better go tell Dawn and Lil." She smiled and her hazel eyes glinted.

When she left, Claire turned to Jennifer. "You're coming on the cruise, aren't you?"

"Of course. Someone needs to keep an eye on Jonah," she said.

"And someone needs to keep an eye on you." Claire ran her fingertips along her unshaven legs. "I can't wait to shave!"

❧

Dawn was the only one who hadn't been told about the cruise. And the reason was while Becky was scouring the resort searching for her, she was scribbling away in her journal in a secluded garden. It was her first and only entry, and it was to her mother-in-law, Edna.

Dear Edna,

I've been thinking about you a lot this trip. Too much, in fact.

They say to start a letter with something nice. So I'll

start with saying thank you for raising my wonderful husband.

Having said that, I have to tell you that you have a problem with boundaries. When I get back this is going to change!!! I'm tired of feeling like a visitor in my own home. It's our home, not yours. I decorated it! I cook in it! I'm living in it!

If I were saying these things to your face, your head would be going back and forth so fast it might fly off. And to tell you the truth I don't think I could say any of this to your face. That is precisely the problem. The other problem is that I shouldn't have to say any of this. Your son should be telling you these things.

Maybe I should be writing this letter to Tommy. You know, he was a good husband before you came along. Kind and decent and loving. His beauty surpassed the sea. I want my man back!!!

I'll tell you what the problem is with Tommy. It's you, MIL! How can he cleave to me when he's cleaving to you?

With all due respect,
Your daughter-in-law Dawn

P.S. You may not believe it, but I actually want to be friends with you.

Dawn took a deep breath. *Now I think I'll go buy her a postcard in the gift shop and try to write something nice. "Thank you for feeding my family all those artery clogging meals," or something like that.* She chuckled.

And everyone thinks I'm sooo nice all the time. *Dear God, if they only knew I'm the same as they are. In the worst way I wish I were perfect.*

18

For two full hours the ladies primped like schoolgirls getting ready for the prom, sharing every inch of mirror in both the bathroom and the bedroom.

Hair dryers were blowing and hair spray was flying and makeup and fragrant lotions were generously applied as they chattered like magpies.

Earlier, Lillian had bounded out of the bathroom flaunting her gaudy, sequined outfit she had been saving for a special night out, bragging that she was going to be a big hit. She had stepped on a curler and slipped, colliding with the dresser. Now she was rubbing her ankle and looking mournful.

"What's wrong, Lil?" Jennifer asked, already knowing the obvious.

"My ankle is hurting."

Jennifer guided her as she hopped into Becky's room. "We have a patient here."

"Sit down on the bed," Becky ordered. She examined her ankle. "It's swelling."

Lillian frowned. "I think I twisted my ankle climbing the waterfall, carrying that heavy backpack."

"Who was carrying your heavy backpack?" Jennifer

mumbled. "And besides, I think crashing into the dresser may have aided the injury along."

Lillian frowned again.

"Well, you're going to have to stay off it for at least tonight. Pack it with ice and lie still," Becky ordered.

Lillian gave her standard puppy dog look. "I don't mind staying here all alone when you go on your elegant dinner cruise . . . all that much anyway."

Dawn and Claire had gathered by now and were looking stunning and like themselves again in their own dinner dresses.

"Well, uh, I'll stay with you," Dawn offered.

Jennifer pondered the message Pastor Bob preached this morning about loving the unlovable. Here was Dawn offering to give up her special evening with no hesitation whatsoever.

I want to be as good as Dawn, Jennifer thought. Besides, Dawn needed to enjoy a night out like this. So before she changed her mind, she said, "No, I'll stay."

"You will?" Lillian squealed.

"Yeah, sure."

Claire eyed her suspiciously.

"Be sure to identify all the birds for me," Lillian said as they were leaving.

"Believe me, I won't be paying attention to the birds," Becky said as she floated out the door.

∽⚬∽

"It was nice of you to stay with me," Lillian said, dressed and ready for bed.

Jennifer sat next to her on the flowery bedspread, looking longingly out the window at the patch of sky. She was thinking about the dinner cruise she was missing.

"It's okay, really." Jennifer tried to sound convincing.

There was an awkward moment of silence. "I've always wanted to bond with you, Jen."

The pressure was on. Jennifer generally avoided high-maintenance types. She smiled to conceal her warring emotions. "You have?"

"Yeah. You seem so smart, so fascinating."

"I've been called a lot of things; fascinating is not one of them. Trust me; I'm not all that fascinating, Lil."

"I miss Martha, don't you?" Lillian asked. One of her typical out-of-the-blue statements.

"A little," Jennifer said.

After she thought about it, the truth was, she hadn't thought about her much. Only at night in her prayers.

It was obvious Martha played a big role in Lillian's life, however.

Jennifer remembered the first day Lillian showed up at Bible study, wearing an outdated peach-colored sweater and a checkered wool skirt, looking lost. Martha had immediately taken her under her wing.

Lillian interrupted her thoughts with a request. "Will you rub my shoulders? I think it would help."

Rubbing your shoulders will help your ankle? Jennifer didn't see the connection. "Yeah, sure, I'll rub your shoulders."

"Wait, can you fluff my pillow first?"

Are your arms broken or something? "Of course." Jennifer was trying very hard.

"You're so nice."

No, I'm not. Jennifer situated Lillian's pillow.

"I wish Derrick was this nice."

"Doesn't Derrick ever rub your shoulders?"

"Never."

Jennifer felt fortunate. Eric gave a great massage. And sometimes they had family foot-rubbing marathons.

She gave Lillian a token shoulder rub. "All done," she said.

"You know, I thought when Derrick became a Christian he'd stop all his bad habits." Lillian rolled her eyes and sighed.

"Bad habits?"

"Like burping and drinking out of the milk carton and forgetting our anniversary and . . ."

Jennifer made a face. "I get the idea."

"He never does anything considerate."

"Unfortunately, Christian or not, we are still human."

Lillian continued. "And he tells me stuff all the time, like I'm bossy and a nag. He says I get on people's nerves. You don't think that, do you?"

Jennifer sighed.

Lillian answered her own question. "I'm not bossy."

Jennifer's full lips tightened. Uncomfortable with the subject, she rerouted the discussion. "There is something I'm curious about, Lil."

"Yes, the rumor is true. Derrick uses Rogaine."

"Rogaine? I don't care about what your husband does with his hair!"

"What hair?" Lillian laughed and snorted.

"What I'm curious about is . . . when you were drowning, Lil . . . did your life flash in front of your eyes?"

Jennifer had considered the possibility that her plane could crash on the flight home. And then wouldn't her family think she was terribly selfish. Of course, she would be in heaven having a great time, so it wouldn't matter.

"I thought about Derrick and the kids. But as far as my own life . . . well, I didn't have a very good childhood."

Jennifer suspected that. Someone seeking attention 24/7 had to have some big issues.

"In fact, I have a terrible, tragic secret churning inside me, but I think I can trust you with it."

Do I really want to know? Jennifer thought and braced herself.

"I'm an identical twin," Lillian blurted out.

"There are two of you?" Jennifer tried to imagine Lillian's poor mother.

"That's right."

"Oh." Jennifer wasn't sure what to say.

"But the tragic thing about it is my mom kept her and I was raised by my grandmother."

Jennifer nodded to show she was listening.

"And later, when she died, I lived in seven foster homes. It would take all night to tell you about it." Lillian bit at her cuticle. "Three nights maybe."

Jennifer felt horrible about her bad thoughts. "That is tragic." Her eyes teared up. Now she understood why Martha probably spent so much time and effort with Lillian.

"Do you think that there was something wrong with me that my mother would keep my sister and not me?"

"I'm sure she had her reasons."

"My social worker used to say that. But I can't imagine giving one of my children up."

"Do you know where your sister is?"

"In Minneapolis."

"That's so close."

"She doesn't know I exist. We almost met once."

Jennifer wanted to ask, but she hesitated. It was probably a long, complicated story.

"Oh, well," Lillian said.

Jennifer wrinkled her forehead in thought. Lillian seemed

so disconnected from her circumstances. "Lil, you talk about this as though it doesn't matter. It does, you know."

Lillian closed her eyes and opened them again. "Martha says the past is the past and we need to leave it alone."

"But the past steps on the heels of the future."

"Wow, that's really profound."

"I didn't make it up."

"Who did?"

"A wise guy somewhere in the world. Or he could be a dead wise guy."

Lillian yawned. "Jen, this painkiller Becky gave me is making me sleepy."

"Painkiller?"

"Tylenol PM."

"Strong stuff."

Maybe it will knock her out and she won't snore tonight.

"I know this is sorta silly. But can you talk to me until I fall asleep?"

"Talk about what?"

"The beach, the sun, pretty things. Stuff from your happy childhood."

"That would have to be the first half when my real father was alive; things went downhill at eleven when my stepfather came on the scene," Jennifer said, surprising herself at the disclosure.

"Do you want to tell me about it?" Lillian's eyes were hopeful.

Jennifer looked away. "Not really. My made-up stories are better. Trevor likes my stories."

"You can pretend I'm Trevor."

"You do a lot of pretending, don't you, Lil."

Lillian nodded. "When I was little I used to pretend I was invisible."

"Like a superhero?"

"I guess so."

Jennifer's eyes glinted. "Alright. I have a story." She smiled at the good memories. "When I was six we lived in this beautiful yellow house with an enormous willow tree with branches reaching—"

"Wait!" Lillian interrupted.

"Do you have something against willow trees?"

"No. I was just thinking about something really sad." Jennifer swallowed hard. "Go ahead."

"I only got breastfed for one day."

"I guess that is sorta sad."

"And only because the doctor made my mother breastfeed me."

"Now that is sad."

After a moment of silence Jennifer continued her story where she left off.

Lillian fell asleep in the middle of her story, despite her attempts to stay awake and listen. Her snoring was the same loud racket, but it didn't matter—for now.

Jennifer pondered the things Lillian had shared. Lillian seemed so helpless, so fragile all of a sudden. Jennifer vowed to be more patient with Lillian. To keep her secret between them.

❧

"So how was the cruise?" Jennifer asked as the crew strutted in the door around eight. Dawn and Claire flung their purses in a pile at the end of Jennifer's bed.

Claire unzipped her jacket. "It was amazing! I tried to bring you back some food, but someone sat on it."

"Thank you, anyway. I guess."

154

"The sunset was so wide and the colors so vivid," Dawn recounted.

"And everything else?" Jennifer once again tried to get past her emotions about Jonah. She smiled at Becky.

"Jonah was amazing too." And with that comment, Becky grinned, maneuvered around the piles of luggage, and shut the door to her superior world.

"Stay for a while and chat," Jennifer said to the door.

"I don't think she can hear you from Cloud Nine," Dawn said.

Jennifer smiled.

"You're being awfully nice," Claire said suspiciously.

Jennifer closed her lips tight. She was tempted to share Lillian's story with Claire and had to remind herself of her vow.

They listened to the lighter but unremitting snoring.

"I'm sorry you had to stay back with Lillian," Dawn said.

"Don't be. I think it touched my soul as much as the sunset could have."

Claire gave her a long, considering look.

Jennifer made an innocent face. "My life is so blessed. Nothing can disturb my peace from now on."

Claire gave her another long look. "What about Miss Jet Plane there?"

Jennifer looked at Lillian's mouth, frozen wide in position. "I'm going to be more patient with her. Love her for the uniqueness of her character. She's been through a lot." She looked back at Claire and gave a deliberate nod. "Yes, I am going to be patient with her if it kills me."

"We'll see how long that lasts," Claire said under her breath.

Jennifer heard but was determined to say nothing back.

19

Four hours later, the gated community at the Sea View Resort had all but shut down. Even the tree frogs and crickets seemed to have gone to bed early.

The only sound that could be heard was coming from Lillian. Her snoring was a constant, noisy wheeze that echoed in the hot, stuffy room.

Claire checked the clock and grimaced. It was five minutes after midnight.

There were plenty of nights at home when Claire stayed awake past midnight staring at the ceiling in the stillness. She mostly thought of her and Alex and how they used to be. The thoughts would grow darker as the hours dragged on.

Claire watched Jennifer's profile in the faint glow of light coming from outside, wondering how she could sleep through this.

How many times Jennifer had awakened her from a dead sleep to ask if she were awake, Claire couldn't count. It was payback time.

"Are you awake, Jen?" she whispered.

Jennifer turned toward Claire. "Of course I'm awake! I have ears."

"I know what you mean." Claire sighed. "So your plan to be more patient 'if it kills me' didn't work?"

"It did for the first hour. But after lying still and feeling my legs tingle, I'm convinced I have restless leg syndrome."

Claire laughed quietly, and then grew suddenly serious again. "You know earlier when you told me Lillian thought you were pregnant?"

"Yes."

"Do you ever regret that you can't get pregnant now?"

"No, of course not." Jennifer took a breath before she spoke. "There was a time after my miscarriage nine years ago that I did . . . but then, it seemed right, just the three of us. And you can't replace a child."

Claire exhaled softly.

"I'm sorry. I didn't mean it the way it sounded," Jennifer said quickly.

"No, it's true. You can't replace a child."

Jennifer shifted restlessly.

"Tomorrow is the anniversary of David's death," Claire said, her throat tightening. "Four years ago."

Involuntarily, the memory flooded in . . .

It was four days before Christmas. Jennifer had dropped by, and she and Claire were having a good time that afternoon. Claire was testing the scented lotions Jennifer had bought her, and Jennifer was devouring the assorted chocolates Claire had special-ordered from Godiva. And, in between, they were jabbering away.

The kick start of a motorcycle in the garage and a sudden roar interrupted their laughter.

"Oh, no! Not on these icy roads!" Claire cried. She knew it was David on his father's motorcycle. He had been determined to ride it ever since Alex had taken him riding that past summer.

Within seconds, the sound of screeching brakes confirmed her worst fear. The next thing Claire knew, Jennifer was calling for an ambulance.

In the days that followed, a tension settled over the Parker house, a tension that was still present.

Jennifer put her hand on Claire's shoulder. Up until this year, Jennifer had gone to great lengths to make sure Claire was never alone on December 21. "I'm sorry, sweetie; I forgot. I've been so caught up in my own world . . ."

Claire gathered her silk nightshirt in a ball and squeezed. "I wonder if I'll ever get over it," she said.

Jennifer took Claire's hand and squeezed it. "Why would you want to? Would you want to get over a Picasso or a Rembrandt, or a sunset?"

"That's a beautiful way to put it." Claire gave Jennifer's hand a squeeze and then released it.

"I have my moments."

"You sure do."

Claire stared at the ceiling, wishing she could see the stars.

"Claire."

"Yes."

"Do you want another baby?"

The question surprised Claire, even though she had just asked Jennifer the same thing.

"No, not another baby, for sure." Her voice faltered. "I-I've thought of taking in foster children, though."

"Really? I didn't know you would want that."

"I know. You should have heard Alex when I mentioned it to him."

"How did he react?"

"To put it mildly, he was mortified." Claire sighed. "He won't even let Lexie get a dog."

"Maybe while we're gone he'll have some enormous transformation and change his mind about it."

"That would be a miracle." Claire's voice betrayed her angst.

"And what? You don't believe in miracles?"

Claire was silent.

"So who's changed?" Jennifer said.

Claire shifted uncomfortably. "What does that mean?"

"What'd you write in my high school yearbook?" Without waiting for Claire to answer, Jennifer quoted, "'I believe in miracles!'"

Claire had a glimpse of time passing—a flash of girl to woman. "Someone else wrote that. Someone young and idealistic."

It was Jennifer's turn to be silent. Claire was thankful that her friend didn't push her any further. Just voicing what she'd been struggling with for so long made her realize how much she longed for that kind of faith again.

"Listen," Jennifer whispered.

"Listen to what?"

"Our miracle. For the first time in three nights Lillian has stopped snoring!"

"Quick, go to sleep," they whispered in unison.

⌒⌟⌒

It must've been about three o'clock when Jennifer woke to Lillian's snoring. After tossing and turning, in desperation she dragged her pillow and an extra bedspread into the bathroom. She laid the bedspread down in the tub, propped her pillow up against the back of the tub, and climbed in. She pulled the curtain closed to shut out the night-light Becky had bought them, and after a few minutes of getting situated, she fell asleep.

The early morning sun shone through the open curtain as Lillian swung out of bed and headed for the bathroom. She was delighted to find her ankle only hurt a little. She looked in the mirror at her disheveled hair and debated about washing it. Swinging the door closed so she wouldn't wake the others, she opted to wash her face at the sink.

After patting her face dry, she looked in the mirror again. *I can't do a thing with this hair.* And with that thought, she reached into the tub, turned on the faucet, and pulled the lever for the shower.

An ear-piercing scream gurgled from behind the curtain. Lillian's heart raced. Images from the movie *Psycho* flashed through her mind as she let loose a bloodcurdling scream in return. She stood staring at the curtain as it jerked back and a soggy Jennifer tumbled out of the tub, her legs wobbling like limp spaghetti.

Lillian reached for the faucet and turned it off with shaky hands. Jennifer grabbed someone's towel from the rack, dried off, more or less, and wrapped it around her shoulders.

"Wh-what are you doing sleeping in the bathtub?" Lillian's eyes were wide with confusion.

Jennifer looked like she was struggling for control. She said through clenched teeth, "I am sleeping in the bathtub because you snore like a buzz saw!"

Lillian pulled on the belt strings of her robe, lacking the words to express how badly she felt. By now, Dawn and Claire were watching from the doorway, waiting for a showdown.

"Well, I know I snore when I'm home, but I didn't think I'd snore here with you guys."

After all three friends gave her an extended stare, Lillian realized her thinking was illogical.

She looked from Jennifer to Dawn to Claire, not knowing

what to do or say. They seemed to want something from her. "What do you think I should do about it?" she asked.

"Maybe you can—" Jennifer stopped. She took a deep breath and said, "Nothing. There is nothing you can do about it."

While Jennifer wrung out her pajama pants and hung up the bedspread, Lillian drifted into the other room, dejected because Jennifer was mad at her. Claire walked by with a change of clothes for Jennifer, and suddenly, Lillian had an idea. She went to get the chocolate bar she'd been saving.

Lillian knocked on the bathroom door.

Jennifer opened it, sporting a rather inhospitable expression. "What."

Lillian displayed a chocolate bar. "Do you want it?" she asked meekly, with her childlike desire to please.

Jennifer's expression softened. "What kind?"

"Belgium dark chocolate."

"Dark. Yum."

Lillian's hand remained extended.

Jennifer laughed and accepted the peace offering.

◈

The gang sat in a circle in the gazebo, unusually quiet, sipping on fruity drinks after breakfast. They were transported into the moment by a passing reggae band playing the *Little Mermaid* theme song in calypso.

When the band moved on, Becky's vibrating cell did a dance on the bench. She cupped the phone in her hand and read a second before she announced, "Here's the update on your families I asked Martha for!"

The group bolted to attention.

Wasting no time, Becky jumped into the meat of Martha's text message. "'Regarding the Holmes.'"

Lillian sat on the edge of the bench.

"'The boys are fine, and Casey learned to tie her shoes.'" Becky looked up at Lillian apologetically. "That's all it says!"

Lillian's eager eyes dimmed. Her nose scrunched. "I thought Casey already knew how to tie her shoes."

Becky went on. "'Regarding the Woodson clan.'"

Dawn squirmed.

"'Your mother-in-law is making a Christmas goose.'"

"Do you know how much fat is in a goose?" she erupted passionately.

"How much?" Lillian asked.

Dawn's tone softened as she asked about the children.

"There's nothing else. Um . . . I guess Martha wanted to fit everyone in," Becky said.

"Thanks," Dawn said meekly.

After a glance at Dawn, Becky looked at Jennifer and then shared the next line. "'The Baker family is fine.'"

Jennifer let out an extended sigh. "That's all I get?"

"I'm only reading what Martha wrote," Becky told her and then turned to Claire with her report. "'The *Nutcracker* was a hit!'"

Claire beamed with obvious pride.

Becky read the next part to herself first and then swallowed hard. "And now, for the shock." She paused. "'Alex is on a Harley on his way to Arizona for a Toys for Tots event.'"

"Read that again, Bec!"

The words came back just as startling the second time around.

"Where is Lexie?"

"Lexie is fine," Becky assured her, having already read the next line. "She's staying with Meagan for the holiday."

Jennifer quickly answered the questioning looks. "That's Lexie's best friend."

162

Claire cradled her head in her hand and then lifted it slowly. "My daughter has been farmed out?"

"I didn't know Alex owned a Harley," Lillian said.

"He doesn't." Claire looked away.

The tension was building fast.

Becky read the rest of the message hastily. "And then Martha ends by saying—get this, ladies—she is managing without us and hopes we don't feel guilty. Which, of course, means she wants us to feel guilty."

"Do you feel guilty?" Dawn addressed the group.

"No, but I feel guilty about not feeling guilty," Becky said.

"Are you okay, Claire?" Jennifer whispered in her ear.

"I am so incredibly mad at my husband right now. My daughter farmed out while he goes on a joyride. I know who it was. That hardware salesman, Daryl, talked him into this."

"I don't care if they want us to call home or not. I'm calling," Dawn said, determination in her voice.

Becky related the bad news. "Well, I hate to tell you all this, but when I tried to call the hospital early this morning I couldn't get through. I called one of my nurses who lives in Bridgeport. She said the phone lines are down from the snowstorm."

"Snowstorm?" Dawn cried.

"Remember those?" Becky said.

Emotions were heating up.

Becky offered a quick solution. "I'll send a text message to Martha asking for more specifics. How's that?"

There was a lengthy pause.

"Look, you guys, you know everyone is fine. Wasn't the point of all this to have a well-deserved break?"

"Yes, the point was for *us* to have a break, not our husbands," Claire said.

"Everybody's fine. Maybe you should leave well enough alone," Becky said.

The ladies brooded.

"Ladies, ladies . . . a vacation in the Caribbean is no longer enough for you? Come on now, don't worry. Be happy."

"It's easy for you to say not to worry. You don't have a family," Lillian said, not meaning anything by it.

It was obvious to everyone but Lillian that Becky was incredibly hurt. It was also obvious that she refused to show it.

She blinked slowly and grabbed her purse. "Guys, I'm supposed to meet Jonah. I'll see you all later." She was gone.

20

To improve the general bad mood, Claire suggested "some duty-free shopping and female camaraderie," even though her funds were limited and shopping was the last thing on her mind, it being the anniversary of her son's death.

Five minutes into their excursion, Dawn vanished in a cooking store that had caught her eye, and Lillian disappeared in after her.

Claire and Jennifer moved on down the colorful row of craft shops and food stands buzzing with tourists, many proudly wearing their new watches and pearls.

Suddenly, Claire halted in front of a shop. She was mesmerized by a sign that said BLUE MOUNTAIN MOTORCYCLES.

"Oh," Jennifer said when she saw the sign.

Claire's words came out in an agonized whisper. "I just realized something, Jen."

"What?" Jennifer put her sunglasses on top of her head and looked into Claire's eyes, wide with visible pain.

"I took away the thing he loved."

"The thing he loved?"

"Alex," Claire said and took a breath before continuing. "Alex gave up his love of motorcycles because every time he brought it up I gave him the evil eye. He knew I blamed him for David."

"Did you?"

Claire's heart pounded with the admittance. "Yes, I did . . . at first. I think you know that."

"I guess I do."

"But then I realized the truth. David may have been only twelve, but he had a mind of his own. If he was bent on something, he was going to get it. And he was determined to ride that motorcycle even though he knew it was off limits."

Jennifer nodded.

"I don't think there was a year that went by that he didn't peek at his Christmas presents, no matter how many times I told him not to. He was going to be a great adult, but a difficult teenager. Alex and I always said that."

"David was his own person, for sure." Jennifer smiled.

"His own beautiful person," Claire said, tears spilling from her blue eyes. And a look of joy spread across her face.

Claire smiled at Jennifer, her expression telling her that she didn't have to say something meaningful in return. Everything had been said that could be said.

The friends squeezed hands and smiled.

Claire looked up to the wide, blue sky and thought of David in heaven.

༄

On the way back to the hotel Jennifer and Claire stopped at Planet Jamaica, an Internet café. It was just a small hole in the wall, with a dim interior, dark wood bookcases and benches, and antiquated computers. But it was cozy and charming, with a friendly and helpful staff.

Jennifer logged on to the computer and checked the email account she had set up earlier. She found her cousin's reply.

"'Re: your suspect,'" she read with extreme interest.

"Suspect," Claire said, looking over her shoulder. "That sounds so criminal."

Jennifer kept her eyes on the monitor. "Rupert tends to be a little dramatic."

"Must run in the family," Claire said to the air.

Jennifer read the next line aloud. "'I need your suspect's middle name.'"

They looked at each other. "You'd think with a name like Jonah Beach . . ." Jennifer shook her head.

"There are a lot of beaches in the world; you'd be surprised," Claire said.

"Yeah, but I didn't know there were a lot of Beaches."

"Absolutely."

"I'll drag his middle name out of him, then," Jennifer said with a smile.

"Or, you could just ask," Claire suggested.

༄

Everyone met up again at one o'clock for afternoon tea on the terrace, including Becky and Jonah, who were comfortably crammed together, their fingers intertwined like vines.

Before anyone had even taken a sip of their English tea, Jennifer brought up the subject of the middle name.

"So, Dawn, what's your middle name?" she asked, leaning forward.

"Uh . . . Elizabeth." She gave Jennifer a strange look.

Jennifer turned to Becky. "And yours is Sue, Becky."

"Not Sue Becky, Becky Sue."

"Right."

Becky jolted in her seat. "That's not something I advertise. How did you find out?"

"I snuck a peek at your driver's license. Not a bad picture." She waved Becky's Coach wallet around.

Becky grabbed it back with a scowl and returned it to her purse.

"I'd watch your wallet if I were you," Jonah advised, and they resumed holding hands.

"My middle name is Jo," Lillian divulged, looking like she expected some sort of reaction from the group.

Jennifer proceeded with her detective work. "And what about you, Jonah? What's your middle name?"

"Mine is Jo," Lillian piped in again. "Like Jo in *Little Women*. She's the one who was the author. Beth was played by Elizabeth Taylor. She looks terrible as a blond, by the way."

Jennifer was not distracted by Lillian's monologue. She waited for Jonah's response.

"What's in a name?" Jonah philosophized.

"A lot is in a name," Jennifer said and tried to think of something convincing to say. "Names express the very fabric of our lives."

Her eyes strayed in the other direction as she thought how that sounded like a magazine ad.

"My middle name is Alise," Claire said, trying to cause trouble.

Jennifer made a face at Claire and flashed Jonah another tight smile. "Unless there's some reason you don't want to tell us what your middle name is, Jonah."

"There is," he said.

Lillian interrupted again. "We're all friends here. Tell us. Oh please, oh please, oh please! I told you mine."

Jonah appeared to be having a titanic struggle within himself, or at least Jennifer thought so. He tried to drink his tea as all the ladies stared at him.

"Okay, it's Clark," Jonah reluctantly uttered.

"Clark. What's wrong with that?" Becky smiled.

"I was named after Superman. It was all my mother's idea." He quickly put on his sunglasses.

"I LOVE Superman!" Lillian said in such a loud voice that the startled woman at the next table spilled her tea.

Jennifer stood up abruptly and said she had something she had to do.

"Where are you off to now?" Becky called.

"You don't want to know," Claire said.

"Have a scone, Claire," Jennifer yelled over her shoulder.

∽∾

Jennifer, having completed her mission of emailing her cousin with Jonah's full name, burst through the unlocked door of her hotel room and tossed her purse in the corner.

"Where is everyone?"

"We're in Becky's room!" Claire called from the adjoining room.

Jennifer smiled, gave a greeting, and went straight for the source of cool air. "Ah, air-conditioning!" she said as she stood near the vent, cooling off.

Becky and Claire were sitting on the tropical-print couch, their hands folded in their laps. Jennifer noted their somber expressions.

"Something terrible has happened," Claire said.

It was apparent Becky had been crying. She took the last tissue from the Kleenex box on the mosaic coffee table and blew.

Jennifer rushed over, squeezed in between them, and patted Becky's shoulder in sympathy. "I knew that beast was going to break your heart!"

"Honestly, Jen, you jump to conclusions quicker than . . ." She sighed. "It's not Jonah. I've been robbed!"

"Robbed? What happened?"

"My earrings have been stolen." She rubbed her ears as if they were still there.

"Those beautiful diamond earrings you were wearing Sunday that belonged to your mother?"

"Yes." She shrugged. "It's my fault; I left them on the dresser and didn't lock my door."

"You should have put them in the safe at the front desk," Claire reprimanded.

Becky shook her head. "I know, you told me that already."

A glum silence filled the room.

"The earrings are insured, aren't they?" Claire asked.

"Yes, they're insured."

"For how much?" Jennifer asked.

"Ten thousand dollars."

Jennifer's mouth dropped open.

"But I don't want the money! They are all I have left of my mother," Becky said.

"Let's report it to the police," Jennifer said.

"I'm going to report it to hotel security first and let them decide whether or not to involve the police."

Becky stood, wiped her eyes with her damp Kleenex, and headed out the door without another word.

21

Alone in Becky's room with Claire, Jennifer ambled over to the trash can. "The maid was in here. See, the trash was emptied."

"So," Claire said.

Jennifer lifted her eyebrows. "It could have been the maid who stole Becky's earrings."

Claire looked skeptical. "Her name is Felicia. I met her and her little boy at church. And I don't think so, Jen. She's been extremely helpful."

"Yes, I met her on the beach. She has been really nice. She washed my bedspread for me after Lil tried to drown me in the bathtub."

"That scene in the bathtub was pretty funny."

"That depends on who you ask."

Claire laughed.

Jennifer remembered seeing a little boy at church. "Was that Felicia's son . . . the one with the physical deformity?"

"Yes, he's so sweet."

"He seems sweet."

"We take our health for granted sometimes."

"Most of the time."

Claire sat back down on the comfortable couch and stared out the window, obviously enjoying the breeze and the view.

Jennifer joined her on the couch, propping her feet on the edge of the coffee table. She listened to the sounds coming from outside for a moment. But her suspicions about the robbery resumed almost immediately. "What about that guy hanging around the bushes with those big clippers? He could be the robber."

Claire turned to Jennifer and blew a sigh. "That man hanging around the bushes was the gardener."

"And gardeners don't commit crimes?"

"The gardener is never the guilty party, you know that."

"Or . . ."

"Or what."

"Not what. Who?" Jennifer tugged at Claire's sleeve. "Dr. Jonah Clark Beach."

Claire looked at her as if she were crazy. "Becky just told me Jonah owns a banana plantation. What does a man who owns a banana plantation want with earrings?"

"He could be lying. Did you notice that he didn't touch his banana at breakfast the other day?"

Claire rolled her eyes in response.

Jennifer continued despite the lack of support. "If he owns a banana plantation, don't you think he'd like bananas?"

"So, maybe he has too much potassium already."

"Besides, I think he has squinty eyes."

"Probably because he was squinting, you goof. Now, would you please leave poor Dr. Beach alone?"

"My cousin will be emailing me concerning his true identity, and then the truth will be known."

"In the meantime, let's lift his fingerprints off his tea cup with your Barbie detective kit," Claire said sarcastically. She felt Jennifer's forehead. "I think sleep deprivation is making you paranoid."

Jennifer considered it. "No, this time it's hunger. Let's go eat at Shakey's Pizza."

"I'm still full from all those scones."

"Please, Claire. The Canadians I was talking to say there's a Shakey's around here somewhere. And I have this unbelievable craving that can only be satisfied with Shakey's pizza."

"You've never even had Shakey's pizza."

"That's why I have to have it." She pulled her toward the door.

On their way out of the hotel complex a breathless Lillian caught up with them. "I just saw Becky and she told me how her diamond earrings were stolen. It's so scary to think we have a thief lurking around here." She scoped the area with her big brown eyes.

"I don't think our lives are in danger," Claire said.

"So where are you guys going?" Lillian asked.

Jennifer folded her arms.

"Uh, we're going out for an early dinner," Claire answered.

"Can I come?"

Jennifer stared into space.

"We're going to be walking a long way. It's not a good idea with your ankle," Claire said.

"My ankle is fine."

Jennifer smiled. "And we want to keep it that way."

Lillian's eyebrows went up. "I know, I'll go get my cholesterol checked at the mobile unit where Jonah is volunteering."

"Sounds like fun," Jennifer said, relieved.

"I'm guessing mine is in the five hundreds the way I've been eating." Claire patted her tummy.

Jennifer posed in thought. "Hey, Lillian, while you're in

Dr. Beach's mobile if you happen to see Becky's diamond earrings lying around . . ."

Lillian's eyes widened. "What would I do?"

"Pick them up."

Claire stared at Jennifer without blinking. "Stop it! You're worse than a child sometimes."

"I am not." Jennifer ran her fingers through her hair.

"You two are just like sisters," Lillian said.

"We know," they chimed together.

∾

Lillian made her way to the mobile unit, a forty-foot trailer with a small waiting area and two examining rooms. Jonah welcomed her with a big smile. He had on a crisp white shirt, a striped tie of green and yellow, and blue jeans.

She stared into his piercing green eyes and grinned. "I'm here to have my cholesterol checked, Dr. Beach. My husband, Derrick, has a terrible diet and his cholesterol is low. I want to beat him."

"I'm happy to see a patient. We've been rather slow today. In fact, I just sent my nurse off for some supplies because we're so slow."

"What kind of supplies?"

"Alright, milkshakes. I sent her off for chocolate milkshakes at Eddie's. Jamaican milkshakes are the best." He laughed, and a ripple of dimples showed.

Lillian wondered if Becky had noticed his dimples. She couldn't wait to ask her.

"Now, follow me into the exam room and take a seat."

Lillian trailed after Jonah, his black Nike tennis shoes squeaking as he led her into the small examining room. She sat in the plastic chair against the bright green wall and eyed the "Heart Health" and "Get Checked for Diabetes" posters on the walls.

"So who sponsors this place?"

"I do."

"You?"

"Yes."

"You volunteer at your own mobile lab. Why?"

Jonah pulled the rolling tray with the supplies over to the chair where Lillian was sitting. He took hold of her left arm and swabbed it with rubbing alcohol. "I do it because it makes me feel good."

He flinched as though he knew it sounded selfish. "We also do osteoporosis and diabetes screenings for those who can't afford it. Most of our patients are hotel employees."

"It's been a long time since I've had my blood drawn," Lillian said. She fidgeted a little.

"Well, I assure you it's not painful. It feels like a pinch," Jonah insisted.

"That's what they say when my children get their shots." Lillian made a face.

"Maybe we should talk to keep your mind off things until you're feeling more comfortable, Lillian. How about if I ask *you* a few questions for once?"

"Sure, dive right in." She chuckled. "Get it? You saved my life."

"Yes, I get it." He laughed lightly. "Becky hasn't mentioned her family. Does she have any?"

"Not that I know of. She did have a very rich father who died and left her a big trust fund. But nobody is supposed to know that," she said. "Not that he died. About the trust fund, I mean."

"Then why do you?"

"Well, maybe everybody does know it; it's just that Becky

doesn't know they know it. We live in a small town. There's this guy who had a nose job and nobody is supposed to know that either."

Jonah wiped the sweat off his brow before he asked the next question. "Are there any men in Becky's life?"

"Felix is the only male in her life I know of," Lillian said, trying to be funny. Then her face contorted as Jonah placed the elastic band around her upper arm.

Had she not been preoccupied, she might have mentioned that Felix was Becky's fussy, tailless cat. Then, again, she might not have. Lillian had a knack for creating misunderstandings.

Jonah inserted the needle and drew her blood as Lillian looked away, humming.

Jonah removed the disposable needle and threw it away. He capped the vial. As he applied a cotton ball on her puncture he asked very seriously, "So I don't have a chance with Becky then?"

Lillian looked at him directly. "Sure you have a shot." She laughed. "Get it. You have a shot; I'm getting a shot."

"Actually, you're not getting a shot. You're having your blood drawn."

"Same difference."

He applied the bandage.

"I was hoping for Superman."

"*You* were hoping for Superman?"

"Yes, Superman." She pointed at her plain bandage.

"Oh, that. We're all out of him." He tidied up the tray.

A woman's voice came from down the hall. "Is anybody here?"

"I'll be right there, May," Jonah said and steered Lillian from the exam room into the lobby.

He said hello to his patient and then stood for an absent moment.

"So when do I find out about my DSL?" Lillian asked.

"When you get back to America and ask your cable provider."

"I mean HDL, or T something something." She blew her thin bangs in the air. "The bottom line, Dr. Jonah, is I want to know if I'm on my way to heart disease or do I still get to eat pizza and Poppycock?"

"You'll get your cholesterol results in a few minutes. If you want to take a seat over there, miss," he said, sounding professional.

"Miss." She frowned at him. "I know your middle name and you're calling me Miss?"

"Take a seat, please." His eyes met hers and he took a deep breath.

"Oh, I get it. Patient confidentiality." She winked.

Jonah led his new patient into the other room.

22

After two minutes of wiggling in the plastic seat, bored to tears, Lillian decided to check out the candy dish she spied on the high counter. She reasoned that standard practice in most mobile lab units was to give a reward after being pricked. She stepped over to it, deciding between the raspberry and lemon jellied candies. That is when she spotted something glimmering on the far counter.

"Becky's earrings," she murmured and impulsively grabbed them. She tore out the door and down the walkway toward her room, nearly knocking over a startled Dawn.

"The chef just taught me how to cut a star apple," Dawn said and smiled.

Lillian displayed the earrings in her open palm.

"What are those?"

"Becky's stolen earrings."

"Let me see those." Dawn took them and, after a short examination, stared at her in shock for a few seconds. "Lil, these aren't Becky's earrings. They're fake. My mother-in-law has a collection of diamond earrings from her ex-husbands. And these aren't diamond."

"I can try to cut a hole in a glass door to be sure," Lillian said, reaching for one of the earrings.

Dawn clutched the earrings. "If you don't believe me, let's get a second opinion." She headed toward the lobby with Lillian in tow.

꘎꘎꘎

The appraiser in the hotel jewelry shop wore big gold earrings, a thick black-and-white pearl necklace, a huge green ring, and a colorful turban. She inspected the jewelry and made an instant determination.

"These are cubic zirconium," she said. "Which one of you ladies had da bad man dat did dat?" She laughed heartily.

"Thank you very much for your help." Dawn pulled Lillian out the door and stared her down, eyes narrowed in concern. "Where did you find these?"

"At the mobile unit where I just got my cholesterol checked."

"You mean they were just lying there on the floor?"

Lillian made a face. "More like on the counter."

Dawn's startled blue eyes rested on Lillian's blank face. "Why on earth would you take something that doesn't belong to you?"

"They were sitting there looking stolen."

Dawn shook her head. "Stolen by who? That's the part I don't understand."

"Jennifer told me to." Lillian tried to justify her actions.

"First off, if she did say that, I think she was being sarcastic. Secondly, if I told you to jump off a bridge would you?"

"That is so seventies!" Lillian rolled her eyes.

"Maybe so, but we need to get them back before we become the thieves! You need to think before you do things, Lil."

"I know, but I have adult ADD!"

"We can only hope nobody noticed them missing," Dawn said, finishing her thoughts and pulling Lillian back through the hotel lobby.

∽⚬∾

While Lillian was returning the earrings to the trailer with Dawn as her lookout, Jennifer and Claire were getting lost.

They'd passed the streets they had shopped previously and moved beyond the town, down the lush, green winding lanes of shops and pottery stands. They found themselves in a more rural area with no tourist-looking types. And still no Shakey's Pizza was anywhere in sight.

The sun was shining intensely, and the heat wasn't making their aimless trek any easier.

"They're pulling your leg! There is no Shakey's Pizza," Claire said resolutely.

"Why would they do that?"

"I don't know. Maybe Canadians are mean."

"There is so a Shakey's Pizza! We're just turned around."

"You mean lost."

"Same thing."

"That's something Alex would say. He hates to ask for directions."

"I have no problem asking for directions." Jennifer grinned nervously. "But those guys on the corner look a little scary."

"Don't worry, I hear 99 percent of the murders are drug related."

"Thank you for that miniscule comfort."

"You're welcome."

They stood on the corner, looking around warily. Jennifer searched for a friendly face.

"I think you've picked the worst neighborhood in all of Ocho Rios."

"I'm sure you're right."

"Let's go back!" Claire clutched her purse.

"You're a sitting duck with your Louis Vuitton purse," Jennifer said in a loud whisper.

"This is not a real Louis Vuitton. It's a knockoff my sister sent me from New York. I'm smart enough not to carry the real thing on vacation."

"I'm sure a criminal is not going to check the tag."

"Let's not stand here talking. Just walk and act like you own the neighborhood." Claire nudged Jennifer along.

"I wouldn't want to own this neighborhood."

A block down, a man approached them. He was wearing a store's worth of shiny gold jewelry and had his arms crossed over a silk shirt that bared his black muscles.

"Ladees, pay money for a watch?"

"No thanks, we're not buying today," Jennifer said and coughed violently, trying to sound contagious.

"C'mon, ladee, your man will love you!"

"My man already loves me," Jennifer said, as they shuffled down the dirt street.

"Use your street smarts," Claire said. "Two women walking alone on a strange street do not engage in conversation with strangers."

"When did I have a chance to acquire street smarts? Like Lakeside has crime." Jennifer rolled her eyes and stopped.

Claire stopped too. "It does. The mayor's son was arrested for stealing a car."

"There was no arrest, he was reprimanded. And it wasn't a car, it was for stealing condiments."

"I heard it was a car," Claire said.

"Nope, it was ketchup."

"How do you know?"

"I know because Eric sold the mayor some insurance. Just

goes to tell you the rumor mill is alive and well in Lakeside."

"I wonder what they're saying about us."

Jennifer suddenly remembered where they were. "This is not the time for speculation, Claire."

The pair continued walking for a few minutes and then stopped, this time on a deserted street, to catch their breath and plan their route, when Jennifer felt a tug on her shirt. She froze.

Claire tried to speak but was unable to get the words out.

The hand remained. Jennifer imagined it slowly creeping toward her neck. She had read an article just last week called "The Village Creeper," and the words from the article captured her imagination.

"The creeper's enormous hand grasped her jugular vein . . ."

Her story line was interrupted when her nostrils were filled with a blast of sweet smells, vaguely familiar. It dawned on Jennifer that a villainous type would be unlikely to smell so sweet.

She turned around . . . slowly to see a smiling woman. "Felicia!" she screeched.

Claire shared her relief with a sigh.

Felicia's flawless complexion was the color of cocoa, and she was dressed in a colorful, short-sleeved cotton dress. The fact that she just happened to be on this street this very instant was no coincidence, Jennifer knew. God was watching over them.

"Now come with me." Felicia herded them past the crowd that was gathering.

"This is not a safe neighborhood," Jennifer said.

Their tennis shoes created a dust cloud as they rushed along.

"Thank you for telling me dat so I can move." Felicia laughed.

A block down, she allowed the ladies a moment to catch their breath after the vigorous walk.

"Thanks for stopping." Claire took a lungful of air.

"She fired her personal trainer . . . in September." Jennifer panted, out of breath as well.

"So you live around here?" Claire asked, changing the subject.

"A couple of blocks away. Just keep walking."

They struggled to keep up with Felicia. "What were you thinking, wandering so far from Sea View?"

"Looking for Shakey's Pizza," Claire said.

"Well, you won't find it around here. Shakey's is miles away. By Burger King and TCBY."

"Frozen yogurt. Oh, I would love some frozen yogurt!" Jennifer exclaimed.

"You come to Jamaica and want American food. Hard to figure." Felicia sighed.

23

In the heat of the afternoon, Jennifer and Claire reached Felicia's bright blue house and stood on her porch, recovering from their fright—real or imagined.

Down the street, children were playing. It sounded like a typical active neighborhood in Lakeside during the summer. As Felicia led the women into her two-room house, Claire and Jennifer looked around slowly. The house was airy and full of color and plants, unlike the unfinished outside. The kitchen was simple, with only a small refrigerator and a hot plate.

Felicia put her straw purse on the wooden dining table and offered them some water. It was cool and refreshing.

When her thirst was quenched, Jennifer commented, "You have a nice place here."

"Thank you," said Felicia.

Claire drifted over to the sunny windowsill to feel the welcome afternoon breeze coming in through the open window. She was unusually contemplative for several minutes as Jennifer and Felicia chatted.

Once a world traveler, Claire had been to many places, as far away as India. What struck her now was that she had only seen the touristy, well-traveled spots the guidebooks had recommended. Four stars and up, of course. Now she realized that her need for comfort may have limited the richness of her travels.

Felicia suddenly appeared next to her. "This, my friends, is the real Jamaica. Not dat hotel you're staying at."

"I'd like to see more of the real Jamaica." Claire turned toward her hostess and smiled.

They spent the next fifteen minutes on Felicia's worn sofa talking about the easy lifestyle of the islands.

"The tourists I talk to say they want to see Jamaica," Felicia explained. "But they don't want to see Jamaica. They want an exotic atmosphere with all the comforts of home, plus some."

"I'm sure you're right, Felicia," Claire said. A hint of chagrin passed over her face.

Jennifer scratched her head. "Don't you ever want to see other places, Felicia? Escape to somewhere different? Away from this predictable weather?"

"We have our storms here too, believe me. But no. I've never thought of it. I'm quite content with things as they are. Life here is simple and happy." Her bright eyes dimmed. "Except one thing."

"What's that?"

"My son has a cleft palate and needs an operation." Felicia picked up some sort of memory book with a sun drawn on it by a child.

"I saw your beautiful son at church," Claire said compassionately as Jennifer nodded.

"When he was a baby, he could not breast-feed. He took his milk from a nipple, da kind dey use to feed baby lambs, and da little man got so chubby." She laughed at the thought as she toyed with the book.

Claire watched her rustle the pages. *Most likely private*, she thought.

"Those who know Thomas and his pure little heart look past his disfigurement," Felicia said.

"But it would be nice if they didn't have to look past anything, wouldn't it?" Claire smiled.

"Yes." Felicia pointed at his picture on a bookshelf in a silver-plated frame. "Dat's my Thomas, alright. Ten and as smart as can be."

"And the other picture . . . Is that your husband?" Jennifer asked.

"Yes, I'm a widow." Felicia stood up and reached for the other silver-plated frame. She smiled. "He was a handsome man."

All three women teared up.

Claire thought of Alex.

Felicia put the picture back with care, turning toward the ladies. "My husband was a Christian and I was not. One night he was in Kingston visiting friends. Afterwards he was chased down by a mob who thought he was somebody else. Dey slashed his throat and left him to die."

The women gasped in horror.

"Dat's when I went to work at the hotel. I met Pastor Bob one day while I was sobbing in da laundry room as he was walking by."

Claire and Jennifer listened intently as she went on for several minutes with her testimony.

". . . and since den da people at da Church on da Beach have been my family."

Silence filled the small room.

"I'm sorry. I had much more in my heart den I knew." Felicia turned to pick up her purse. "I'm walking you back to da hotel now," she said.

The ladies rose to leave.

∽◦∾

The streets didn't appear as scary to Jennifer on the way back to the hotel. The people not as terrifying. Felicia introduced them to several of her curious friends.

The man with the gold jewelry ended up having some very funny jokes, and a woman ran out of the house to share her boiled green bananas with them.

When they arrived at the gate to the hotel, Felicia gave one last warning. "Now don't be leaving da gates without knowing where you're going! If you have something you want to see, I'll be your escort!"

"Thank you so much, Felicia," Jennifer said, and Claire echoed her appreciation.

They hugged her and exchanged one last smile.

As they watched Felicia walk away, Jennifer shook her head. "I am so embarrassed about how I acted. My perception was so tainted by my—I hate to say it—prejudice."

"Now don't you feel terrible about suspecting Felicia?" Claire asked.

"Yes," Jennifer confessed. "I feel terrible about a lot of things right now. I'm beginning to see how small my problems are in the grand scheme of things."

❧

Desmond, the security guard, stood in the threshold of Becky's room wearing a uniform of black pants, a white collared shirt, and black closed-toed shoes. "I'm sorry I'm late. But you wouldn't believe my day. First, a man exploded in a tirade over some papers missing from his room, which turned out to be in his briefcase. And den dere was a mix-up with room keys. I didn't get in da sun all day."

"Well, I'm glad you found my note and you're here now," Becky said.

Desmond stepped in and his dark eyes scanned the room.

"So I received your information," he said as he looked around. "Dese robberies are beginning to vex me. We gonna catch dat thief."

Dawn stopped what she was doing. "There's been more than this one robbery?"

"A rash of 'em. Someone's got da red eye."

"I have some Visine," Lillian offered.

"He means someone is envious, you goose," Jennifer said, amused.

"Dat's right."

The women gave him space as he began a thorough examination of the room.

"Dis is da seventh pair of earrings dat's been missing," Desmond said when he was done. He took some notes and left.

"Bedtime, everyone," Becky said a minute later, and went into her private bathroom closing the door behind her. The other ladies left, but Jennifer lingered as Becky showered.

Finally, Claire came in after Jennifer. "C'mon, girlfriend. Back to the nanny's quarters."

Jennifer was obviously eyeing the turned-down satin sheets. "Becky won't mind. I don't take up much room." She crouched, in an attempt to appear smaller.

Claire held her arm and pulled.

Jennifer resisted. "Oh, please don't make me go in our room. I want to be long-suffering. Honestly, I do. But I need some sleep, and Lillian's snorefest is making me crazy."

"Look, I'm tired too. But this is Becky's room and she needs her space."

"I need my sanity and my beauty sleep."

"You're so beautiful, Jen, you'll look great exhausted or not."

"So I'll be beautiful but crazy."

Lillian, in the adjoining room, was listening to every word and feeling terrible.

∽

It was, Claire commented, the most perfect weather yet, and everyone agreed, except Lillian.

She was lying head down on the table, listless, as the others were relishing their sumptuous breakfast buffet.

"What's with you, Lil?" Jennifer asked, after swallowing a piece of mango.

Lillian sat up and rubbed her eyes. "I tried to stay awake all night."

"Why?"

"So I wouldn't snore."

"Oh." She realized Lillian had overheard her comments last night, which explained why she had gotten a decent night's sleep for the first time this trip. She tried to think up something clever to say but then stopped herself. There was no point to it. "I'm sorry," Jennifer finally said.

"No, I am. I'm the one ruining everyone's sleep," Lillian said and lay back down on the linen tablecloth.

"Lil, you snore?" Becky asked.

"Does she snore!" the group erupted in unison.

Lillian sat up with a start, a sheepish expression overtaking her face. "See what I mean."

The group looked at one another, shamefaced.

"What about sleep apnea surgery, Bec?" Dawn directed her question at the expert.

"Right now they do it the old-fashioned way. By cutting out tissue with a scalpel."

"Gross." Lillian cringed.

"If I were having the surgery and could afford it, I'd wait

until the new laser technique is perfected," Becky continued.

"That doesn't help me now!" Lillian's curly head went back down.

Jennifer felt bad about the whole thing.

The conversation dragged along tediously as the group engaged in small talk in between bites.

Jennifer felt so bad about Lillian, she'd lost her appetite. She watched the others eat.

After a while Jennifer was bored. She realized Lillian's playful energy ignited the group. It wasn't as much fun without her constant jabbering about all those useless facts stored in her brain. How the average pencil can draw a line that is thirty-five miles long, and such.

"There's a full moon tonight," Dawn said.

"Yup," Claire said.

"That should be romantic," Becky added.

"Uh huh," Jennifer said.

And then it was too quiet again.

Lillian would have had something interesting to say about the full moon, Jennifer thought. Some mistaken fact or crazy story. Something she'd picked up in home schooling her kids that had no merit but was entertaining nonetheless.

"Full moons are so pretty," Dawn said after she swallowed.

"They are. They really are," Claire agreed.

Jennifer had to do something to perk up Lillian. *That's it,* she thought. "Maybe with the full moon you won't snore as much tonight, Lil."

There was no response from Lillian.

Claire looked at Jennifer. "I'd love to hear your logic on this one."

Jennifer tried to think up something that sounded scientific. "I'm thinking it may be possible that the change in gravity with the full moon tonight could, uh . . . rearrange the . . . uh, nose air flow . . . uh . . ." She prodded Becky along with a raised eyebrow.

Becky picked up on Jennifer's good intentions instantly. "I suppose the change in gravity could reduce the upper airway size." She winked.

"So, Lil, you probably won't snore as much tonight," Jennifer said, sounding conclusive.

Lillian lifted her head. "Jen, I wasn't born on the side of a barn, you know."

"Goodness, I hope not," Dawn said. "The whole town would have witnessed it."

Lillian's one-track brain was so focused on Jennifer's comment she didn't hear Dawn. "You're just saying that to make me feel better."

Jennifer suppressed a chuckle. "Maybe so, Lil, but I just want you back to your old self." She stared at her, thinking of how to say what she wanted to say. "I'm willing to suffer through some snoring to see you bound out of bed like Tigger tomorrow morning. Your silence is making me crazier than your snoring."

Lillian almost cracked a smile. "I'll take that as a right-handed compliment," she said.

"I think you mean left-handed."

"No, I'm right-handed."

Jennifer grinned. "No, I mean it, Lil. I would rather lose sleep and have you back to yourself."

"Really?"

"Really."

Lillian smiled as she lay down again.

❧

The ladies welcomed Jonah's unexpected appearance at the table a few minutes later. He greeted them, pulled up a chair, and sat down next to Becky. Their eyes met and they smiled wide.

He was dressed in a holiday shirt with a large poinsettia on the front. And though he appeared to be in a mood as festive as his shirt, he was as tired as Lillian. He too had been up all night, not because he'd been trying to stay awake, but because he'd been thinking of Felix and how to prove to Becky his merits over his competition.

As soon as they finished exchanging smiles, Becky spilled the story of the robbery in sixty seconds.

"I'm not surprised," Jonah stated. "These hotel robberies have been going on for a while. In fact, yesterday my nurse was missing her earrings, and she feared the worst."

"But she found them later, right?"

It was Lillian's voice. Jonah looked over at her, wondering why she was suddenly wide awake.

Dawn looked down at her fingernails and gulped. "Yes, how did you know?"

Lillian wrung her hands nervously. "Well, when I lose something I usually find it."

Jonah dismissed Lillian's odd reaction, thinking how strange women could be sometimes. "By the way, Lillian, you left without your cholesterol results." He took a paper out of his back pocket and handed it to her.

She read it hastily and carelessly. "I'm gonna die!" she wailed. "My DSL is off the charts. Four hundred and thirty-two."

Jonah found Lillian to be slightly overreactive.

Becky grabbed the paper from her and read the numbers for herself. "That's not your cholesterol. You are patient number four thirty-two. Your cholesterol is only one sixty. That's really low."

"Here, have some butter on your crumpet, Lil." Jennifer pushed the butter dish toward her.

Jonah leaned forward and kissed Becky's cheek. "I'm sorry about your earrings, Rebecca. Honestly."

"Thank you," she said, and they held hands.

~⁊⁊~

After breakfast, Dawn led the way down the beaten path to their room and unlocked the door, her three friends following close behind. She suddenly stopped and turned to the others.

"We've been robbed!" she cried as she dropped the key on the bed table. "My iPod is gone!"

Lillian searched the room. "And my digital camera!" she cried.

Claire and Jennifer looked at each other. "The door was locked," Claire said.

"Not the dead bolt," Jennifer pointed out. "It would be easy to pry the door and lock apart with a credit card . . . so I read in *True Crimes* magazine."

"Are you sure you didn't leave your iPod by the pool or somewhere else?" Claire asked Dawn.

"I'm positive. It was here on the dresser where I always leave it. Along with the USB adapter, which is also missing."

"My jewelry is still here," Lillian happily announced, referring to her huge, chunky costume jewelry collection.

Claire plopped on the bed, and Jennifer plopped down next to her.

"You know what I'm thinking." Jennifer's forehead had creased with a frown.

"Not again." Claire threw her a wary look.

"I'm thinking 'you-know-who' is our primary suspect."

193

"Who is you-know-who?" Lillian asked, as she rummaged through the drawers.

"That's preposterous!" Claire objected.

"That sounds like something you-know-who would say."

"Who is you-know-who?" Lillian tried again, and stuck her head under the bed.

They ignored Lillian and looked at each other.

"Motive, my dear. Motive," Claire said with a smirk.

"Motive?"

"Diamond earrings, an iPod, and a broken digital camera. This is a diverse thief," Dawn remarked.

Lillian's head reappeared. "Diverse is right," she spouted. "That thief took the Chia Pet I traded for a pair of Spanx!"

"Do they still make Chia Pets?" Dawn asked.

"Of course they still make Chia Pets. That's like asking if they still make Pet Rocks."

"Do they still make Pet Rocks?"

"I've seen them in Goodwill."

Jennifer and Claire looked at each other again.

"Oh, right. You-know-who has a million uses for a Chia Pet." Claire scowled at Jennifer.

Jennifer gave a brisk nod.

"Will you stop?"

"I'll stop after I check my email and find out you-know-who is who you-know-who says they are. If you know what I mean." Jennifer let loose a devious laugh.

"Who is you-know-who?" Lillian asked one last time.

"She wants to know who you-know-who is, Claire. What do you think?"

"I don't know. But it appears to me you-know-who took your chocolate."

Jennifer's eyes widened. "And right out of the ice bucket. Now that's low."

24

A couple of hours later Jennifer and Claire returned from Planet Jamaica. Jennifer had checked her email, which was nothing but spam.

When they were near the end of the street, Jennifer's eyes settled on a blond figure. "Is that Pastor Bob making that racket?"

Claire turned her head in the direction of the noise and squinted.

"A version of him, anyway."

"Repent, you sinner!" he yelled through a large, bright red megaphone, in a fire and brimstone style of a stereotypical Hollywood street preacher.

They made their way down the busy street and stood before him with a bewildered look as people passed by, treating him as though he were invisible. For the sake of the gospel, Jennifer wished he were.

He was standing on the same trunk he'd preached on Sunday, dressed in fatigues, looking very different than he did in his Sunday best. The preacher was so caught up in his street preaching he didn't notice Jennifer and Claire at first.

"Ladees, how nice to have my practitioners in my audience," he said as he stepped down and put his megaphone aside.

"I think you mean parishioners," Claire stated.

"Whatever," he said.

The women looked at each other with incredulous expressions.

Jennifer's voice shook. "Bob, I don't think your, ahem . . . subtle approach is working."

His expression changed. "We're in a war! The wicked shall be as stubble! The fire shall burn them up!" he yelled, looking to the passersby who, in turn, looked anywhere but in their direction.

"This is a different preaching style than you had on Sunday, Pastor Bob," Claire said.

"Ah, yes, Sunday," the preacher smiled. "Be kind to the unloved."

"Yes, what happened to all that kindness?" Jennifer asked.

"I like to go easy on them once a week. After all, the Bible says, 'More flies are taken with a drop of honey than a ton of vinegar.'"

"That's not in the Bible. Thomas Fuller said that." Claire peered at him. "He also said, 'If it were not for hope, the heart would break.'"

Bob tilted his head. "I haven't read that sermon on the Internet."

Jennifer studied Bob for a moment. Somehow his face seemed sharper than it did the other day. His nose pointier. His eyes—one blue, one green—closer set. His whole appearance had a nerdish quality that Jennifer hadn't picked up on Sunday. If Becky were here Jennifer would be embarrassed that she had wanted to fix them up.

"Where did you go to seminary, Pastor Bob?" Claire asked.

"I don't believe in seminary. I believe the Holy Spirit calls you to preach."

"And how did he call you?" Claire looked at him sideways.

"On a surfboard in Florida. A killer wave too. He said, 'Go and help those wretched Jamaicans.'"

The blood drained from Jennifer's face at his condescending attitude.

Claire was speechless.

The conversation stalled, so Pastor Bob went back to his preaching.

"So what do you think of Bob now?" Claire asked as they crossed the street. "A good match for Becky, eh?"

"Okay. So I was way off on that one."

"How way off?"

"A couple of thousand miles." Jennifer shook her head, still unsettled. "But . . ."

"But, what."

"What if he's our robber?"

Claire put her hand on her hip. "Just because he's a jerk doesn't make him a thief."

"I can't help but have my suspicions. Did you notice his big, jagged scar?"

"You mean his chicken pox scars." Claire sighed. "You'd have suspicions about a Pet Rock." She tossed her head toward the shops. "Keep walking."

"Now all we need to do is spot someone with a pink iPod, diamond earrings, and a broken digital camera," Jennifer said.

"Don't forget the Chia Pet." Claire shook her head and added, "I never did understand the fascination with those things."

They walked by a T-shirt store with huge sale signs on the windows.

"Wouldn't it be great if the thief stole Lillian's wardrobe? It would be like they were wearing a blinking light." Claire snickered.

"And whose clothes would she borrow?" Jennifer wanted to know.

Claire grabbed Jennifer's arm. "Wait. Hide!"—she slowed their pace— "That guy over there has an iPod."

"That's Dawn's friend, the chef. That would make sense."

"It would?"

They crept closer.

"Darn, it's blue," Claire said.

They exchanged a look.

"That one's pink," Jennifer said, noticing the woman in the purple T-shirt coming out of a store.

They sauntered over. "Excuse me, ma'am. But where did you get your iPod?" Jennifer asked.

"The same place dat everyone else does."

"Where's that?"

"Apple.com. And free shipping too, if you order before Christmas."

The ladies stared at each other and laughed.

With a puzzled look, the woman shook her head as she walked away.

∽⚬∽

The afternoon was still brimming with possibilities, yet Jennifer and Claire were lazily relaxed in comfortable hammocks under a thatch hut. Palm trees dotted the beach around them. They were close enough to the ocean to wash the sand off their feet.

"It's a perfect day for parasailing," a passing tourist called.

Jennifer smiled serenely. "Thanks, but we're content right here." She didn't budge from her prone position.

Claire stretched and turned to Jennifer. "What's wrong with us? Everyone else who comes to the Caribbean has all these bold adventures. Even Lillian is using her Spanx money to take a snorkeling lesson. After her nap." She swung one leg over the other.

"Well, I don't have Spanx money. I plead poverty." Jennifer removed the straw hat from her head and covered her face with it.

"So if you had the money, you'd be out there whipping around on a Jet Ski?" Claire asked in a skeptical tone.

Jennifer lifted the hat from her face and sat up. She watched a Jet Ski bounce in the water for a minute. "That looks scary!" she stated emphatically.

A woman in a bikini passed.

"But I might go swimming . . . if I had her perfect figure," Jennifer said.

"So you're as vain as me?"

"Vein as in V-E-I-N. But since I got Trevor out of the deal, I'll live with it." She glanced at Claire and smiled. "Enough of this futile talk. Now hand me one of those chocolate truffles."

Claire sat up to reach for a chocolate on the other side of her. "It's liquid chocolate now," she said.

Jennifer puckered her lips. "You'd think if they can invent a digital Smart Pan like Dawn bought—which I need, by the way—they could invent chocolate that doesn't melt."

"I have a caterer who delivers my meals prepared and frozen for the week."

"I'm sick of chocolate anyway," Jennifer claimed.

Claire threw her head back with a laugh. "I've been waiting for this day."

Jennifer cracked a smile. "Trust me, it's only temporary."

Becky appeared in the thatch hut, startling them. She wore shorts and a tank top and looked soft and feminine all in pink.

"And speaking of perfect figures," Jennifer murmured.

"Good afternoon. Are you girls enjoying yourselves this beautiful Jamaican day?"

"Bec, we want to tell you again how much this trip means to us," Claire said.

"You are very welcome." Becky smiled and her white teeth looked even whiter against her tanned skin.

All three of them smiled.

Becky sat down next to Jennifer in her hammock. "Now for the invitation of the year. Do you guys want to stay at Jonah's house for the rest of our trip?"

"His house?" Claire asked.

"We would each have our own private room with a sweeping ocean view of our own private beach . . . and a maid. No more view of the block wall. It would make me feel better." Becky looked from one to the other, waiting for their reaction.

"I might actually wear my bathing suit," Claire said.

"So Jonah invited us out of the blue," Jennifer asked suspiciously.

"Not exactly. Lillian told him her snoring was driving you guys crazy."

"Well, she's not lying there," Claire said.

". . . and also that she was creeped out about the robberies and was afraid to stay here. To tell you the truth, I'm not all that crazy about it myself. I locked all my valuables in the safe at the front desk."

Jennifer looked doubtful.

"We could decorate his banana plant for Christmas?" Becky said.

"Tree," Jennifer said.

"Plant," Becky said.

"Whatever," Claire said.

"He's not one of those bad banana plantation owners who ruins people's health with pesticides, is he?" Jennifer said.

"I think he raises bananas for fun."

"He raises bananas for fun? I've heard of raising llamas for fun, but bananas?"

"What if we want to come into town?" Claire asked.

"I've rented us a van and put you guys on the insurance. You can use it any time without even asking."

"Hmmm." Claire weighed the offer.

"Please, I'm dying of curiosity to see his place, and I don't want to go alone." Becky stood up. "See you out front in twenty minutes. My rental car is the blue Dodge Caravan." She walked away.

"Okay, but if I see a hatchet lying around . . . ," Jennifer warned.

"Whatever that means," Becky called over her shoulder.

Claire's clear blue eyes brightened in mischief. "Have you considered donating your brain to science, Jen?"

"I'd like to be dead first, thank you."

"Maybe Mr. Beach and his hatchet could arrange that," Claire said and then lay back in the hammock for a few more minutes of bliss.

25

After a tour of Jonah's lavish seven-bedroom estate, Becky and Jonah had left Claire and Jennifer on the balcony with four types of banana drinks the maid had prepared.

It was a paradise on a scenic hillside above Ocho Rios overlooking a wide, open ocean. The view was as green as the rain forest. "A little slice of heaven," Becky had called it.

"And you thought Jonah was making all this up," Claire said in a know-it-all voice.

"Okay, okay, so he doesn't need Becky's diamond earrings. His floors are practically diamond."

"And I haven't seen a hatchet yet." Claire put her hand on her hip.

"So he's a wonderful man and Becky should marry him and move to the islands." She rested her elbows on the balcony railing.

"You really should see a doctor about your personality disorder." Claire flashed a smile.

"We have a doctor on the premises," Jennifer said.

"So you're saying you believe Jonah is a doctor," Claire asked, sounding relieved.

"I've ruled him out as the diamond thief, but I still wonder why he would retire so young."

"I'm sure there's a logical explanation."

For a few minutes they listened to the waves lapping on the rocks below.

Jennifer broke the silence. "If Becky did marry him and moved here, we could visit. And that wouldn't be a bad thing."

"Could you live here?" Claire wondered aloud.

"If I did live here, which I'm not planning to do in this century, I would build a skateboard ramp for Trevor over there." She pointed to an open stretch of land. "And maybe a Krispy Kreme factory for Eric over there." She smiled. "What about you, Claire? How about a horse riding arena for Lexie and a dirt bike trail for Alex?"

"Why not."

"You've forgiven him for becoming a Harley boy, haven't you?"

"What does anger ever get you but a red face?" Claire shook her head and sighed. "I was thinking about the old days and how Alex used to shine his Kawasaki until it sparkled."

"That Kawasaki was the most over-insured motorcycle in Minnesota thanks to my insurance-selling husband."

Claire laughed and went on with her original thought. "One night I found him in the garage at three a.m. staring at the thing with a rag in his hand."

"And . . ."

"And . . . he looked so adorable."

Jennifer smiled so wide her cheeks looked like apples. "I think you guys are going to be just fine."

"'If it were not for hope, the heart would break.'" Claire stretched her arms and took in the sunshine. She took a sip of her banana drink before she spoke again. "For some reason this trip has restored my hope."

Jennifer put her arm around her best friend.

"And I owe it all to you, Jennifer, and your childish, petty, selfish, discontented—"

Jennifer pulled away and sneered playfully. "Flattery will get you nowhere."

❧

On the opposite side of Jonah's luxurious home, he and Becky stood on the deck holding hands and staring at the view.

"So what's it like living in paradise?" Becky asked, wrinkling her forehead and exposing her worry lines.

"Sometimes lonely. But mostly unadulterated, magnificent splendor," Jonah replied, sounding like he'd answered the question a hundred times before.

"So really, what are you doing living here in Jamaica? Getting away from the trappings of modern civilization?" Becky stared into Jonah's beautiful green eyes.

"You saw that Cary Grant movie too? *Father Goose*, wasn't it?" He smiled.

"You have satellite TV?"

"Of course."

"Do you get the Hallmark Channel?"

"Yes."

"Do you watch the Hallmark Channel?"

"No, I watch *Doogie Howser* reruns," he said and laughed.

"Really, Jonah. Why did you come to Jamaica to live?" she pressed.

"I told you, I inherited this place from my father eight months ago."

"So you packed up and left your career as a doctor just like that?"

He didn't answer, but his face showed anxiety.

"Living abroad is a big decision," Becky said.

Jonah laughed, but it was a tense laugh. "Okay, I can see you want the better, exciting version."

"Just the real one." Becky's hazel eyes grew serious.

Jonah fidgeted, appearing hemmed in by the question. After a moment's pause, he said dramatically, "I came to get away from the pain and horrors of disease."

Becky couldn't help wonder what Jonah was hiding. What if Jennifer was right? She hadn't had this kind of emotional intimacy with a man for years. There was a doctor she had thought she loved during her nursing program. And since then, only bad dates and constant disappointment.

Jonah leaned on the balcony and changed the subject. "Didn't you just say you quit pediatrics?"

"Yes." Becky felt her own anxiety now.

For a moment they silently reflected.

Jonah finally spoke. "There is something to be said for safe distances."

"Safe distances?"

"Yes."

"I'm not sure what you're saying, Jonah."

"I'm saying I can do my volunteer work and come home and feel as though I've done some good for the world . . . without the heartbreak."

Becky studied Jonah's profile. She wanted to know the rest of the story but decided to drop it for now. If there was anything all those singles ministry meetings had taught her, it was to take things slow.

〜〜

During the fabulous seafood dinner that evening, Jonah's maid came in and handed Jennifer a message. The front desk at the Sea View Resort had called.

Jennifer started reading the note out loud. "Call your cousin . . . Rupert." She folded the note and looked up, embarrassed.

"You can use my phone," Jonah offered.

"But it's long distance. California," Jennifer said.

"I'll write the country code on a piece of paper," Jonah insisted and went for pen and paper.

All eyes were on Jennifer as she put down her glass of Perrier and stood up, avoiding Becky's glance. She felt like a pot ready to boil from the pressure she was feeling.

∞

As the call rang through in Jonah's study, Jennifer thought how evil she was to suspect Jonah of anything. Especially being the hotel robber. What a ludicrous thought.

Her cousin picked up the phone.

"Rupert, this is Jennifer in Jamaica. Did you call me?"

"I wanted to tell you about your Mr. Beach, and my server is down for repair."

"He checked out all right, didn't he?"

"He doesn't exist."

"What?"

"There is no Doctor Jonah Clark Beach. There is no Jonah Beach period."

Jennifer took a deep breath. "So what does that mean?"

"For one, he's not a doctor."

"And for two?"

"It could be one of his aliases."

"Why would someone have an alias?"

"To hide his criminal background would be my first guess."

"And your second guess?"

"He could be hiding from something."

"Like what?"

"An ex-wife he owes alimony to, or embezzlement. Practicing medicine illegally? Fraud." He paused. "Like that no-good ex-stepfather of yours."

"Please don't mention *him,* especially not at Christmas."

"Anyway, whatever the reason, Jamaica is a good place to hide."

Jennifer's suspicions were aroused all over again. She thanked her cousin for his expense and his trouble and offered to return the favor.

"You can return the favor by allowing us to stay with you for a couple of weeks this summer."

"Of course."

There was a voice in the background.

"Oh, Karen wants to know if you have a mall in Minnesota."

"Only the largest mall in the United States."

Jennifer said good-bye and sat for another minute, thinking about what Rupert had told her. She decided not to say anything to anyone about Jonah for the time being.

A heavy sigh escaped her as she stood. She wished she'd kept her nose out of it in the first place. If she could only be more like Dawn, who looked for the best in everyone, then life wouldn't be so complicated. But she wasn't Dawn.

26

After a luxurious night's sleep (due mainly to Lillian sleeping at the opposite end of the house in her private room), day five of the vacationers' stay in Jamaica looked to be trouble free.

The five rested women were unusually happy and chatty this sunny morning. They sat in comfortable Adirondack-style chairs in Jonah's marble-floored sunroom overlooking the lovely grounds. There were ferns around the room, and the table was exquisitely set and as colorful as Lillian's outfit. The music in the background was lively, yet not distracting from the meal, which was as good as or better than the hotel food.

The uniformed maid brought out a silver tray with a stack of banana pancakes and individual pitchers of warm syrup and set it on the white lace tablecloth with a ready smile. And this was just the beginning of the buffet. There were cereals, juices, fresh fruit, home-baked breads and muffins . . .

When Dawn ended her prayer of thanks, Becky breathed in the scent of freshly cut tropical flowers beautifully arranged as the table's centerpiece. She smiled. "Now this is how I imagined Jamaica."

Dawn raised her chin. "Then you have a great imagination. It's certainly more than I expected it to be."

After a lull in conversation, Becky said in a soft voice, "I miss Jonah."

Only Claire heard her and asked where he was.

"He's in town this morning," Becky answered.

Claire whispered in her ear. "I've never seen you so giddy. It must be love."

L-O-V-E. Becky spelled in her mind. Four letters she dare not speak aloud. The word scared her, the feelings scared her. The idea of change scared her. But being alone ten years from now scared her even more. Her thoughts seesawed back and forth. She'd only known Jonah for a few days, and at times, it seemed as though he were hiding something.

Lillian's contented sigh pulled Becky back to the present. "Enjoying yourself, Lil?"

She shook her head. "You know, this may never happen again. Not in our whole lives."

"What may never happen again?" Becky raised one waxed brow.

"Free time?" Dawn asked.

"Having a maid meet our every whim?" Jennifer said.

"Our own room with a sweeping view of the sea?" Claire grinned broadly.

Lillian shook her head and then cut a piece of pancake and waved it on her fork. "No, banana pancakes with this incredibly sticky, gooey, sweet syrup."

The group roared in laughter.

The maid returned to set an ornate teapot on the table in front of Becky.

"Joy, what kind of pancake syrup is this?" Becky asked.

"Mr. Beach orders it in specially. I'll check."

In a minute Joy was back with the bottle and read the label. "Log Cabin," she said and then excused herself.

"Thank you very much," Becky said and chuckled.

Once again everyone at the table caught the humor except Lillian, who seemed to miss the irony of the situation.

Lillian took another bite of her pancake and swallowed. "This Log Cabin stuff is so good. It's better than the generic brand for sure."

"You can buy it at the market in Lakeside," Becky said.

"You mean the international market with all those fancy groceries you shop at?"

"No, like at the People's Market on Second and Main." Becky laughed.

"Cool," Lillian said.

"Here, here!" Becky cried and tapped her glass with a silver spoon. "A juice toast to appreciating what we already have back home."

❧

Later that morning, Jennifer and Claire rode the golf cart down the long driveway and waited at the high stone gate for Felicia to arrive with their clothes. Jonah had hired her to launder them.

Jennifer stared at the high stone wall with massive pillars. "It's a beautiful fortress, but intimidating."

"Just think of the history," Claire remarked.

"It may not be a very good history, Claire. This place has to be a hundred and fifty years old. Who knows what kind of mistreatment went on?"

"That takes some of the fun out of it, doesn't it?" Claire admitted.

Jennifer peered at what she thought would be a panoramic view of beautiful houses and green lawns like she had seen adjacent to the resort. Instead the neighborhood was bright-colored stucco houses, plain and run-down.

A little barefoot boy showed up at the gate and put his face to the bars. He had big black eyes and long eyelashes.

"Hi there," Jennifer said.

He folded his arms and stood there, in a shirt and jeans that were patched and old, but he did not speak.

Both women smiled, but he would not smile back.

Jennifer reached in the shirt pocket of her sundress and gave the little boy some candy.

He ate it with gusto and extended his hand for more.

Jennifer shook her head. "No more, I'm sorry."

The little boy looked so lonely and sad standing there, Jennifer decided to go back for more chocolate and ran up the driveway.

By the time she was back, several more children were gathered at the gate with the little boy. Jennifer gave them all her chocolate—over twenty pieces.

As she watched the children through the bars, she realized she'd thought mostly of herself this entire vacation. She'd told herself that she deserved a carefree time. Away from the underprivileged children's party. Away from all her stress and her problems.

In truth, her heart had grown stone cold, like the wall separating her from the children.

The spokesman of the group, a small boy with a contagious smile, asked for more chocolate, breaking into Jennifer's long reflection.

Felicia showed up, balancing a large basket on her head, just as Jennifer was trying to explain to the children that was all the treats she had for them today.

Felicia shooed them away.

Jennifer shook her head sadly as Claire opened the gate for

Felicia and shut it behind her. Felicia stepped in and dropped the load of laundry on the back of the golf cart.

Claire looked around. "We thought your son might be with you."

"He's waiting down da hill because he's embarrassed."

Jennifer almost asked why, and then remembered.

"Thank you, Felicia, for doing the laundry. Can we pay you?" Jennifer asked.

"Jonah already did. He is a very generous man."

"Leave the laundry here. We'll take care of it," Claire insisted.

"Alright, if you're sure," Felicia said.

It was then Jennifer noticed something. Felicia's large earrings glinted in the sunlight. *Those are Becky's earrings*, she thought and was shocked. She wanted to say something, but what could she say without accusing Felicia directly?

"God bless you, den," Felicia said.

"God bless you too," Claire said.

"See you later," Jennifer said with a loopy grin.

The second Felicia left, Jennifer grabbed Claire's arm. "She has Becky's earrings on."

Claire pulled away. "You don't know what you're saying! That doesn't make sense."

"I know they're Becky's earrings. They're the size and the same brilliant cut."

"I did notice them," Claire said. "But this is over the top, Jen."

Jennifer started to sweat. "And another thing. I wasn't going to tell you about this because I was trying to give Jonah the benefit of the doubt."

Claire moved in closer.

"Jonah Beach doesn't exist."

"If he doesn't exist, then how is it that he and Becky are on a hike today? Besides, I thought the point was Felicia wearing Becky's earrings."

Jennifer blinked. "You just don't get it, do you, Claire?"

"Apparently not," she said.

⁓

Outside, the blue canvas had turned to twinkling stars against a black velvet drop. Inside, a string of white lights glowed. The ladies were showered and ready for bed, crowding the couches in their pajamas and enjoying the goodies covering every inch of the coffee table.

"Smile," Lillian said, as she took another picture with Becky's picture phone.

"What time is it?" Jennifer popped another piece of chocolate in her mouth.

Claire pointed to the clock. "Ten minutes after nine."

Jennifer's brown eyes grew pensive in contemplation. Jonah and Becky had been gone since early that morning. "Maybe they went off and got married," she speculated.

"And I'll bet Pastor Bob performed the ceremony on his surfboard," Claire joked tersely.

Jennifer took a sharp breath and gave her a look.

"He's so skinny, you'd think a good wave would knock him over," Dawn commented.

Lillian headed the discussion in another direction. "If I were home, we'd be wrapping presents for our children. Derrick would be playing with the kids' toys and wanting to keep them for himself."

"Oh, no, don't start," Jennifer said.

"We'd be stringing popcorn," Dawn said, staring at the lights. "Stirring the hot chocolate to a frothy foam and baking Christmas cookies to a golden brown."

"With your mother-in-law?" Jennifer narrowed her eyes.

"Oh, yeah, her," Dawn replied faintly. Her expression suddenly changed to one of misery.

"I wonder if Alex got to see Lexie's play before he went zooming around the Southwest on his Harley," Claire said, looking hypnotized.

Lillian made a heaving sigh before she blurted out her next sentence. "I think we made a huge mistake in coming." She paused, immobilized. "Martha was right!"

There was a deafening silence, long and eerie. Much like that morning three weeks prior when Jennifer had brought up the subject of Christmas stress.

Dread came over the entire group. Even Jennifer got to thinking about home.

A voice from the hall broke the silence. "She usually is. But in this case I'm afraid she wasn't." All heads turned.

Lillian's eyes grew wide. "I just heard Martha's voice!"

"We must be hearing things," Dawn said, looking around at the others.

They rose all at the same time and forced their stunned bodies down the hall.

There was Martha standing in the hallway, wearing a colorful cotton sleeveless dress with her auburn hair in a casual new style.

Lillian was the first to react. She buried her face in her hands and then lifted her eyes. "Martha!" she shouted. And then she practically jumped into her arms. "I can't believe it's you!"

❧

Jonah and Becky were right behind Martha. "We've done our good deed." Becky smiled, satisfied.

"Or you did, anyway." Jonah smiled back at her.

Becky shed a few tears herself as she watched the reactions as they welcomed Martha. "I can't believe Martha called me."

"Why are you so surprised?" Jonah asked.

"She was so opposed to this trip, and here she calls me saying she wants to come."

"Sometimes the things we fight are the things we really want the most."

"That's true."

She wondered if Jonah was thinking about the same things she had been wrestling with. She had pushed the thought of true love away, but it was what she wanted most.

"I don't think anyone will notice if we slip out for a few minutes." Jonah slipped his arm around Becky's small waist and whisked her back out the door into the balmy night.

⟨⟩

On the couch in the airy living room, a few minutes had passed, and the initial shock and surprise had turned to tremendous joy.

"I can't believe how different you look, Martha," Lillian said and hugged her again.

"I hope that's good," Martha said. She looked around lovingly at the group. "There is so much I want to tell all of you," she said.

"Tell us about the party first," Lillian insisted.

Martha touched her shoulder. "Let's save that for later."

Lillian frowned at her.

"I will tell you this, though. Every one of your husbands took part in the party."

"If that's all we've accomplished by taking this trip, that's enough for me," Dawn said.

Jennifer nodded in agreement. "I think we'll be more appreciated now that they know what we do."

Claire's face took on a faraway look.

Martha stood up and walked over to her. "Alex is working things out, dear."

"I know."

"He gave me this to give to you."

Claire's eyes showed apprehension.

Martha reached for something in her enormous hand-bag she was clutching. "It's a video of the *Nutcracker* performance."

Claire took the tape and started crying. When she caught her breath, she said in a whisper, "Thank you, Martha. Thank you," and took off down the hall en route to the TV room.

Dawn and Jennifer smiled on her account.

A little light flickered in Martha's brown eyes. "I have another surprise."

"You're surprise enough, Martha," Jennifer said.

A head peered around the corner.

"Lisa, come on in!" Martha yelled.

All five foot ten of Lisa's toothpick form appeared in the room.

The ladies gasped and laughed at the same time. They waited for Martha to explain.

"Well, Becky paid my way, and so I paid Lisa's way."

Martha put her arm around her. "I needed her to keep me in line."

"But, Lisa, what about your children?" Dawn asked.

"They're with their father," she said with a tinge of sadness in her green eyes.

27

The two ladies had settled into their bedrooms and joined the others in the living room. Lisa had the table jammed with seven shades of nail polish and assorted accoutrements essential for female foot pampering, and the six women were wiggling their bare toes on the coffee table.

"Lisa, tell us about yourself," Dawn encouraged.

"I'll tell you about Lisa," Martha piped in. "We've gotten to know each other quite well." Martha touched her shoulder. "She is an amazing young woman."

The group listened intently. Lillian squirmed uncomfortably. She wondered why Martha would bring the church's cleaning woman with her. As far as she knew, Martha didn't even know her last name.

"Lisa has three beautiful sons who think she is the coolest mother on earth. And she manages to take care of them on her meager salary, which will be remedied shortly," Martha added.

Lisa's pale complexion brightened.

Lillian's complexion faded.

Jennifer leaned forward. "How did you two get together?"

"Becky's cell phone," Martha replied.

Jennifer smiled. "I knew you were pushing those buttons, Lisa."

"I was pushing buttons, alright. Martha's buttons." She flung her long hair as a grin spread across her face.

Martha's mouth turned down at the corners.

Then Lisa laughed and Martha laughed, and all the ladies joined in, except Lillian.

Lisa straightened the straps of her yellow tank top. "You know how I'm always singing and dancing with that little worn dust rag of mine?"

"No," Lillian said. Her frown deepened.

"Well, I am." She laughed. "Anyway, one day I was singing, and Martha started singing with me. And we found out we have perfect harmony."

"One, two, three. Harmony," Martha shouted, and she and Lisa sang "Our God Is an Awesome God" with passion.

Lillian was bamboozled at this new Martha, so unlike the reserved Martha she knew. What had happened to her?

"And there's more news." Martha grinned. "We're going to stay here another week after you leave."

Lillian's face twisted in jealousy. The others drew a communal sigh of elation.

"The unbelievable news is that my husband suggested it," Martha said.

"Knowing Harry, that *is* a miracle." Claire looked at Martha, gauging her reaction.

"I went on strike. Refused to fix him breakfast." Martha straightened her collar and smiled a little.

"You went on strike?" Jennifer's voice mirrored the surprise Lillian felt. "Obviously, you forgot to attend your own Bible study on submission," she teased.

"I've realized there are gray areas," Martha said.

Lisa stood up and swayed like one of the island palms. "Yah mon." She did a jig.

The other women joined in, and to Lillian's surprise, Martha did not object.

"Come on, Lillian," Lisa encouraged.

"I'm not sure if Christians dance." She watched Martha, who was starting to sway.

"'Then David, girt with a linen apron, came dancing before the Lord with abandon.' Second Samuel chapter six," Martha quoted properly and then turned to Lisa. "Put on that Christian reggae CD you brought, honey."

∽↫

The next morning the house was full of such energy that all the women (except Becky who stayed up half the night talking with Jonah) were on the beach at eight o'clock wearing Sponge Bob T-shirts Lisa had given them.

Jennifer pulled Claire down the beach for a private conversation.

Lillian followed, oblivious to their desire for privacy. "We're going for a jog. C'mon, guys."

Lisa yelled from the surf. "Come on, you domestic goddesses. Get your lazy butts over here."

"She said the 'b' word," Lillian said, shocked.

Claire shook her head. "That Lisa. She's such a kick."

"She's one of those people everyone likes," Jennifer said.

"Almost everybody," Lillian said.

Jennifer looked at her. "What's wrong, Lil?"

Lillian pursed her lips.

"Is it animal, vegetable, or mineral?"

"Would a tall woman who stole my best friend be animal or mineral?"

Neither one knew what to say to her.

"Your mascara is running." Claire reached over to wipe the smear.

Lisa ran up and loomed over Lillian's petite form. She tugged at her arm. "Let's go before we turn into grandmothers."

Lillian gave a helpless shrug as she was dragged away.

"Poor Lillian," Claire said when they were out of earshot.

"Never mind Lil right now. We have our own matter to attend to."

"What?"

"Felicia is walking around with Becky's earrings, and those earrings have sentimental value."

Claire put her hands on Jennifer's shoulders. "Let's tell Becky and see what she wants to do about it."

"I want to be sure first."

"You said you were sure."

Jennifer's brown eyes were intent. "I want to be absolutely sure. Let's go visit Pastor Bob."

Claire swept her blond hair off her cheek. "Why would we want to visit that creep?"

"As weird as he is, he's still her pastor. Maybe he can talk her into turning herself in. I'd rather not involve the police."

"I still think it would be better to let Becky handle it her way."

"Let's change. I'll drive the van."

"I would stand here and argue with you except that you always seem to get your way."

"Not true. The next time you want something we'll do it your way."

Claire dug her flip-flops into the sand. "That, Jen, is the funniest thing I've ever heard."

◦⋈◦

Jennifer knocked on Pastor Bob's door.

He opened it, looking scruffy. His hair was disheveled, and he was wearing short shorts and a plain white T-shirt that said "Procrastinate Now" in big red letters.

"We hope we're not disturbing you, Bob," Jennifer said, "but we need to talk to you."

Claire nodded unenthusiastically.

Standing in the small living room, Jennifer couldn't help but glance through the door to Bob's cluttered bedroom. His bed was unmade and his dirty clothes and comic books covered the floor. On his laziest day, Trevor wasn't this disorganized. She wondered what Claire, who had no tolerance for smelly messes, was thinking.

"Can we sit in the kitchen?" Claire suggested through clenched teeth.

They followed Bob into a small kitchen/dining area and sat down around a card table.

"It looks better in here than it smells," Claire said and frowned. "Sorry, I didn't mean to make it sound like—"

"Hey, it's cool. I took a bath last night," Bob said.

Jennifer didn't agree. The breakfast dishes were still on the table, dirty dishes were piled high in the sink, and the trash can was overflowing.

Both women raised their eyebrows.

Bob lit a scented candle.

Claire thanked him profusely and then took a deep breath.

"So, what are we talking about here, ladies?" Bob eyed his visitors with apprehension.

"It's about Felicia," Claire said.

"Tell me the whole story."

As Jennifer finished, Bob rubbed his fingers over his fuzz. "Felicia, huh. I'm not surprised."

"We are!" Claire exclaimed.

"Her kid needs an operation."

"Yes, we know about that. But what does that have to do with anything?" Claire said, looking rather shaken.

Bob dropped his head and then raised it to look them in the eye. "Ladies, ladies, are we not naïve?"

"Well, *she* is," Jennifer teased Claire and elbowed her friend. Claire rolled her eyes.

Bob continued with his theory. "Felicia needs the money for her son's operation. She'll probably wear the earrings for a few days and sell them on the black market."

"Black market!" The thought stunned Jennifer.

"The interest rates in Jamaica are killer and she can't afford a loan, if she could even get one."

"You could cosign for her," Jennifer quickly suggested.

Both of Bob's mismatched eyes dimmed. "Do I look like I could cosign for anyone?"

"No," Jennifer admitted.

"She also may have taken some other items too," Claire informed the preacher.

"Like what?"

"An iPod, a digital camera, and—" Claire stopped before she got to the Chia Pet. It sounded too ridiculous.

"Possibly as Christmas presents for her son." Bob scratched his white T-shirt under his arm.

"Her son. Oh, Claire, this is terrible. What would happen to her son if she served jail time?" Jennifer was wishing they hadn't come.

"Would you take him in, Bob?" Claire asked.

"Of course he will. 'Love the unlovable; help those who cannot help themselves,'" Jennifer quoted from his sermon.

"Did I say that?" Bob asked, eyes darting back and forth.

"Yes," Jennifer said.

"Having a kid around would sorta cramp my style," Bob said, furrowing his bushy eyebrows.

"You need to practice what you preach." Jennifer gave a photogenic smile, but she was having second thoughts about Claire's suggestion already. She looked around, wondering what kind of place this would be to raise a child. If Jonah wasn't a phony, he would be a much better prospect.

Bob tapped his finger on the table.

"Will you at least talk to her?" Claire asked.

"I don't know."

"Please!" Jennifer said.

"I think it would be better if you left it alone," he said firmly.

"But wouldn't that be unethical?" Claire almost knocked over a dirty glass on the table.

"Your friend could get the insurance money, Felicia's kid could get the operation, and everyone would live happily ever after, like in the fairy tales."

"But life is not a fairy tale," Jennifer said.

"My life is," Bob claimed.

Jennifer wondered how he could say that with his slim subsistence.

"You need to simply forgive," Bob said assuredly, as though it were an easy and obvious solution.

"Look the other way and it will all disappear," Jennifer said, sounding cynical. "That was my mother's philosophy and guess where it got her?"

One of Bob's eyebrows went up. "Where did it get her?"

"Never mind." Claire quickly changed the subject. "Do you miss the States, Bob?"

"Only one thing."

"What?" Claire asked.

"Krispy Kreme doughnuts."

Jennifer shook her head. "What is it with men and dough-nuts?"

∽⌒∽

As soon as they were in the van with the door shut, Claire sighed in exasperation. "He wasn't much help."

"What was I thinking?" Jennifer hit herself on the fore-head.

"He's a looney toon for sure."

"And his spiritual advice? We'd get better advice from the Psychic Hotline." Jennifer shrugged. "What are we going to do?"

"Wait. Let's just wait," Claire said with confidence.

"No way."

"You said next time we'd do it my way, and I say wait! Let's get back for Jonah's barbecue and pretend everything is normal."

"Alright. We'll do it your way."

"Good."

Jennifer shook her head. "I knew I shouldn't have said that."

∽⌒∽

Back at the banana plantation, Jonah turned another jerk-spiced chicken breast on the barbecue and then, once again, summoned his courage. Courage that had failed him three times before. He straightened his posture and prepared to ask Becky the question that had been plaguing him since Lillian had talked to him that day in the mobile lab.

"Can I ask you something, Becky?" He turned to her, think-ing how much he liked everything about her.

"Feel free," she smiled.

"About Felix?"

"Oh, you heard about Felix, did you?" Becky laughed.

"From Lillian."

"Ah, Felix, the perfect companion," she said.

Jonah ran his fingers over his freshly shaven face, crushed.

I have to prove my merits over this Felix character, he thought again.

"How long have you two been . . . uh."

"Felix has been hanging around for three years now. He showed up on the doorstep one day, and he's had me under his spell ever since. The crazy fur ball."

Fur ball. A hairy guy, eh. Jonah imagined his competition to be large and broad shouldered, with an army of flannel shirts in his dark, wood closet and size fourteen shoes crowding the floor. He would have strong, large hands with dirt under the fingernails.

Jonah sighed and pulled the cross on his neck. "So he's quite a guy, your Felix?"

"He's the kind of guy that keeps you feeling merry." Her hazel eyes brightened. "You know the tune."

Jonah didn't but forced a laugh anyway.

The night before, he had shared the truth with Becky about his reasons for leaving his physician practice, which had everything to do with fear and disappointment. They had a deep discussion about it, and she said she completely understood. He wondered now if she was being honest with him. Why would she be discussing another man with him so casually unless she'd changed her feelings for him, or had he misread her feelings to begin with?

"You know, Jonah, Felix watches the Hallmark Channel with me, and you only watch *Doogie Howser* reruns."

The humor escaped Jonah.

"I could learn to love the Hallmark Channel."

"*Dr. Quinn Medicine Woman* even?"

"Can we start with *Gunsmoke*?"

"That's not the Hallmark Channel. That's TV Land." She hit him on the shoulder playfully.

Now he was really confused.

28

By the time Jennifer and Claire showed up around eleven thirty, the scent of barbecue wafted through the air of Jonah's ample courtyard and brought the neighborhood children to the side gate.

"Those children out there, Jonah," Dawn asked as Jennifer and Claire approached. "Whose are they?"

"Neighborhood children, I guess. I don't really pay attention. Except when they trample my greenery to death."

"Can we invite them in?" Dawn asked gently.

"You can't help them all, you know. And besides that, if I had them in, they'd be hanging at my gate all the time."

"And what's wrong with that?" Lisa asked.

Jonah shook his head reluctantly. "It would mean I would have to look into their eyes."

Martha broke into the conversation. "And what would happen if you looked into their eyes?"

Jonah was already beside himself after Becky's comments about Felix. He was utterly depressed at this point. "It would remind me that I am a failure," he said decisively and walked away.

The comment floored the group.

Jennifer stared at Becky. "I'll talk to him," she said.

"It's complicated, Jen."

Still, she walked after him.

⁂

"Jonah," Jennifer called softly as she trailed him to the French doors and out onto the balcony.

He reluctantly turned around.

"Jonah, I wanted to apologize." Jennifer crossed the balcony to join him at the railing.

"For what?"

"Let's not play games. You know I haven't been very charitable. And here you are letting us use your house anyway."

"I understand why you're a little protective about Becky." He sighed. "Well, maybe I don't."

"Neither did I . . . at first." Jennifer felt her heartbeat speed up, a cold panic creep over her. "It has to do with my father."

"Your father?"

"Ex-stepfather actually." Jennifer knew she couldn't go on without sounding resentful, and that was not her purpose. "Let's just say I have some issues with him that I'd rather not go into."

"I understand," Jonah said thoughtfully. "I was raised by my stepfather, and he wasn't a very good role model. In fact, I only recently found out about my real father a little over a year ago when my mother died."

"That must have rocked your world," Jennifer said.

"My world was sufficiently rocked as it was."

"Are you talking about . . . why you quit being a doctor?"

"Yes, I am." Jonah averted his gaze, obviously struggling with his emotions. "One day a little pale, freckled-faced guy I had been treating died. If I were a betting man I would have

228

bet on him living to be one hundred. I did everything I could for him—" He halted midsentence.

"Have you shared this with Becky?"

"Unfortunately I did. Which may have complicated matters."

Jennifer spoke cautiously. "So the little boy died and . . ."

"His family threatened to file a malpractice suit, despite all my efforts." He looked out at the ocean. "They never did file, but a few weeks later I used the plane ticket my long-lost father sent me and came to visit. My real father."

"And . . ."

"The rest of the story started out happy enough. We spent a lot of time together here in Jamaica, and my father introduced me around as his son, Jonah Beach. The name stuck."

I'm a full-blown idiot, Jennifer thought.

"It sounds better than my legal name, Jonah Quest."

"I hear you." Jennifer closed her eyes and opened them slowly.

"Obviously, Beach was my biological father's name. I still need to make it official."

Jennifer cringed. "Was?"

"I inherited the estate from him when he died. I knew him for only a few months. And I'm not sure I really knew him."

"That was very generous of him to leave the place to you."

"One might think so. I did. Then I found out he was a con artist."

That sounds annoyingly familiar, Jennifer thought.

Jonah took a breath and went on. "That's how he managed all this. He used child labor and harmful pesticides to run this plantation."

"I've read about that kind of thing," Jennifer said.

"That's why the plants are dying. I refuse to use pesticides. And I don't know what I'm going to do about laborers when it comes time to harvest."

Jennifer had no answers for him.

After a long silence Jonah finally said, "So, two fathers and both of them failures."

"I suppose you could interpret it that way on the surface," Jennifer said.

Jonah's mouth thinned, exposing his vulnerability. "Why am I telling you all this?"

"Because God is using you to speak to me, Jonah. You see, my circumstance is similar. But with you I can see God's handprint all over it. I think it's time to let go of the past."

"But the past steps on the heels of the future."

She laughed. "True. Except . . ."

"Except what?"

"When God is in the picture. Then it's another thing altogether."

Jonah smiled.

"Shall we go back to the barbecue? I have an apology to make to our friends."

❧

After the barbecue was over, Jennifer used Jonah's phone to call Desmond and bring him up to date. "I thought you should know," she ended the explanation.

Silence on the other end.

"I'm thinking," Desmond said after a long pause. "Felicia won't be working again till next week. She's taking off for da holidays." He sighed. "We may need to involve da police. If they catch her with da diamonds, there will be no alibi, no matter how convincing her story."

"Please give us a chance to try to get her to turn herself

230

in. If she doesn't, Desmond, we promise we'll involve you," Jennifer pleaded.

"It has to be soon. I'm not going to make an arrest on da holiday."

"You mean Christmas?"

"Christmas and Boxing Day."

"Boxing Day?"

"The twenty-sixth of December. It's a public holiday here in Jamaica."

Jennifer laughed nervously. "It sounds like a holiday my husband would like to celebrate."

"It has nothing to do with fighting. It has to do with spending time with people you care about . . . and sometimes thanking those who serve you with a tip, bonus, or gift basket."

"Like your mailman?"

"Or your friendly security guard type." He laughed his full laugh.

❧

Jennifer dangled Becky's keys in front of her face in the long hall. "We're borrowing your van again," she announced.

Becky wrinkled her forehead. "Are you still investigating Jonah at the Internet café?"

Jennifer put her hand on Becky's shoulder and smiled. "That investigation has concluded. You have to promise me you'll marry the man and be happy for the rest of your life."

Becky looked at her in disbelief. "Are you Jennifer Baker from Lakeside, Minnesota, or an imposter?"

"I'm the real deal. And I'm going to get your diamond earrings back, which is why we need the van."

Becky wondered what Jennifer was up to. "If you're going to the pawn shops, Jonah and I already did that."

"We're not."

Becky shrugged. "Well, I can't waste any more time trying to figure you out. Not when my head is filled with poetry and my heart with music."

∽

"Do you watch the television show *Alias*?" Jennifer asked Claire as they sat in the van in front of Felicia's house ready for their investigative work. It was almost two in the afternoon.

"No, why?"

"I thought it would be convenient if one of us had state-of-the-art audio recording equipment that looked like a banana we could carry and get Felicia's confession on tape."

"I think a banana would rot."

Jennifer couldn't answer. She had just fixed her lipstick and was smoothing it out by rubbing her lips together. She turned to Claire. "Remember, act natural."

Claire stared at her strangely. "Sure, Mrs. Gloop. But maybe you might appear more natural if you wiped that chocolate off your lips."

"Who is Mrs. Gloop?"

"Augustus Gloop's mother . . . you know, from *Willy Wonka*."

"It's not chocolate. It's lip gloss that smells like chocolate. Lisa brought it for me from the mainland. Ha."

"But it's brown," Claire said.

"Chocolate brown lipstick is the trend."

They fell silent. Jennifer watched the children playing in the street. "I wish I had brought some chocolate for the kids. I love giving out chocolate."

"You seem to think that chocolate is the answer to all the world's problems," Claire said and smirked.

"No, Jesus is," Jennifer said. She was overcome with sudden guilt at how trite that must have sounded. "I think we should pray."

"We should." Claire nodded in agreement.

They held hands and prayed for guidance and peace and even a miracle. Jennifer's hand was still shaking when the prayer was over.

Claire released a long breath and smiled. "Well, are you ready to go in?"

"Was Moses ready to part the Red Sea?" She immediately shook her head, knowing it made no sense.

"Ohmigosh, you're turning into Lillian."

Jennifer laughed. "I'll take that as a right-handed compliment. That girl is starting to grow on me."

"Well, let's hope your attention span is a little longer than hers. Let's go!"

"I'd rather follow the advice on Bob's T-shirt."

"I forgot what it said."

"Procrastinate Now!"

They took their time walking to Felicia's front porch.

"Felicia," Jennifer called through the screen.

Felicia appeared in less than a minute and opened the door with her ever-present smile.

"Come in," she invited.

"No, thanks," Jennifer said.

Felicia was still wearing the earrings. Claire and Jennifer looked at each other with wide eyes, taken aback.

"Are you sure you don't want to come in?" Felicia asked.

"No," Claire said.

Jennifer took a deep breath. "Felicia, we're here because—"

Claire interrupted. "To give you some money." She spontaneously pulled two bills from her wallet.

Jennifer was stumped.

Felicia took the money hesitantly.

"So your son will have a good Christmas," Claire added.

Felicia smiled radiantly.

The head of Felicia's little boy appeared from behind the couch, and he scurried across the room.

Felicia looked over her shoulder. "Thomas, you shy little thing," she said. "Excuse me, one moment."

When she was out of earshot, Jennifer whispered, "What are you doing, Claire?"

"It sounds too horrible to go right out and say, 'Felicia, are you a thief?' Besides, her little boy is so sweet."

"Yes, he is. But we're not here for her son; we're here for Becky."

"Jennifer, please don't be mad about it."

Her face creased in thought. "How can I be mad? I know that was the last of your money."

Felicia returned, smiling and holding a picture she handed to Claire. "Thomas just drew dis picture. He says you are da tree and da fruit are your presents."

"Wow, that's almost profound," Claire said.

"Thomas is a bright boy." She turned her head and called. "Aren't you, Thomas?"

Thomas said something so quietly they couldn't hear.

Felicia shook the ladies' hands. "Thank you for making dis Christmas special."

"You're welcome," Claire said.

Jennifer half smiled and then reminded herself that this matter had not been resolved. She was going to ask Felicia where she got the earrings. Her mouth opened, but the words would not come out. She changed her mind.

29

The children in Felicia's neighborhood smiled and waved as Claire and Jennifer got into the van and drove away. As Claire concentrated on driving, Jennifer asked, "What are we going to tell Becky about all this?"

"Marry Jonah and he will buy you dozens of diamond earrings," Claire said, her eyes fixed on the road.

"I still can't believe it was Felicia. I know she's wearing the evidence, but I don't believe it."

"I know, I know. It also doesn't make sense that she would wear them around us when she knows Becky is our friend."

Jennifer gasped. "Stop the car!"

Claire obeyed without asking questions. When she was at a complete stop in front of a pottery shop, she said, "This better be good."

"I just remembered something. Something crucial to this case."

"Is that what this is, a case?"

"Claire, this is serious. I just remembered Bob had a Chia Pet on his windowsill."

"Oh, yeah, that sounds *extremely* serious."

"I saw it as we were leaving yesterday and didn't think anything of it 'til now. But it's the same one that Lil had. The one that was stolen."

"So, just because he has a stupid Chia Pet, he becomes the diamond thief?"

"I'm telling you that Chia Pet hasn't been released to the public. It's a special collector's item for club members only. Lil was telling me about it at the barbecue."

Claire looked doubtful.

"It's the same company that makes the Clapper. The owner's vacationing here."

"The Clapper? They still make those?"

"Yes."

Claire tapped her French-manicured nails on the steering wheel. "So, where's all the other stuff he steals?"

"He's hiding it. We need to do a thorough check of his house without him there."

"You mean break in?"

"Not exactly break in. We can use a credit card like Bob probably did to break in our room."

"My credit card is at Jonah's house."

Jennifer was beginning to feel flustered. Claire just wasn't getting the urgency of the situation.

"One more question, Jen. Why didn't he hide the Chia Pet?"

"Bob is a weirdo. He probably couldn't wait to watch it grow. It already has a few sprouts on it."

Claire slapped her hand against the steering wheel. "This is a ridiculous conversation."

"I can't help that."

Claire stared straight ahead as they sat in silence.

Anxiety bubbled inside Jennifer as she reviewed the evidence in her mind. When she came to a conclusive decision that Bob was the culprit, she couldn't hold in her emotions. "That no-good-dirty-rotten-criminal!" she nearly yowled.

"Remind me to never make you mad," Claire said.

"I'm not mad, I'm furious!" Jennifer cried.

"We still don't know for sure, Jen."

"Why don't we?"

"There is one problem with Bob being the guilty party."

"What's that?"

"Felicia is wearing the earrings."

"Because he's pinning it on Felicia, see. Bob gave them to her to make her look like the guilty party."

"And . . ."

"He's going to exchange them with fakes later."

Claire wasn't completely convinced. Jennifer, on the other hand, was intensely focused. "Drive to the hotel parking lot so we can talk to Desmond."

⤜⤛

There was a note on the door when the ladies reached the hotel security office.

Jennifer peered in the window and saw only darkness. "He's never here," she complained.

Claire shrugged. "Maybe he doesn't need to be here. Who wants to sit in a stuffy office when you could sit in the sun at the—"

"Pool," they cried in unison.

Poolside was where they found Desmond sipping on a Ting. He was in a jovial mood, as always.

"We thought we might find you here," Claire said, more amused than annoyed.

"It is a tough job, but somebody has to do it," Desmond said and smiled wide, showing all his gleaming teeth. He was wearing island casual wear—a colorful shirt, shorts, and sandals.

"So why aren't you in uniform?" Jennifer asked.

"My cousin owns da place," Desmond said and took another sip of his soda.

"And he lets you dress like that because you're a relative?" Claire asked.

"No, I only dress like dis when he's gone. He makes me wear dat stupid uniform with shoes dat hurt. I'm tellin' you." He smiled again. "So have a seat in my office."

"Where?" Claire asked.

"Grab a lounge chair."

Jennifer and Claire sat down, and Jennifer explained it all to Desmond.

He sat up straight and pulled out his briefcase. "Let's get to work, ladies."

"What kind of work?"

"Detective work. Persistent observation will get you everywhere."

Desmond's brown fingers riffled through paperwork.

Claire and Jennifer waited impatiently but enjoyed the sun.

"Dare," he said ten minutes later. "I have a list of all da missing items. Now let's go and intimidate da man."

Jennifer inhaled sharply. "I have to tell you, Desmond, Bob is about as intimidating as Napoleon Dynamite."

"Who's dat?"

"He's in a movie that has a cult following back home," Claire explained.

"And he's an action figure too now."

"Really?"

"I saw it on Target.com." Jennifer laughed. "There's Napoleon in a prom suit, and even a Pedro action figure. But my personal favorite is the tetherball champ action figure."

"Are you a closet fan or something?"

"I just seem to stumble across these things by mistake."

"Well, let's hope all this isn't an embarrassing mistake."

Desmond had been trying to keep up with the conversation. "Is tetherball a popular sport in America?"

"If you're a high school nerd, I guess," Claire said.

Jennifer's expression changed. "And speaking of nerds . . ."

Desmond scratched his head. "Do you know where dis Bob character lives?"

"As a matter of fact, we do," Claire said.

∽✿∾

The detective team parked a couple of shacks away from Bob's run-down dwelling.

"First, we need to determine if he's home," Desmond said, and his thin, tall body inched toward Bob's shack, the ladies following single file, close behind.

"How do we determine that?" Claire whispered.

"We'll knock on da door," Desmond said as they reached the sidewalk. He clutched the list of stolen items in his hands.

"What if he answers?" Jennifer said in a small voice.

He came to an abrupt stop. "Oh, dat could be a problem since he knows you. And I am sure he's seen me."

"At the pool," Jennifer added with a sweet smile.

"Quick, let's hide behind dat shed."

When they reached the steel shed, Desmond crouched down and the ladies followed suit.

"If I knock, he will see me. If I throw a rock at da door, he'll come out. Stay here and don't move." He left the ladies in their squatting position and picked up a rock. He ran over to the house and hurled it in the direction of the door.

There was a crash as he cringed and ran back to the startled ladies.

"Was that crashing sound the window?" Claire asked.

"I guess he's not home," Desmond stated. "He would be out by now."

"I guess not," Jennifer agreed.

"We'll have to break through da door," Desmond whispered.

"Or you could go through the window you just busted," Jennifer said.

"True."

They crouched as Desmond scratched his curly black head and thought things out.

A minute later Claire complained, "Whatever we do, I think we look suspicious crouching on the ground like this. Besides, my legs are getting tired."

"She fired her personal trainer in September," Jennifer explained.

"And look who's talking. Miss I-can-do-two-sit-ups," Claire shot back.

Desmond bit his lip. "You two are just like—"

"Don't say it," Jennifer whispered.

"—sisters."

"You said it." Jennifer rolled her eyes at Desmond.

‿✧‿

The three sleuths didn't need to go through the window. Bob's door was unlocked. Jennifer held on to the Chia Pet as she looked through kitchen cabinets. Claire was searching the bedroom for the items on the list. Desmond was cleaning up the broken glass.

All three met in the small living room to finish their search. Desmond was following Claire around when she stopped suddenly and put her hands on her hips. "Wait, this is way too far-fetched. We're not going to find any jewelry in here."

"He may be stupid, but he's not that dumb," Jennifer agreed.

"And don't forget we already know where one pair of earrings is. On Felicia's ears," Desmond pointed out.

Jennifer winced. "I know, an hour ago this was all so clear. But now I'm having second thoughts about this junior detective work."

"Especially since it stinks like rotten seaweed in here," Desmond said, obviously repulsed by the odor hanging in the air.

Claire grimaced. "More like clothes that haven't been washed in a decade."

"Besides, we could be lying on the beach right now," Jennifer said.

"And I could be at da pool," Desmond smiled lopsidedly.

"Wait, Desmond, this is your job," Claire reminded him.

He shrugged. "I only took it because my cousin said it would be a good opportunity to meet women."

Jennifer looked at her new friend. "He could've at least made you the manager."

"Are you kidding? Da hours are too long," Desmond replied.

"We need to focus." Jennifer was beginning to get nervous. "Or Bob might come back."

Desmond looked out the window with an intent expression.

"What?" Jennifer asked.

"Follow me," Desmond said. "I think I just figured something out."

He led the women to the shed where they had been hiding. "Dis is too obvious," he said, lowering his voice. "A heavy-duty steel padlock, a well-lit area with flowers planted by da window so it looks homey. Aha."

"And you're thinking his stash is in there?" Jennifer asked.

"Yeh."

"There's only one problem, Desmond," Claire pointed out.

"What?"

"I'm pretty sure this is the neighbor's shed," Claire said. "These flowers are the same as theirs." She pointed to the tidy shack next door that had a small flower garden in front.

"So, it's not in da house, and he has no shed."

"Think about it, guys. Bob doesn't need a shed to hide those small items," Jennifer reasoned.

Desmond rethought the scenario. "You're right. He could hide dem somewhere in a small case of some sort," he surmised.

"Let's just give up. We gave it a Lakeside Tigers' try and failed," Claire said.

"It was a stupid plan, and this is Christmas Eve," Jennifer said.

Desmond conceded. "How about a quick bite to eat at Reginald's in town? My treat."

"Can you afford it, Desmond?"

"Are you kidding? Not on my salary." He grinned. "But my cousin owns da place."

30

As they walked up to the restaurant door, an annoying cry came from across the busy street.

"Listen. Is that Pastor Bob?" Claire said.

They all turned toward the street.

"Repent, you sinners," another howl blasted over the reggae coming from the shop next door. By now, all three saw where he had set up camp down the street, red megaphone in hand.

"Our number one suspect and we cannot do a thing about it," Desmond said, disgusted by the situation. He started to open the restaurant door for the ladies.

"That little trunk is like his pet," Jennifer said, still watching her adversary.

A Jamaican man walking by overheard and put in his two cents. "He's never without dat stupid box. The locals here call it his pulpit. A pulpit with a lock?"

"What if . . . ," Claire said and stopped.

"What if what?" Jennifer leaned in closer.

"Bob uses that trunk to hide the stolen goods." Claire finished her thought.

Desmond let go of the door and stepped toward them. "Dat makes good sense. It is unusual for a preacher to lug a trunk around." Suspicion spread across his handsome face. "Where did Bob go to seminary?"

"He didn't," Jennifer said. "He was called to preaching on a surfboard. Supposedly God told him, 'Go help those wretched Jamaicans.'"

Desmond's eyes bulged. "Dat makes me so mad!"

Jennifer gave him a sympathetic nod.

Desmond put his finger in the air. "You say this loser likes doughnuts."

"That's what he said." Jennifer gave a weary smile.

"I have a plan."

"In this plan can we stand up instead of crouch?" Claire begged.

❧

Desmond's plan was put into action.

"Oh, Bob," Jennifer called. "A tourist from the ship has some Krispy Kreme doughnuts he's giving away."

Just as expected, Bob flew off his trunk and stood in front of Jennifer.

"Man, I've been dying for a Kreme for ages. Where are they?"

"Follow me," Jennifer said and waved her finger.

Bob followed, nearly tripping over his big feet.

In the meantime, Desmond skillfully opened Bob's locked trunk with a screwdriver, as Claire served as the lookout.

As suspected, the jewels were taped inside the lining of the trunk, along with all his other stolen goods, including some items not on Desmond's list.

A pair of cubic zirconium earrings was also there, as expected.

Desmond gave the thumbs-up signal to Jennifer on the other side of the street.

"Close your eyes first, Bob," she said.

The dim-witted thief was so crazy with doughnut lust that he carelessly obeyed.

"Wait, what are you doing?" Bob opened his eyes and yelled as the handcuffs were placed on his wrists.

"Repent, you sinner!" the crowd yelled as the policeman Desmond had called over made the arrest.

"Dere is something I always wanted to do," Desmond told the policeman, who just happened to be his uncle.

At the policeman's go-ahead, Desmond yelled, "Spread-eagle, buddy!" And then frisked Bob's pockets.

"Hey, what about the Krispy Kreme doughnuts?" Bob asked.

Jennifer couldn't believe how clueless he was. "I have a question for you, Bob," Jennifer said.

"What?" He sneered.

"What were you doing with all that money from stealing all that stuff?" Jennifer hoped it was for the church, as bad as that sounded.

His voice matched his deadpan expression. "It was for a new surfboard."

"A surfboard? How much can a surfboard cost?"

"The one I want costs a grand."

"But you stole seven pairs of diamonds, probably over forty thousand dollars."

"Ten pairs." Bob looked around. "Ooops."

"Where's a hidden microphone when you need it?"

"What?"

"Nothing." Jennifer shook her head, exasperated.

"Listen . . . dudette, I was going to have the diamonds embedded in a surfboard."

"That makes a whole lot of sense."

"I thought so."

Jennifer looked at him in astonishment. "Did you ever think you could've used cubic zirconium, and no one would have known the difference?"

"A cubic z board would never make it into the Surfer's Hall of Fame."

"And neither will you." Jennifer nodded contemptuously.

"Whoa, dudette, those are harsh words."

Jennifer *almost* felt sorry for him.

"I wanted something that would last. Riding a gnarly wave doesn't do it for me anymore. You understand?"

"No, I don't. You had something that would last." She looked at him. "Or did you?"

"Well, I guess I'm not sure."

"You better be sure if you want to store up treasures in heaven."

"Where moths and rust cannot destroy them . . ."

Jennifer walked away, shaking her head.

✺

"Do you mind if we wait in the van?" Jennifer said to Desmond with a frown. "I don't have the heart to be there when you take the earrings from Felicia."

"Me neither," Claire said, with her hands on the wheel.

"I wonder how Bob was going to switch the earrings with the cubic zirconium," Jennifer speculated.

"You have to remember he's very crafty and Felicia trusted him," Desmond said.

"This is going to be so hard on her," Claire said, almost crying.

Jennifer choked back her tears.

"I have a plan, a good plan," Desmond said. "How 'bout if I buy Felicia some cubic zirconium earrings in da gift shop over dere. No one will know da difference, and she'll save face."

"You're a good guy, Desmond," Jennifer said.

"Yes, I know dat."

Claire smiled knowingly. "And that Felicia is a beautiful woman."

Desmond smiled, indicating his agreement.

"We'll deliver a box of chocolate on Boxing Day for all this good service," Jennifer said and laughed.

"Actually what I'd really like is one of dose flashlights dey sell on American TV dat doesn't need a battery, you just shake it."

"I'd like one of those myself," Jennifer said.

∽༚∾

"So, here are your earrings, Becky." Jennifer dropped the treasured jewels in her palm.

Becky stared at the gleaming diamonds and made an attempt to say something. When words failed her, she hugged Jennifer and Claire, and then walked away.

"And Dawn, your iPod, and Lillian, your digital," Jennifer said, and dropped the items on the table.

Dawn was so surprised that all she could do was offer a weak "thank you."

Lillian checked out her camera. "It's working!" she exclaimed and took a picture of Jennifer.

"Great," she said, knowing she was a sweaty mess.

Lillian wasted no time in asking about her Chia Pet.

"Your Chia Pet already has hair so we decided to let Bob keep it. It'll keep him occupied in jail."

"In jail?"

"For the robberies."

"I guess it'll be a long time before he's hanging five again."

"You mean hanging ten?"

"I guess. What does that mean anyway?"

"Uh . . ."

"Hey, maybe I'll buy him a Chia Pet from the Madagascar collection and send it with a Bible."

"He's a preacher, Lil. I suspect he has a Bible."

Lillian frowned. "He's a bad, bad preacher."

"No one is beyond redemption," Dawn said on a positive note.

Jennifer sank in the floral couch.

Claire dropped next to her and laid her head on her shoulder.

"So do you feel a deep sense of accomplishment?" Claire barely got out.

"I feel as though I've had enough adventure for a lifetime." And Jennifer sighed.

"This is the oddest Christmas Eve I've ever had." Claire sighed too.

~⚬~

Lillian decided to write about the events of the day in her fuzzy tulip journal. But when she had the blank page in front of her, she went in a completely different direction than she expected.

She could no longer fight the feelings. The words flowed out like a torrent.

To My long-lost Mother,

Why did you give Me up? I don't understand why. What was it about My sister that you liked better than Me?

I want to ask you why I had to live with people who didn't want Me around. Why you raised My sister and went to her graduation instead of Mine. Not to Mention My wedding and the hospital when I had My babies. The babies I breastfed for More than a day.

Did you ever think that I might miss my sister? Even though I have everything, sometimes I feel like something is missing in my life. Sometimes I want to share secrets or a bag of Poppycock with her. I don't even know her name. I want her to see my children.

Jennifer (she's one of my very best friends) said that I shouldn't pretend it doesn't matter. She's right. It does matter. At least to me.

I'm telling you that you hurt me. You will never know because this is just a piece of paper. But I'm saying it because it's true.

Now that I said all that, I want to say that I still love you. I love you because God loves you. And because you gave birth to me like I did to my children. If you didn't have me they wouldn't be here. So I have to love you and forgive you. Or forgive you and love you. I'm not sure what comes first, the egg or the chicken.

Anyway, all is well with my soul.
Sincerely,
Lillian Jo Holmes of Lakeside, Minnesota

≈≈

Later, around nine, after the amateur sleuths finally had their dinner and some time to recuperate, Jennifer told the full membership of the Christmas Club the whole amazing story.

"I can't believe that. A pastor." Martha shook her head.

"He may have started out right, but he didn't end well," Claire remarked.

"The sad thing is, he didn't even mention his parishioners." Dawn sucked in her cheeks.

"He wanted the diamond surfboard so bad he didn't even care about those who needed him," Claire said.

"Diamond surfboard? That would be hard to surf on," Lillian said.

"Not the whole surfboard . . ." Jennifer took a deep breath and exhaled. "Never mind. Can we change the subject, please? I'm starting to get depressed."

"Why?" Claire asked.

"Don't you see? The running theme here is disappointing people who need you. And that's exactly what we did. Those children at the underprivileged party needed us, and so did our families. I thought I had this all figured out, but now I'm more confused than ever."

Martha looked around at the group. "Jesus was perfect love. He loved his disciples, yet he took time away."

"To be with the Lord," Jennifer said.

"Well, maybe in some way this was about you being alone with the Lord. I'd like to think that," Martha said.

"So would I. But the truth is, we let a lot of people down . . . ," Jennifer's voice was subdued, ". . . a lot of children down."

"Next year we won't," Becky promised. "It's a good thing we do and we should be proud."

"Martha, can you please tell us about the party now?" Lillian begged, as she squeezed in even closer to her on the couch. "Everyone is here. Please, you promised."

Martha touched Lillian's knee. "We'll start with Derrick then."

Lillian smiled.

"He was terrific as Santa. You should have seen him sharing the Christmas story, the children's eyes wide with wonder."

"He loves being Santa," Lillian said.

"Eric and Tommy helped out too."

Dawn's expression reflected skepticism.

Jennifer looked surprised. "Funny, Eric usually misses the party with some excuse."

"He brought a truckload of Krispy Kremes left over from his office party," Martha said.

"Now that sounds like my husband," Jennifer said, mildly amused.

"He took off work every day to visit your friend Marge at the nursing home."

"Wow! That does not sound like my husband."

Martha looked at Claire. "Your Alex was something else, Claire. He arranged a toy drive in three days."

Claire's blue eyes twinkled.

Martha took a sip of cocoa and went on detailing the highlights.

When she was finished, the group released a happy sigh.

"You know, I thought this vacation was going to be about relaxing. Instead it's been about seeing the things in my life that I've never seen," Jennifer said.

"We've all changed," Dawn said, trying not to cry.

Lillian beamed. "I feel it in my soul."

"This is the biggest makeover I've ever had," Claire added.

Lisa, who had been quietly listening up until now, stood to get everyone's attention. "Ladies. Speaking of makeovers . . . I have tattoos." She looked at Martha.

Martha hesitated, her expression dubious. "Sticker tattoos, I hope."

"No, a man with a big needle is hiding in the other room." Lisa laughed. "Of course, sticker tattoos."

"I suppose sticker tattoos would be permissible." Martha laughed with relief.

Lisa laid an open box full of stickers on the glass coffee table. "Lil, you want to pick out the first one?"

Lillian smiled at Becky and then picked the tulip on top. "I have an aversion to tulips."

"I don't think that's what she means to say," Jennifer said to Becky as she headed over to the sticker box.

"Lillian," Lisa said to Lillian's bent form.

"What?"

"Would you like to share a room with me tonight?"

Lillian looked temporarily spaced out. "Probably not."

"Well, okay," Lisa said as she scoured through the sticker collection.

Lillian stared at her intently. "Well, you see, I have this problem."

"Uh oh." Lisa's green eyes were unsure.

"I snore."

"You snore?"

"Like a . . . a . . ."

Jennifer pulled out a rainbow sticker. "Is 'buzz saw' the word you were searching for?"

"Derrick says I sound like a pack of wild pigs rooting in a garbage dump."

"That's not true, Lil. The trash can maybe." Jennifer grinned and reached over to give her a playful poke.

Lisa smirked.

"I know. It's okay, Lisa. Everyone feels the same way," Lillian said.

Jennifer patted her shoulder. "We love you."

"I snore too," Lisa said and turned to Martha who was searching through the stickers. "And Martha has been very patient about it."

"Dear, I can sleep through anything."

Lillian smiled.

The four of them continued searching through the stickers.

"So, Lisa, didn't you say your sons liked *Spiderman*?" Lillian asked.

"The older one. The youngest likes *Toy Story*."

"What about the middle one?"

"He likes *Stargate*. But I won't let him have it."

"Is that the collection with that skinny guy with the big brain head?"

"Yep. Thor."

"The Napoleon action figure is Dynamite too," Jennifer threw in.

They paid no attention to her.

Lillian and her one-track brain was on a roll. "Did you know Hasbro just put out a new . . ."

Jennifer fought back the urge to laugh as Lillian expounded on the latest action figure releases.

❧

"Wake up, it's Christmas!" Lillian ran out of her bedroom at 7:00 a.m. "Wake up, wake up, wake up!"

She ran around the sofa like a flash and into the kitchen. "Wake up, Dawn!"

Dawn stood at the long counter, mixing bowl in hand. "I'm already awake, Lil. And you should be quiet or you'll disturb the whole household." She shook her head in amusement.

"I couldn't wake Lisa up. She's still snoring like a foghorn, or maybe a freight train . . . or a sawmill."

"I get the picture," Dawn said.

Lillian froze and stared at Dawn in her red apron, her blond hair up in a bun.

"The maid has the day off," Dawn explained.

"So you're fixing us breakfast? Oh, goodie."

Dawn looked around the kitchen, smiling. "I love this

kitchen. Just look at this counter space. I would be happy every day of my life if I had a kitchen like this."

Lillian returned the smile as she danced around. She ran to the window and wiped it off as though the window panes were covered in condensation and she was expecting to look out to a white field.

"No snow out there," Dawn chortled and wiped the flour from the biscuits off her nose.

"That's okay. It's still Christmas." Lillian tore off down the hall.

"Don't hurt yourself in your footie pajamas," Dawn warned. "The marble can be slippery."

Lillian opened Jennifer's door and pranced in. "Wake up, sleepyhead!"

Jennifer moaned and then turned over. "You're under arrest for disturbing the peace."

"But it's Christmas morning, Jen."

Jennifer stared blearily at Lillian, whose eyes were wide with wonder.

Lillian erupted again. "Candy canes, hot cocoa, cookies, and presents and presents and presents—"

"Let me guess. You're a tape recorder on full speed." Jennifer rubbed her eyes.

"Have you forgotten what it feels like to be a child? To look at those presents under the tree and feel like you are the most special person in the world."

"I guess I have," Jennifer said. "Since our children aren't here, I was hoping to sleep in for once in my life."

Lillian settled on the edge of Jennifer's bed and turned serious a moment. "The truth is, Jen, I don't have anything to remember. Anything good, anyhow. In the foster homes I was in, we were lucky to get an orange and a handful of walnuts in our stocking. And sometimes the oranges were rotten and the walnuts had worms."

"Even half asleep that sounds tragic."

"It was."

"Look, Lil, I'd love to talk, but I'd love to sleep better."

"Sure."

"I love you, though. And I mean it."

Lillian laughed. "Of course you meant it. Why wouldn't you mean it?" She blew Jennifer a kiss and out the door she went.

❧

After having their hair braided by a woman on the beach, enjoying a fabulous breakfast Dawn had lovingly prepared, hearing Martha read the Christmas story, and opening presents, the members of the Christmas Club sat around in the large, airy living room watching Lillian sleep.

"The Energizer Bunny ran down her batteries. I can't believe it," Jennifer said.

"I can't believe she's not snoring," Claire said.

No one said anything for a long time.

"We look like someone just died," Lisa finally said.

"I am not dying in this terrible hairstyle. Whose idea was this?" Jennifer grumbled as she touched her braids.

"Yours," Claire said.

"I don't think so," Jennifer said.

"Lillian's!" the whole group declared at once.

Lillian remained undisturbed.

"What's wrong with us?" Claire erupted. "I've heard of post-Christmas letdown, but it's still Christmas."

"We're supposed to be celebrating the birth of Christ. Joy to the world," Martha said, but not in a preachy way.

"We're ingrates," Jennifer concluded.

"I don't think so," Dawn said. "I think Christmas is about giving, and when it's not, some of the magic disappears." She looked suddenly sad. "The other day at our barbecue . . . I can't help but see the faces of those children at the fence. Their hands outstretched and their little eyes speaking love to you."

Jonah, who had been sitting on a stool in the far corner observing the women silently, left the room.

"I think we upset Jonah," Jennifer said.

"He's been upset off and on for the last couple of days," Becky said. "He's going through something. Men are complicated."

"We're all complicated." Claire looked out the window.

Silence hung heavy in the humid air.

"I can't get my mind off those children," Dawn said again, and then brightened in thought. "Hey, what if we pool our money and buy some gifts for them."

"I have lunch money for the airport tomorrow. I wouldn't mind skipping a meal," Claire offered.

"She gave all her money to Felicia," Jennifer explained.

Claire twisted her hair. "What about the chocolate Jonah gave us? Do you think he'll mind if we give it to the kids?"

"We can ask him," Becky said.

Jonah reappeared in the room, wearing jeans and a white oxford shirt. A flush spread over his cheeks.

Becky looked at him, concerned. She got up and went over to him.

"Ladies, I'm sorry to interrupt."

"As our host, you are perfectly welcome to interrupt," Martha said.

"Circus Jamaica will be here in a few minutes, and so I'm going to need your help to set up."

"What?" Becky squinted.

"The circus will be here shortly," he said matter-of-factly.

"You ordered a circus for us?" Dawn looked at Lillian's sleeping form. "Lil will be happy."

"That's a generous present, Jonah," Becky said, putting her arm across Jonah's back.

"It's not for you."

"Who, me?" Becky said.

"It's not for any of you," he said, maintaining a placid look.

Dawn stood up and clapped. "It's for the children!"

❧

The courtyard was being transformed into a circus.

"Oh goodie, the Bouncy Boxing Ring!" Lillian shouted.

"Jonah, this must have cost you a fortune," Becky said.

"My father's money was ill gotten, and I want nothing to do with it. It belonged to the community and it should go back to the community." Jonah sounded resolute about the whole thing.

"What is he talking about?" Lillian asked.

"Let it alone, Lil," Jennifer said and pulled on one of her tiny braids, thinking the style looked good on her, and only her.

"Now, I need some of you to go into the neighborhoods to hand out flyers . . ." Jonah went on with his organizing and instructions, giving a glimpse of the type of doctor he had been.

❧

Within the hour, the circus tent was up. A cotton candy machine was producing pink sugar. Funny clowns were running around with buckets and seltzer bottles, and the other circus performers were in the makeshift dressing rooms getting ready for their acts.

No detail had been overlooked. Martha made sure of it.

As the children waited at the gate for the festivities to start, the women inserted gospel tracts in each child's goodie bag.

"Ho-ho-ho and Merry Christmas!" a man came out in a Santa suit on stilts to welcome the children.

Throughout the afternoon, all the children in attendance had their faces painted and a balloon in hand. They watched the performance and festivities with enthusiasm. Not a single child was without a smile.

"I have an extra pair of Spanx," Lillian told Jennifer when the circus was winding down. She looked around and then looked up at the stilt walker.

"Are you married, Mr. Stilt Walker Person?" she called.

The stilt walker stopped and balanced himself. "Yes, I am. Is there any particular reason you ask?"

"I have a gift for your wife."

"She's the one over there in yellow with the long black hair," he said and tottered away on his sticks.

Lillian smiled at Jennifer. "Now where is she?" She looked around some more.

Jennifer flinched. "I see her."

"Where?"

"She's the one wrapped in—"

"Wrapped in what? Plastic?" Lillian asked. "What?"

"In snakes," Jennifer said, wrinkling her nose. "Under the sign that says LORETTA THE SNAKE CHARMER."

❧

The circus was being dismantled and the performers packing up when Felicia came to pick up Thomas. Jonah was telling him a story and Becky was watching with a sappy smile, when Felicia touched her on the shoulder.

"Becky. Do you remember me?"

"Of course, Felicia. Thank you for cleaning my room all those days. I know I can be picky."

Becky could see Felicia was embarrassed when her eyes magnetized to Becky's diamond earrings.

"Look, Felicia, it wasn't your fault about my earrings."

"I know dat. I know." Still Felicia looked uncomfortable.

"I'm worried about you." Becky touched her shoulder. "What will happen to the church?"

"You know Desmond?"

"Yes, of course."

"He has a relative who is a minister in Kingston. An excellent preacher who wants to move to a smaller city. Desmond thinks he's gonna come. So we'll be okay. Maybe better."

"I'm sure of it." Becky nodded in agreement.

"You can't look to man. You must look to God."

"I'm sure of that too."

Becky looked intently at Felicia as she felt a tug in her heart. She decided to follow her hunch. She took off her earrings, put them in Felicia's hand, and cupped them closed.

"I want you to have them."

"No, I can't." Felicia pulled back, opening her hand.

But Becky held on to Felicia's hand as she spoke. "I don't do anything I don't want to do. Ask Jennifer here."

Jennifer had just come up behind Felicia and had seen the exchange. "She's telling you the truth," she said.

"I'm not much of a jewelry person anyway." Becky smiled gently.

Jennifer said nothing at that.

"Your son needs an operation and these will pay for it. You go to the jeweler on Third Street, and he'll give you a good price. He was admiring them the other day."

Felicia was speechless. Clutching the earrings, she stared at Becky and then impulsively reached out to hug her. There were tears in Felicia's eyes as she stepped back and walked away, shaking her head in astonishment.

Jennifer looked at her friend. "Bec," she whispered.

"Don't you say a word, Jen. Not a single word. This is not a big sacrifice for me," she said quietly. "My mother is written in my heart. Not in a piece of jewelry. Those little rocks will change Felicia's life."

"And her son's," Jennifer said and walked away toward the gate where the children were exiting.

∽∾

"Wait! Wait!" Jennifer called spontaneously as she ran out the gate and onto the dirt road after the barefoot little boy with the long eyelashes she had befriended at the gate. "Can I give you a hug?"

Jennifer squeezed the little boy tight, and it was apparent by his humongous smile that he loved it.

Another child joined the hug, and another, until it was a group hug.

Claire showed up with Lillian's digital camera and flashed a picture.

When the children were gone and the road was deserted, Claire asked, "So what was that all about? A hug without chocolate?"

Jennifer stopped and stood stock-still. "You know, you're right, Claire."

"Right about what?"

"I prefer to give out the chocolate instead of giving a hug. I knew they would love the chocolate, but I wasn't so sure they would love me."

"Certainly, children love candy, Jen. But they sometimes honestly just want love."

"I guess I never thought love was enough." Jennifer shook

her head. "I don't mean I never thought of it. I guess I think sometimes that love is about performance. I feel like I let people down. That if I don't give enough, people won't love me. And then I get burned out."

Claire nodded. "I'll bet that has to do mostly with your stepfather and wanting his approval."

"I think you're right." Jennifer smiled. "But for once I'm not going to let him ruin my Christmas."

Claire returned her smile. "Good for you."

"Maybe next year we'll have all this figured out, and then we'll have the perfect Christmas."

"I highly doubt it."

"The year after?"

"Perfect only exists in heaven, Jen," Claire said.

"Then that means your David is having the perfect Christmas."

"I think you're right for once."

"For once. C'mon, girlfriend, give me more credit than that."

"I give you a lot of credit."

Jennifer took Claire's hand and smiled. "Let's go help with the cleanup. It will make me think I'm at the underprivileged children's party."

"We are, in a way."

They walked back to the party in silence.

32

The time had come to say good-bye to Jamaica.

"The morning went by fast." Dawn's comment was meant to lessen the tension. It was the only thing anyone had said for several minutes.

The ladies had left Martha and Lisa at the estate nearly three hours ago. No one woke up Lisa, but Lillian had insisted on waking Martha to say good-bye. She hugged Martha around the neck.

"I miss your big fur coat," Lillian said.

"Everything is going to be fine, my dear. You're stronger than you know."

"I think you're right," Lillian agreed.

Martha gave the other travelers a hug and assured everyone that their families were fine. Pastries and coffee followed, and then the walk in the dark to Jonah's Land Rover.

Now at the airport waiting for their departure, all the women were dealing with confusing feelings.

Lillian was feeling introspective. "It feels like the day after summer camp. You know, when you come down the mountain and the party is all over."

"Where did you go to summer camp?" Dawn asked.

"I guess I didn't go to summer camp."

"Well, it's a good analogy, Lil."

Lillian started to feel sorry for herself. Thoughts of her deprived childhood surfaced, but after a minute, she pushed all those weighty thoughts aside. *Martha said I was going to be okay,* she told herself.

"You know what, Dawn?"

"What?"

"I think Lisa needs some of Martha's attention now. She's got it hard being a single mother. I'm really blessed, you know."

Dawn paused and looked at her. "Yes, you are. We all are."

⊷⊶

Becky and Jonah were off to the side, holding hands and having their own conversation.

Jonah had been quiet the whole drive up. He had talked about the mountain scenery—which they couldn't see in the dark. He had talked about the weather—a boring subject in Jamaica. He had talked about everything except the feelings he was avoiding.

"It's like you've cut me off all of a sudden," Becky said when she couldn't stand it any longer. "As though I were a leprous limb. What's wrong, Jonah?"

Jonah said nothing.

She grabbed his limp hand. "If you're struggling, Jonah, I'll struggle with you. I understand why you quit being a doctor. And I don't blame you. I went through the same thing," she said, grasping at straws.

His eyes brightened as he turned to look at her. "Are you saying you want our relationship to continue?"

Becky looked surprised. "Yes!"

A smile tugged at Jonah's mouth.

"Will you come visit me in Lakeside?"

"I'd like that very much."

Becky leaned toward him and put her other hand on his arm. "I want you to meet Felix."

Jonah's smile turned to ice.

"What's wrong?"

He struggled to keep control. "Actually, I don't think it's a good idea for me to come. Continuing our relationship doesn't seem like a good idea either." He loosened his fingers from their entwined hands.

Becky pulled her hand back. "Why?" She stared at him. "Jonah, I thought we both wanted something more than just some vacation fling."

"Sometimes being alone is better."

"What kind of an answer is that?"

"A truthful one."

Becky looked away, hurt.

Jonah looked away, hurt.

"You'll have your hands full with Felix," Jonah finally said.

"My lap anyway."

He was angry at himself for giving up on their relationship and, now, angry at Becky for her insensitive response.

"He sits on your lap?" he asked in an incredulous tone.

"When we watch the Hallmark Channel together. I told you," Becky responded defensively.

"A little too crowded for me, I'm afraid."

"Well, okay, I get the message, Mr. Manners. You don't have to be so obvious about it. Thank you so much for all you've done for everybody." She reached down and grabbed her purse. "Good-bye."

∽⚬

Becky marched over to Jennifer and blew her bangs in the air. "Love is completely overrated."

"Honestly, I thought he was the one," Jennifer said.

"He said something about it being too crowded. Maybe he doesn't want children. I don't know. I think your first instinct was the better one. Guys who are too perfect never are as perfect as they seem."

Jonah was walking away by now.

"Good-bye, Jonah, and thank you!" everyone, except Becky, yelled and waved.

"No problem, mon," Jonah called as he looked over his shoulder and hurried away.

❧

After another round of silence, Lillian scanned the group. It was easy to see this group needed cheering up. "Did I ever tell you about my dog, Blue?" she asked.

No one answered, so Lillian cleared her throat and started in. "It was in the middle of summer. No, wait, winter . . ." She stopped. "Or was it fall? Yes, fall. November is in fall, right? Because the first day of winter is the shortest day of the year. And that's December the . . ." She snapped her fingers trying to recall.

Jennifer could no longer keep a straight face. She burst out laughing, and the other ladies followed suit, lightening the mood. Even Becky shook her head and smiled.

❧

"Really, Jonah, there is no problem with you staying in your own guesthouse. We don't need that much privacy," Martha assured him in the brick driveway of his house.

"Thank you, but I'd rather stay at the mobile lab at the hotel. There's a comfortable cot in there."

265

"We don't want to put you out," Lisa said, as she pushed her braids out of the way.

"I *want* to be alone."

"I thought you and Becky might get together permanently," Lisa said. Her green eyes grew anxious for the explanation.

"You told me, Jonah, that Becky was the best thing that ever happened to you," Martha said and looked him straight in the eye to make her point.

"She was."

"Then why did you let her go?" Lisa pressed.

"One word: Felix." Jonah exhaled slowly.

"Felix! That's drastic. I mean I can understand if you're allergic, but there are medications. My son is allergic." Lisa looked apprehensive.

"I'm not allergic to anything."

"Then what are you talking about?" Martha asked.

"Felix."

"You've lost me," Lisa stated.

"You've lost me too," Jonah said with a shake of the head.

"You do know Felix is a cat," Martha said.

Jonah looked shocked.

"You know"—Lisa started to sing the cartoon theme song—"'Felix the cat. The wonderful, wonderful cat. Whenever he gets in a fix, he reaches into his bag of tricks.'"

"Uh oh."

"What? Is it my voice?" Lisa stammered.

"I'm in a fix. I wasn't very nice to Felix's owner." Jonah slumped into a nearby chair.

Joy, the maid, came out humming.

"Are you a Felix fan too?" Lisa asked.

"Yes, I am. I grew up with Felix. When I was young I lived

in Boston." She paused. "There's *Felix Saves the Day*, and *Felix Hits the Deck . . .*"

"My personal favorite is *Felix in Love*." Lisa smiled wide.

Jonah whacked himself in the head. "That explains a lot," he muttered to himself.

Lisa and Joy started in together with Joy's lead. "'You'll laugh so much your sides will ache, your heart will go pitter pat. Watching Felix, the wonderful cat.'"

"All this makes me want to go home and watch *Felix the Cat Saves Christmas* with my boys," Lisa said and gave a big sigh.

"It makes me want to go home and cry," Jonah said.

"You are home," Joy said.

"If it makes you feel any better, Jonah, I made the same mistake about Felix," Martha said, trying to comfort him.

"Thank you, but it does not."

33

Minnesota was dark and cold when the ladies stepped off the plane into the frigid air. The travelers' mood seemed to match the atmosphere.

The first two flights had been all right, but the four-hour layover in between them was unending. And the last flight out of Minneapolis were pure torture. A stuffy ride packed in tiny seats on a puddle jumper, most of the trip in silence. A one-ounce bag of stale pretzels the extent of the snacks.

Harry, Martha's husband, picked them up at the Lakeside Airport. "How was your flight?"

"Long. Really, really long," Becky said as she took her place in the front seat of the van.

"I'll drive you back to the church, but I'm not answering any questions at this time of night," he grumbled.

"That's okay. We don't feel much like talking," Becky said.

When everyone was seated, Claire's voice in the back broke the silence. "Becky, on behalf of all of us, thank you for the trip. We have really grown from this experience."

"You're welcome," she said weakly.

"I know I've grown." Jennifer forced a laugh. "At least one dress size."

"Jennifer, now that we're the same size, we can trade clothes all the time," Lillian said.

"Hopefully, I won't be this size for long," Jennifer said, but had to smile at Lillian's comment.

A melancholy quiet settled over the van again.

The ladies were each lost in thought as the miles passed. Becky was thinking of Jonah, or more accurately, trying not to think of him. The others were thinking of their families.

All the fun they had, all the lessons they learned, seemed to pale in comparison to the fact that was now seeping into their tired souls: they had missed Christmas with their families. They couldn't get it back, and they couldn't seem to get past it now.

They hadn't read the Christmas story, sung carols, or unwrapped presents together. They hadn't blown out the candles on the Happy Birthday Jesus cake or called their relatives who lived far away.

It was bad enough that they had missed the underprivileged children's party. But missing the family traditions was demoralizing. With it they had missed the warmth, security, and closeness—the things that make up families.

Harry drove into the dark church parking lot. "It's a couple of minutes until midnight," he said, pulling up next to the side door.

"And all our families are sound asleep in their beds," Dawn said.

"And we missed Christmas," Lillian moaned.

They sat in silence.

Finally, Becky patted Harry on the back. "I'll take it from here, Harry. The keys to my van are in the church kitchen anyway."

Harry said something quietly that Becky didn't hear. "What did you say, Harry?" she asked.

"How's Martha?" he mumbled.

"Oh, Martha is fine. She's getting very tan."

"And tattoo—" Lillian said, but Jennifer put her hand over Lillian's mouth.

"She's getting a snooze, you say?" Harry asked.

"Mm-hmm," came Lillian's muffled reply.

Harry climbed out and unlocked the side door of the church. He mumbled something about leaving the luggage to him, and the ladies stepped in the hall. He took the baggage out of the van and piled it in the corridor. And then before they knew it, they heard his tires spin in the snow.

"Someone turn on the light!" Becky demanded.

"I can't find the light switch," Claire said, fumbling in the dark.

"Stop! I hear something," Dawn said. There was panic in her voice. "It could be a mouse."

"You paranoid rat freak," Jennifer said, and only the two of them got the private joke.

"Wait, I hear it too," Claire whispered.

Lillian gasped. "Me three."

Becky shushed the group. "Just listen."

Lillian ignored the directive. "There was this contestant on this show in England. After staying awake for two hundred thirty-five hours he hallucinated that he was being chased by a giant mouse."

"This isn't the time for stories," Claire said.

"Besides it would be impossible for someone to stay awake that long." Becky's voice sounded like she was emotionally spent.

Jennifer unbuttoned her coat. "It's toasty in here. I think someone left the heat on."

"Forget this! I'm getting my keys from the kitchen." Becky pushed her way through, and the other ladies followed.

"Stop pushing," Jennifer said as they stumbled into the fellowship hall.

"Merry Christmas!" The call erupted and a mob descended on the ladies as the room lit up like a Christmas tree. And then more and more lights came on.

"We saved Christmas for you!" Jacob, Lillian's son, yelled.

The colored lights of the Christmas tree reflected dozens of happy faces as the braided ladies of the Christmas Club were cheerfully reunited with their families and friends.

Becky had seen enough of the family reunion. She didn't belong here. She slipped out without anyone noticing.

Jennifer's eyes adjusted. "Eric Baker, you wonderful man, you." She hugged her husband.

He kissed her and touched her face. "I'm happy to see you, baby—braids and all. My office party was a hit!" he said, as though he wanted his wife's approval. He pounded his checked sweater-vest. "Bring Krispy Kreme and they will come." He snapped his fingers. "And speaking of Krispy Kremes, I better get them out of the car or they'll be as hard as rocks."

He sped off.

"Where is that rascal son of mine?" Jennifer called above the happy clamor.

Trevor came up and hugged her. "Mom, I have a present for you."

He handed her a package and helped her tear it open.

Her face scrunched in uncertainty. "What are these?"

"Five advent calendars. In case you still have the same self-control problem next Christmas."

Jennifer cracked up. "You may never understand women, honey. But you will always know that I love you!"

They hugged again and she looked over at Claire, who was hugging Lexie.

Lexie's face glowed like an angel. "Oh, Mom. I missed you so much! I need you, Mom. I need a mother. My mother."

"And I haven't been much of one lately." Claire felt her throat close as she held back tears.

"Yes, you have. And Daddy's been great too."

Claire didn't know how to respond to that. She'd envisioned Lexie being mad at her father. And calling him Daddy was something new.

Lexie barely stopped for a breath. "Daddy bought a huge Christmas tree and we decorated it together before he left on his new motorcycle. It's a really pretty shiny blue. He wrote me this really wild letter too. Something happened to him. I don't know what."

Claire beamed in surprise.

"Oh, no, there goes Noodles," Lexie said and got down on her hands and knees.

"Noodles?"

"My puppy. Daddy bought me a puppy. I didn't have to beg or anything. I better go find him before he rips up something." She looked over her shoulder as she crawled off. "Oh, yeah, read your letter that's hooked to the tree."

Claire ambled over to the tree, pulled off the envelope with her name on it, and ripped it open. She stared at the handwritten note before she summoned the courage to read it.

Dear Claire,
    I realize that I have let the poetry seep out of my life.
    With David's death I shut down. In doing so, I forgot who I was.
    I blamed myself for his death. And then I blamed you. And in the end I realize that no one is to blame.

I want to change and I hope this trip will help me change.

Maybe you think I didn't hear you when you asked about taking a foster child in. I did hear. I am considering.

I have never stopped loving you, not for one moment.

Your loving, Harley-maniac husband, Alex

P.S. You would look really cute in leathers on the back of my bike. Details to follow.

"A new kitchen!" A scream blasted from across the room. It was Dawn's excited voice.

Dawn's two matched daughters were jumping up and down with her.

Tommy smiled widely as he pulled out the architectural plans he had designed. "I thought it was about time I designed our own kitchen."

"Honey, you don't know what this means to me," Dawn said and kissed him again.

"I think I do." Tears welled in his dark eyes. "Dawn, I'm sorry. I didn't realize. Or maybe I didn't want to realize. She treats me like a child," he said and took in a deep breath.

"What?" she asked, even though her intuition told her.

Tommy looked at his children. "Girls, why don't you two go—"

Dawn took over. "Find your presents in my suitcase. The ones wrapped in pink." She held hands with her handsome husband.

"Mother left in a huff this morning," Tommy admitted.

"She did?"

"She left in a huff when I told her that, uh . . ." He looked down.

Dawn leaned closer, squeezing his hand. "You told her what?"

"That I preferred sharp cheddar on my omelet."

Dawn could see genuine remorse in Tommy's face. She almost felt sorry for him. She wanted to burst out laughing in relief, but instead she smiled tenderly. "Can we go back to being the way we were when your mother does come back?"

Tommy grinned. "I hope you mean before my mother came to live with us."

"That is exactly what I mean." Dawn held her smile.

"The next project on my list is the mother-in-law quarters in the back of the property. Or should we do that before the kitchen?"

"No, after," Dawn said graciously. "Give Edna some time to cut the apron strings."

Derrick stood behind the podium on the side of the room and asked for everyone's undivided attention. He and Lillian and their children had already shared a private moment. Lillian had no idea what he was up to.

"Everyone, we have a special unveiling tonight," Derrick announced.

"What is under that white sheet? It looks like a statue," Eric said, sharing a smile with his wife.

"It wasn't there a few minutes ago," Claire said. Heads nodded in agreement.

"This is my present to Lillian. It's something I ordered all the way from Minneapolis."

"It can't be season two of the *Gilmore Girls* on DVD," Lillian said, feeling great as the center of attention.

"And a superhero couldn't fly in this cold," Jennifer murmured.

Derrick went on. "I want to say that sometimes you think you're not appreciated, Lil. And . . . well, that's probably be-

274

cause it's true. But I've learned more in these last several days about what you do. I'm ready to throw in the towel."

The other men echoed his opinion, and all the ladies were pleased.

The statue sneezed.

"What is that?" The question passed through the room.

Derrick stepped off the podium and pulled the sheet off. There was a collective gasp.

Lillian gasped several times. She looked like she would hyperventilate.

"It's her twin sister," Jennifer yelled in delight, and everyone gasped again.

"Lillian has a twin sister? I can't believe it," Claire wailed. She looked at Jennifer. "You don't seem all that surprised that Lillian has a twin."

"Well . . . uh." Jennifer simply gave her a satisfied smile.

"You mean there are two of them?" Dawn said as the three huddled together in a kinship they now shared.

Lillian and her sister hugged for several minutes.

"Martha did this for you, honey," Derrick explained over the tears, including his own. He laughed. "And let me tell you, in the few hours I've known Carol, well . . . you two are going to be hard to tell apart."

Dawn slipped away again with her family, and Jennifer and Claire held hands and cried.

Claire noticed Becky was missing. "Where's Becky? We need to do a toast for her."

"Maybe she had a hot date with Felix," Jennifer said to lighten the situation.

"She had a very hot date in Jamaica." Claire shook her head. "I still don't know what happened there."

"Some people think being alone is less complicated, I guess."

They watched all the action. All the laughter, the hugging, and the attention the children and husbands needed.

Jennifer blew a kiss to Eric across the room. "Being alone may be more complicated." She smiled. "But give me chaos and confusion any day of the week."

"Three hundred sixty-five days of the year?" Claire asked.

"Well, maybe not 24/7. I think we deserve a getaway every now and then. Just not at Christmas again." Jennifer grinned.

"I love you, Jen," Claire said over the racket.

"I love you, Claire," Jennifer said.

"Merry Christmas!" they shouted together.

❧

Felix was not there when Becky returned home just before 1:00 a.m. It was hard enough to deal with ending the relationship with Jonah, and now her feline friend was missing. She didn't want to go to bed yet, despite her exhaustion.

After pulling out her tiny braids, taking a hot shower, and trying to unwind, she called for Felix again. She was convinced he would never come back. That she would be alone for the rest of her life.

She really couldn't blame Mrs. Rauls for the disappearance. She knew her neighbor had a slight case of dementia when she asked her to watch Felix. The box of Friskies on the counter indicated that she had not followed the instructions to feed Felix the premier cat food in an ice cream dish.

Becky pictured herself once again in her bench swing—an old lady with blue hair staring into space, living on meaningless memories. As she scanned through the pictures on her phone, she vowed she would keep the memory of Jamaica in her heart forever. That was until she came to a picture of Jonah. The memory of him and what she'd thought was the beginning of something special hurt so badly that she tossed her phone across the room.

Maybe Jennifer was right to begin with. Most people are miserable at Christmas.

But she knew that was not true. The scene in the church was evidence of that.

She wrapped herself in her robe and went to the kitchen to make a cup of tea. Becky told herself that tomorrow was another day.

As she waited for the tea to steep, she uttered a simple prayer. "God, help me to appreciate my current circumstance. I see so many hurting people in my work. Thank you that I have you as my hedge. Even more, that you are the same, yesterday, today, and tomorrow."

34

The phone rang a holiday tune, waking Becky from a dead sleep on the couch. It took her until the third ring to realize her cell was across the room on the carpet, right where she'd thrown it.

She rolled off the cushions, her legs tangling in her robe, and tottered across the room to stare at her phone as though it were the enemy. When it continued its rendition of "Jingle Bells" in spite of her stare, she punched the ON key.

"Hello," she said in a craggy voice.

"Have you gotten your present?"

"Who is this?"

"It's Martha."

"Martha in Jamaica?"

Becky looked around the room, groggily. The log in her gas fireplace was glowing. Obviously she was in Minnesota.

"Did you get your present?" Martha asked again, much too cheery for the early hour.

"I'm sorry, Martha." She yawned. "I'm not awake yet. What present?"

"I believe it's on your doorstep."

She checked the wall clock and watched the pendulum swing. Like her emotions, she thought.

"It's nine o'clock. UPS doesn't deliver before ten. You didn't need to send me anything. Really."

"Believe me, you'll like this present," Martha said.

"What time is it there?" Becky scrunched her forehead. "And this call is costing someone a lot of money. Are you at what's-his-name's house?"

There was no answer.

"Martha?"

There was static on the other end.

"Martha . . . I can't hear you." The call was lost.

"Thanks for the present," she said and threw the phone on the couch. "I only hope it's not bananas. I am so sick of bananas. Anything with bananas. And especially men who supervise the production of bananas."

Becky warmed herself by the fire. "Felix," she called. It had been his habit to sit on her feet to warm them in the mornings.

A glance at the Friskies box on the counter reminded her that he was missing. Wasting no time, she threw on her Ugg boots and a big coat and hurried to the door, opened it halfway, and called, "Felix! Felix!"

A man in a massive hooded down jacket and heavy gloves stood on her doorstep. For a second she thought he might be the delivery man.

Until she opened the door all the way and he opened his mouth.

"Good morning, have you seen my pet jellyfish milling about?" he asked.

She nearly fainted when she recognized Jonah.

"What are you doing here?" she croaked.

"Swallowing my pride," he said and tried to warm his

cold body by jumping up and down on the snow-covered porch.

She moved to shut the door in his face, but he put his boot in the doorway, bags under his eyes from the red-eye flight.

"You dumped me," she charged.

"I have an explanation."

"And I have morning breath."

"I don't care about your morning breath."

"You don't?" She longed to trust his words.

"No, I don't," he replied in a raspy baritone.

Becky almost softened but felt she couldn't take the chance. "Jonah, nice of you to fly all the way to Minnesota for nothing, but I don't have time for you or anybody else. Felix is missing, and I'm going looking for him as soon as I am properly dressed."

"I thought Felix was your boyfriend and that's why I said what I did," Jonah said quickly.

Her jaw dropped. "Felix, my boyfriend?" She laughed. "That's an absurd conclusion." Her face was a mixture of emotions.

"Maybe so, but I honestly did."

Becky's mind raced back to their last conversation, and it started to make sense. She stood dumbstruck in the open doorway.

As she tried to regroup her feelings, she saw Jonah pull off a glove and take a box out of his pocket. He opened it to show a ring.

She hugged herself.

"Will you marry me?"

She laughed again, this time with a rather hysterical quality.

"I look half dead, my hair is an absolute mess, and you're proposing to me?"

"Yes."

Becky closed her eyes and smiled. Every fiber of her being was telling her this was for real. Even though it was freezing, her face felt suddenly hot.

"When do you want to get married?" she asked, opening her eyes.

"Now. Before I freeze to death." He started stomping his feet in an effort to regain circulation.

"But, Jonah, your house."

He put the ring back in his pocket since she hadn't taken it and slipped his glove back on, rubbing his hands together to warm them.

"The Circus Jamaica owners bought my property on contingency."

"Contingency?"

"The contingency being the money from the sale of the bananas, which will be harvested by a reputable company, goes in a fund for the neighborhood children to get free lessons for the rest of their lives." He coughed. "Oh, I'm homeless, by the way." He huffed and watched his breath vaporize.

"Are you going to marry me for my money?" she said, a speck of doubt still left in her.

"I said I was homeless, not penniless."

"Don't pretend you didn't hear about my trust fund."

"Okay, I know about your trust fund. But guess what . . . I'm independently wealthy, sweetheart," he said, faking some ridiculous accent.

"You mean your father's money?"

"I mean my money. The Yahoo stock I bought in the nineties rose about one thousand percent since I bought it, and my Apple stock isn't doing bad either."

"I get the idea."

"If you let me in I'll tell everything, and then some. And

if you don't, then I will become a block of ice and you will have to melt me before we can get married."

A figure meowed at their feet.

"Felix!" Becky reached for the cat, thrilled to see her feline friend. "Oh, Felix, you naughty, spoiled fur ball."

"I take it this is my competition." Jonah reached out and scratched Felix behind the ears.

"Meet Felix." She kissed the top of Felix's head.

"He's the kind of guy that makes you feel merry, eh?"

"I did say that, didn't I?"

Jonah nodded his fur-capped head slowly.

"And I'll bet you don't know the Felix cartoons."

He continued to nod his head. "I lived in England until I was eleven."

"Oh, I can see how that could lead to a misunderstanding."

Jonah reached one gloved hand and lifted Becky's chin so he could look directly into her eyes. "Exactly."

They kissed with Felix between them.

"Your lips are cold," Becky said after a long exhale.

"I'll have to get used to the cold. Martha says the hospital is looking for a doctor. And I'm thinking of coming out of retirement."

She pulled him through the doorway.

The three figures hiding behind the bushes erupted in a sigh of contentment and then stood up.

Jennifer rubbed her gloved hands together. "I think we're going to be holding a wedding," she said in a singsong voice and then turned to Lillian and the other woman who looked like a mirror image of Lillian. "It's too bad Dawn and Claire couldn't be here."

Lillian turned to her twin. "Dawn's busy cooking. And Claire . . ."

She looked back at Jennifer for an answer.

"She and Lexie are flying to Arizona to be with Alex. The Biltmore Resort and Spa. I believe a motorcycle ride may be on the agenda."

"Things on the mainland are just fine, mon." Lillian chuckled.

"I still can't picture Claire as a motorcycle mama, but anything for love," Jennifer said and smiled.

They looked at Becky's brick house one more time before they started down the sidewalk to Jennifer's SUV.

"Carol, how about we go home and have some pancakes with Log Cabin syrup?"

Carol looked at Lillian. "Okay, but first let's have a snowball fight."

"Right here, now? Would that be fun?" Jennifer asked, smiling at the two, hugging her body to stay warm.

"Of course," Lillian said, apparently immune to the cold.

"Definitely," Carol agreed.

Jennifer's head went back and forth trying to tell the two fuzzy brunette heads apart.

"Carol, I know how to make a perfect snowball," Lillian bragged. "You have to have the right temperature and moisture—"

"It has to be slushy and wet," Carol interrupted.

"No, if it's too wet it won't stay together," Lillian disagreed.

"I don't mean too wet," Carol clarified.

Jennifer watched them intently.

"You scoop it up in both your hands gently," Lillian said.

"No, firmly," Carol argued.

"I was going to say gently but firmly," Lillian claimed.

"But you didn't," Carol pointed out.

"Know what, you guys?" Jennifer asked.

Both women looked at Jennifer and together said, "What?"

"You two are just like sisters."

The twins exchanged looks.

"People have been telling us that since yesterday," Lillian said.

Jennifer hugged Lillian. "I love you, Lil. I really do."

"Of course you do. Why wouldn't you?" Lillian smiled.

"So, back to the perfect snowball," the twins said in unison and laughed.

"Well, you have to roll it around," Lillian started.

It seemed to Jennifer in that moment, standing in the cold, listening to the winter sounds, and sharing the moment with friends, that things on the mainland (and in Lakeside, Minnesota, in particular) were just fine, mon.

Debbie DiGiovanni is the author of three previous novels, including *Reality Queen*. She lives with her family in sunny Southern California where she is happy to be keeping warm after a ten-year sojourn in Montana.

Holiday humor and heavenly hope

Revive your true Christmas spirit with outrageous humor and practical solutions to make your holiday season less stressful and more enjoyable.

Don't miss this **laugh-out-loud** book
from popular speaker and author Rhonda Rhea!

Ɍ Revell

Available at your local bookstore

www.revellbooks.com

for the crazy Christmas rush!

The people of Christmas Valley always celebrate Christmas to the fullest extent. But this year their plans are turned upside down when an unconventional couple arrives in town ready to deliver a baby.

*Don't miss this charming retelling
of the nativity story from Melody Carlson!*

℞ Revell

Available at your local bookstore

www.revellbooks.com